Knit to
Be Tied

Knit to
Be Tied

Maggie Sefton

BERKLEY PRIME CRIME, NEW YORK

MYS
Sefton

BERKLEY
PRIME
CRIME

An imprint of Penguin Random House LLC
375 Hudson Street, New York, New York 10014

This book is an original publication of Penguin Random House LLC.

Library of Congress Cataloging-in-Publication Data

Names: Sefton, Maggie, author.
Title: Knit to be tied / Maggie Sefton.
Description: First edition. | New York : Berkley Prime Crime, 2016. | Series:
A knitting mystery ; 14
Identifiers: LCCN 2016003764 (print) | LCCN 2016008747 (ebook) | ISBN
9780425282502 (hardback) | ISBN 9780698405837 ()
Subjects: LCSH: Flynn, Kelly (Fictitious character)—Fiction. | Knitters
(Persons)—Fiction. Murder—Investigation—Fiction. | BISAC: FICTION /
Mystery & Detective / Women Sleuths. | GSAFD: Mystery fiction.
Classification: LCC PS3619.E37 K63 2016 (print) | LCC PS3619.E37 (ebook) |
DDC 813/ .6—dc23
LC record available at http://lccn.loc.gov/2016003764

FIRST EDITION: June 2016

PRINTED IN THE UNITED STATES OF AMERICA

10   9   8   7   6   5   4   3   2   1

Cover illustration by Chris O'Leary.
Cover design by Rita Frangie.

Penguin
Random
House

This fourteenth book in the Knitting Mysteries is dedicated to my mother—Benny Herndon Conn. She passed away last year in 2015 at the age of ninety-five. She was a remarkable woman in my eyes—a strong and brave woman in a time when women were often docile. My mother was a single, divorced, working mother in an "Ozzie and Harriet" world—the 1950s. She was and has always been a role model for me. I'm so glad she was my mother. I miss you, Mom.

Cast of Characters

Kelly Flynn—financial accountant and part-time sleuth, refugee from East Coast corporate CPA firm

Steve Townsend—architect and builder in Fort Connor, Colorado, and Kelly's boyfriend

KELLY'S FRIENDS:
Jennifer Stroud—real estate agent, part-time waitress

Lisa Gerrard—physical therapist

Megan Smith—IT consultant, another corporate refugee

Marty Harrington—lawyer, Megan's husband

Greg Carruthers—university instructor, Lisa's boyfriend

Pete Wainwright—owner of Pete's Porch Café in the back of Kelly's favorite knitting shop, House of Lambspun

LAMBSPUN FAMILY AND REGULARS:
Mimi Shafer—Lambspun shop owner and knitting expert, known to Kelly and her friends as "Mother Mimi"

Burt Parker—retired Fort Connor police detective, Lambspun spinner-in-residence

Hilda and Lizzie von Steuben—spinster sisters, retired schoolteachers, and exquisite knitters

CAST OF CHARACTERS

Curt Stackhouse—Colorado rancher, Kelly's mentor and advisor

Jayleen Swinson—Alpaca rancher and Colorado cowgirl

Connie and Rosa—Lambspun shop personnel

Knit to
Be Tied

One

"That's a good boy," Kelly Flynn said to her Rottweiler, Carl, who bent his black head to the side, eyes closed, as she rubbed the sweet spot behind his ear. "Ooooo, yes," Kelly crooned as Carl sank down on the concrete patio in the cottage backyard.

Carl began his own doggie version of harmony as the wonderful ear rub continued. The better to fully experience ear rub ecstasy, Kelly figured. It was a good thing, because she also noticed that Carl's nemesis, Brazen Squirrel, was skittering across the top of the chain-link fence surrounding the cottage's part-shady, part-sunny backyard, which looked out onto a city golf course.

"Don't look now, Carl, but your pal Brazen has a friend. Or maybe a girlfriend," Kelly teased as she spotted a brownish gray squirrel racing right behind Brazen on the fence top.

The mere mention of his nemesis was enough to interrupt even the most ecstatic of ear rubs. Carl's black head jerked up and swiveled to check out the backyard. Brazen had just leaped onto a dangling branch of the huge overhanging cottonwood tree that stood right at the edge of Kelly's yard and the golf course. The second squirrel was about to launch into the air as well when Carl launched himself, racing toward the fence, barking threats to the saucy intruders. He charged into the fence with both feet just as the brownish squirrel started to jump. By this time, Carl's head was near the top of the fence. His deep baritone bark clearly startled brownish squirrel so much that the little creature jerked in mid-jump, missing the branch, and fell to the ground.

Carl's angry barking intensified, but Brazen Squirrel suddenly scampered down the overhanging tree branch as he loudly scolded Carl, while safely being out of reach. Brownish squirrel beat a hasty retreat up the huge tree trunk, Kelly noticed, and didn't turn around until he or she was safely on a higher branch.

"Look, Carl, you scared that new squirrel to death," Kelly said, pointing above. Brownish squirrel peeked through the leaves.

Not the slightest bit contrite, Carl kept barking at his chief nuisance, Brazen, and Brazen chattered back angrily in return. Kelly smiled at the Dog vs. Squirrel soap opera. It had been playing out in the trees overhead for years now. Generations of Brazen and his relatives had taken part.

Kelly looked across the golf course to the outlines of buildings in Fort Connor's Old Town and to the mountains in the distance. The foothills, as the locals called them, were the edge of the Colorado Rocky Mountains, and the snow-crested peaks rose up behind. Usually snow-crested, that is. Since it was August, most of the snow on the peaks had melted except on the north-facing sides. There, the sunshine never penetrated enough to melt their glacier-like frozen faces.

"Keep those squirrels in line, Carl," Kelly advised her dog as she slid the patio screen door closed. She'd taken care of her clients' accounts earlier in the day and returned any phone calls. She deserved a break. Besides she needed a fresh cup of coffee, eyeing the empty glass pot sitting beside the coffeemaker on her counter.

That decided it, and Kelly grabbed her large over-the-shoulder bag on the sofa near the desk in her cottage office and headed out the front door. Years before, when Kelly had returned to her childhood home of Fort Connor, the cottage had been her home as well as her office. Her aunt Helen's funeral had brought Kelly back to the town she grew up in. But little did Kelly know at the time that the sad occasion would actually change her life forever by introducing all the wonderful people she'd met who knew her aunt.

Pausing at the flowerboxes lining the sidewalk to her cottage, Kelly checked the annuals growing there. Fully in bloom in late summer and brash in their dramatic colors. Bright orange daisies, sunny yellow marigolds, and fiery red salvia.

She started across the gravel and dirt driveway that separated her beige stucco, red-tile-roofed cottage from the larger look-alike farmhouse that sat on the shaded corner of two busy Fort Connor streets. Huge cottonwood trees surrounded what once was the farmhouse for Aunt Helen and Uncle Jim's sheep farm. Years and years ago, those two busy streets were merely country roads on the edge of a bustling northern Colorado city.

Now, shopping centers and fast food restaurants lined the other side of one street alongside a big box store. Apartments were diagonally across the street. And trendy craft breweries dotted the other street, which led directly into the oldest part of Fort Connor's Old Town. The commercial heart of town sat beside the Cache La Poudre River, which flowed through Old Town Fort Connor.

The House of Lambspun knitting shop came to life when Aunt Helen had to sell her former home and move into the cottage. As a CPA, Kelly had handled her aunt's finances from a distance after Uncle Jim's death. Since her aunt was an avid knitter and fiber artist, Helen told Kelly she was actually happy a friend had taken over her memory-filled farmhouse and transformed it into a paradise of fibers of all kinds. Yarns for knitting, crocheting, spinning, and weaving filled the rooms. Large spools of thread for all kinds of stitchery lined the walls as well. And the memories were still there, Helen always said.

When Kelly returned for her aunt's funeral, she stepped inside her aunt's favorite knitting shop for the first time—and found the friendship and warmth that she lacked in her busy corporate CPA life back East. Kelly had moved into Aunt Helen's cottage and made it—and Lambspun—her home.

Kelly walked between two parked cars in the driveway

and looked across the patio café at the back of the Lamb-spun shop. Pete's Porch Café was closed now since breakfast and lunch were over, but she noticed someone sitting at a shady table beneath the cottonwood trees beside the tall stucco wall that surrounded one side of the shop and curved around the corner of the back patio. The girl appeared to be studying, because she had a book open on the table in front of her and a notebook beside.

A perfect place to study, Kelly concluded as she walked toward the entrance door of the Lambspun shop. A black wrought iron table and chairs sat in the shaded nook beside the shop's covered entryway. Brick flower boxes and the garden captured the bright August afternoon sun. It was hot, summertime hot but manageable, Kelly thought as she heaved open the large wooden door to Lambspun.

Stepping inside the slightly air-conditioned foyer, Kelly spotted shop owner Mimi Shafer arranging a display of ribbon silk scarves across the open cabinet door of an antique dry sink in the corner. She turned at the sound of the tinkling bell over the entry door and smiled.

"Well, hello, Kelly. I saw your car outside so I knew you were inside the cottage and working on your client accounts. I figured you'd drop by here this afternoon."

"You know me too well, Mimi," Kelly said, fingering a sleeveless top that hung from a ceiling display. "Or my habits at least."

"I simply pay attention to your schedule, Kelly," Mimi said, continuing to drape multicolored scarves over the dry sink cabinet door.

"Did you finish that charity project you were working on

the other day?" Kelly asked as she glanced over the colorful piles of yarns and fibers that filled the foyer and spilled over into the adjacent larger room.

"You mean the local Salvation Army project? Yes, I finished one afghan and am starting another. There's always a need when flooding or wildfires occur and people are displaced. I want to finish them before fall when our busy season starts." She placed the last scarf beside the others, creating a rainbow of colors. "There now. That should do it. I wanted to put out these little scarves that my teenage girls' knitting class finished last week. They each knitted up two scarves, one for themselves and the other to put in the shop to sell for charity. All proceeds will go to the Disaster Relief Fund."

Kelly walked over to the dry sink, its unfinished surface a perfect background for the colorful ribbon scarves. "I remember my first ribbon scarf years ago. When I was beginning to knit. I still have it, you know. I use it as a belt for my jeans." She fingered the scarves.

"Goodness, that was several years ago, wasn't it?" Mimi glanced into the larger central yarn room, filled floor to ceiling with bins of colorful yarns and fibers.

Kelly paused and counted back. "Seven years ago, in fact."

Mimi turned to Kelly, her blue eyes wide. "Oh, my word, you're right. It has been seven years since you came back to Fort Connor for Helen's funeral. That's hard to believe."

"Time flies, as they say," Kelly said with a grin. "Sometimes when I'm walking over here from the cottage, something catches my eye. The garden patio outside the café in the summer, when everything is so green. Or just looking over at the front door of Lambspun and remembering when I opened it for the first time. That makes me think back, and it's amazing how many things have happened since I first came to Lambspun and met everyone. All of you."

Mimi's blue eyes suddenly grew moist. "Ohhhh, Kelly, that's beautiful," she said softly.

"Oh, no, I've made Mother Mimi cry," Kelly teased. "Forgive me for waxing poetic. I won't do it again."

Mimi reached for a tissue in her pocket and dabbed at her eyes. "Oh, don't mind me. I loved it. I love happy memories. And making new memories. Like now, with Megan and Marty and little Molly."

"The little firecracker?" Kelly said, laughing at the image of Megan and Marty's nine-month-old daughter with a mop of red curls. "Oh, that reminds me. Megan told me at our ball game last night that she was going to drop in today and bring Molly."

Mimi's eyes lit up, no trace of tears anymore. "Wonderful! I just *love* that baby!"

"She's more a toddler than a baby now. When we were all over there at Megan and Marty's house last Friday night, Molly came charging out into the living room. Man, can she go fast on those little legs. She's going to be a heckuva base runner when she gets older."

Mimi laughed her musical little laugh. "Oh, Kelly, leave it to you to picture Molly playing ball."

"Believe me, she's going to be a natural. Both her parents are athletic. Mark my words, as they say," Kelly teased.

The front doorbell tinkled again and retired Fort Connor

police detective Burt Parker walked into the foyer. His friendly face spread with a grin when he saw Mimi and Kelly together. "Well, well, two of my favorite women," he joked as he walked over and gave Mimi a kiss on the cheek.

"Kelly just told me Megan's dropping by today with Molly," Mimi said, giving him a hug.

"Oh, great. Two more of my favorite women," Burt said with a grin. "You can't have too many beautiful women around, I always say."

"Oh, pooh," Mimi said with a familiar wave of her hand as she went to retrieve her empty box of yarns. "What did that store say? Do they have any of the special thread we need for the tatting classes?"

Burt shook his head. "I'm afraid not. And I've already called the rest of the stores in Northern Colorado. It looks like I'll be taking a trip to Denver to check out those suppliers."

Mimi cocked her head to the side. "You know, I think I'll go with you. We can stop for lunch at that café we discovered the last time we went down there."

"I think that's a great idea," Kelly chimed in, uninvited. "I love to see you two break out of the routine and do something for yourselves. You deserve it." She gave a definitive nod of her head.

"Well, you heard that, didn't you?" Burt said to Mimi. "I guess we have our marching orders."

"Why don't you check out the list of shops and give them a call," Mimi said as she started through the curved opening to the loom room.

The largest weaving loom in the shop, the Mother Loom

as Kelly called it, sat right in the middle of the room that led toward the front of the shop and the counter. There, Lambspun staff handled the customers and their purchases, while other staffers sat at the winding table, winding fat balls of yarn from loopy draped skeins of wool. Hanging on the walls were examples of every kind of fiber art imaginable. Exotic shawls, sweaters, scarves and mittens, sleeveless summer clothes and hats from soft-rolled edge baby hats, to collapsible cloches and floppy-brim felted hats.

"I'll do that," Burt said as Mimi headed toward the front of the shop. "You have a game tonight, Kelly? Or is it Steve's team? I can't keep you folks straight."

"Steve and the guys are playing tonight," Kelly said as she walked into the main gathering room of the shop.

A long dark wood library table dominated the length of the room, which had windows facing toward the golf course on one side. Everyone called it the knitting table. An assortment of all sorts of items spread across the middle of the table. Scissors, plastic stitch markers, knitting needles, crochet hooks, odds and ends of yarn, and a teapot, usually empty after a busy morning of classes and afternoon lessons. The other three sides of the room were filled with shelves piled high with yarns. One large section was stuffed with books and magazines on all things fiber. Whether you wanted to knit, crochet, spin, weave, or dye yarns, you could find a book to help you. Kelly often marveled at the variety of techniques and instructions for all types of fiber art and activity.

Kelly dropped her shoulder bag onto the table, which was unusually empty for a summer afternoon. "Early August, and it's family vacation time," she observed. "A couple of the girls were missing from my softball clinic yesterday."

"You're right. It's that time of summer when families try to squeeze in a vacation before the junior and senior high school fall sports' teams start mid-August practices." Burt jerked his thumb behind him. "If you'd like some coffee, Jennifer left a pot sitting on the café counter before they closed up."

"You read my mind, Burt," Kelly said as she followed him through the central yarn room and wound around a corner to the hallway that led toward Pete's Porch Café.

The breakfast and lunch café was darkened now but Kelly spied a thermos on the counter in front of the grill. Unscrewing the top, she sniffed the rich aroma of grill cook Eduardo's strong brew. She poured a black stream into her empty mug. "Ahhhhh, yes. That's better," she said after taking a big sip.

Burt laughed softly, watching her. "You know, Cassie has learned how to make the coffee so you can't tell Eduardo didn't make it."

"You're kidding," Kelly said as she replaced the thermos and walked toward the hallway once more.

Burt followed after her. "Nope. Jennifer says Cassie watched Eduardo make the coffee over and over, observing him carefully, before he let her make it. Pete said they were all surprised how good it was. Except Eduardo. He just grinned."

"That sounds like Cassie. She's at her tennis lessons now, right?"

"Yes. I dropped her over there and stayed to watch.

Brother, those kids in the class have gotten really good this summer. Their shots just whiz over that net."

Kelly turned and walked back into the central yarn room. "I'll have to go see one of her classes before school starts. I could tell her skills had improved whenever I saw her play a tennis match. It's such fun to watch young kids learn new skills in sports and watch them gain confidence."

"That's what makes you a good coach, Kelly," Burt said, giving her a fatherly pat on the shoulder. "As for Mimi and me, we're simply amazed at how fast Cassie is growing up. She's as tall as Mimi now. And . . . and she's filled out. Well, you know. It brings back memories of watching my daughter grow up all those years ago."

Kelly gave Father Figure Burt a big smile. "Cassie's growing up, for sure. And this must be the day for memories. Mimi and I were reminiscing earlier about that year when I first showed up at Lambspun's door. Or rather, outside in Pete's Café. I remember Jennifer waited on our table when Mimi and I sat in the patio garden. That was seven years ago, Burt."

Burt's eyes widened and he shook his head. "Ohhhhh, don't get me started on bringing back all those memories, Kelly. We'll be here past closing."

The doorbell's tinkle sounded, and Kelly saw friend Lisa Gerrard walk into the foyer. A young brunette woman who looked faintly familiar accompanied her.

"Hey, you two," Lisa called to them with a big smile as she walked into the central yarn room. "I brought one of my grad student friends to see the shop. She wants to start a knitting project."

"Well, she's come to the right place," Kelly said as she walked around the round maple wood table, which was piled high with soft balls of blue and green and purple yarns along with open magazines with patterns marked. She noticed that Lisa's friend was still in the foyer, clearly admiring all the yarns and fibers displayed there.

Lisa beckoned to her friend, who was stroking some of the merino wool and silk combinations, clearly entranced. "Nancy, come and meet my friends."

Nancy glanced up and quickly joined Lisa. "Wow, I can't believe everything here," she said, wide-eyed as she looked around the central yarn room.

"If this is your first visit, I suggest you take your time and stroll around," Burt said. "There are several rooms to the shop and they're all chock-full of fiber." He gestured around him.

"Nancy's in the same graduate psychology program I am at the university." Lisa pointed toward the empty knitting table in the main room. "All the pattern books are in there. So why don't we get started."

"It's nice to meet you, Nancy. This is an unbelievable place," Kelly said with a smile. "I think I saw you sitting outside in the garden at one of the corner tables. It looked like you were studying."

Nancy's pretty face lit up with a smile. "Yes, that was me. We have to use every bit of spare time we can find to keep up," she said, gazing about the central yarn room at the kaleidoscope of color surrounding them. "This is just beautiful. I had no idea."

"I hope to see you here again, Nancy. Enjoy yourself," Burt said as he headed toward the front of the shop.

Lisa had already ushered Nancy into a place at the knitting table and was perusing the bookshelves. Kelly followed after them. "What's the project you're working on, Nancy?"

Nancy gave a shy smile then glanced away. "I'm starting a baby sweater, and I've never knitted any baby clothes before. Only sweaters for myself. So I figured I'd call on Lisa for help." Her smile returned, brightening her face again.

"You'll do great, Nancy," Lisa said, book in hand. "Since you've already done adult sweaters, you're familiar with most of the techniques. This book will help a lot. It's a step-by-step approach."

"Oh, just what I need," Nancy said, setting her small backpack on the table.

Kelly decided not to distract newcomer Nancy with any more conversation while she was trying to learn. Instead, another idea presented itself. Maybe this was a good time to pick out a yarn for one of those charity afghans Mimi was making. She could have it finished by fall, in time for the cold weather. Kelly took another big sip of the rich Cassie-made coffee and headed back into the central yarn room, where she proceeded to lose herself in the wonderland of color.

Two

"**Wooooohooooo!**" Cassie yelled, jumping up from the bleachers the moment Greg's bat made contact with the baseball and sailed high over right field.

"Way to go, Greg!" Lisa shouted over the cheers of the surrounding friends and family members that crowded the City Park ball field bleachers.

Standing beside Lisa, Kelly added her cheers then yelled, "Home run!" as the ball sailed past the fence.

"Boy, I'd love to do that!" Cassie said, then let out another "Woooohooo! Over the fence!"

"Keep working and you will," Kelly promised, and they settled back on the bleachers again. "You'll get stronger as you get older, too. More muscles."

"What is it Megan does?" Crooking her right arm up and flexing, Cassie laughed. "Check it out."

Both Kelly and Lisa laughed. Lisa leaned back against the bleachers. "It's a combination of your muscles getting stronger and your height and weight. All sorts of things go into making a good batter."

"So if I get taller, I'll bat harder?" Cassie looked at Lisa with an inquisitive expression.

"Well, that's part of it. You also have to be coordinated so your batting motion is smooth. Yours is looking good, so not to worry."

"Cassie's been doing really well in my batting clinics each year. Her swing has gotten much stronger." Kelly glanced to Cassie. "You'll be hitting it close to the fence by next summer, I bet."

"Really?" Cassie's face lit up. *"Awesome!"*

"Totally," Kelly said with a sly grin to Lisa, who just shook her head at Cassie's favorite descriptive word.

"Okay, explain this. Megan's short but muscular. She's tough, and she can knock it just over the fence. But skinny Marty can knock it way over the fence, almost out of the park." She pointed to Marty, who was at home plate now.

Marty swung at the fastball. "Steee-rike one!" yelled the umpire.

"Marty may be skinny," Lisa observed. "But he's got a great motion and he's tall. And he's got muscles. Not as big as Steve's or Greg's, but big enough." Lisa grinned.

"Who're you guys talking about?" a teenaged boy's voice said from the side of the bleachers.

Kelly turned and watched Eric Thompson, rancher Curt Stackhouse's grandson, climb effortlessly over the bleacher rows to reach them. Long legs. Fourteen years old like Cassie, both of them growing like the proverbial weeds.

"Here's another long drink of water," Kelly said as Eric plopped himself onto the bleacher in front of Kelly and Lisa and next to Cassie. "Have you grown another inch since I saw you last? It's only been a month."

"Uhhhhh, maybe." Eric gave her a little grin.

"Yeah, he has," Cassie piped up. "Every time I catch up with him, he passes me," Cassie said, shaking her head.

"That's because he's a guy. They're usually taller," Kelly observed good-naturedly.

Cassie just made a face. But Eric grinned and said, "That's what I tell her, but when I do, she throws things at me."

Kelly and Lisa both laughed, recognizing typical fourteen-year-old behavior. "What does she throw at you?" Lisa asked. "Nothing heavy, I hope."

"French fries mostly," Eric teased, glancing slyly at Cassie.

"Oh, I bet you really hate that, don't you?" Kelly played along.

Eric just grinned. Cassie, meanwhile, reached over and scavenged through Steve's leftovers in a nearby white plastic container. Finding a limp French fry, she tossed it at Eric, who snatched it from the air and popped it into his mouth.

"Steee-rike two!" the umpire called.

"Uh-oh," Kelly said, turning her attention to the field.

Just then a strong female voice called from the front of the bleachers, "Knock it out, Marty!"

Kelly and friends looked down and saw friend Megan cheering her husband as she returned from the concession stand. Other friendly cheers and shouts rose up. Marty was a dependable batter and a greased-lightning base runner. Kelly had seen him steal two bases in one inning on a regular basis. Fast feet.

The ball flew from the pitcher's hand, and Marty swung again. This time, he connected with a crack of the bat, and the ball soared up, up, and away. Kelly and everyone jumped up cheering as Marty was halfway to first base before the shortstop got to the ball. Down below, Megan was jumping up and down, French fries drifting to the ground.

Plop. The ball landed right in the shortstop's glove. Marty was out.

"Awwwwwwwww!" Cassie complained.

"Darn it!" Lisa yelled.

"Bad luck," Eric said, leaning back onto the bleachers. "Next time."

"Yeah, next time," Cassie echoed.

Megan climbed over the bleachers and settled right in front of Cassie and Eric. "Who wanted the taco? Was it you, Lisa? And Cassie, here's your hot dog." Megan handed over the hot dog smothered in mustard and ketchup and relish. "Cassie, hand Lisa the taco, please."

"Sure thing," Cassie said before taking a big bite of the juicy-looking hot dog. She handed Lisa the paper-wrapped taco while she munched the big bite.

Kelly caught Eric eyeing the tempting ballpark treat and was about to get one for him when Megan handed over another fully loaded dog. "Here you go, Eric. I always get an extra hot dog because I know someone will want it."

Eric's face lit up. "Really? Gee, thanks, Megan!" He eagerly accepted the scrumptious-looking treat. And like Cassie, didn't waste any time before taking a huge bite.

Kelly decided she couldn't stand the temptation any longer. "Okay, that's it. I have to have one of those," she said, rising from the bleacher row.

"Isn't that Steve coming up to bat?" Lisa said, nibbling the edges of her taco. Compared to the fully loaded hot dogs, the taco was positively dainty.

"I'll cheer him on from the concession stand," Kelly joked as she used her long legs to clear one bleacher row after another until she reached the ground. Her boyfriend, Steve, was settling into his stance.

"Outta the park, Steve!" Kelly yelled as she headed for the concession stand. Then she noticed friend Jennifer and boyfriend Pete walking toward her. Jennifer held a container with soft drinks and Pete had a huge bag of popcorn. "Hey there, you two. Cassie said you were here at the game."

"Yeah, we got stopped by Mimi and Burt. They were leaving early," café owner Pete said.

"They're going to take a day trip to Denver tomorrow," Jennifer added. "Take some time to see a theater production maybe."

"They offered to take Cassie to see her grandfather while there, but I didn't want them to spend their time doing that. They deserve some time together," Pete observed sagely.

"Definitely. Both of them are always working."

"How's the game going?" Pete asked, peering at the field. Steve had just popped a foul ball and was jogging back to home plate.

"They're even right now, but their pitcher is really sharp.

So I don't know if the guys can pull off a win this time. Greg hit a homer, but Marty struck out."

"Steee-rike one!" the umpire's voice called.

"Uh-oh," Jennifer said, staring at the ball field.

"That's Steve at bat," Pete observed. "He'll hit it out."

"I sure hope so," Kelly said, watching the pitcher catch the baseball thrown from the catcher. "That pitcher has a wicked fastball. The best I've seen in this league. Must be a newcomer because I haven't seen him before."

The pitcher began his windup and let fly. The ball whizzed toward the plate. Steve swung hard . . . and missed. The ball was safe inside the catcher's mitt.

"Steee-rike two!" the umpire called.

"Wow, he is fast," Pete said, looking surprised.

Kelly watched Steve stretch the bat behind his shoulders, then take a couple of practice swings before settling into his stance again.

The pitcher retrieved the tossed ball again, wound up, and whipped it toward home plate. This time, Steve swung and connected, sending the ball toward left field.

Kelly, Jennifer, and Pete all broke into loud cheers as did the fans on the bleachers behind them. Steve barely made it to second base as the left fielder sent the ball to the second baseman.

"Wow! That sure made up for the strikes," Pete said with a grin.

"It sure does. Now it's a ball game." She jerked her thumb toward the bleachers. "Lisa and Megan are there with Cassie and Eric. Do you want me to get you guys something from the concession stand? I'm starving for a hot dog."

"Naw, I'm good," Pete said. "Jen, do you want anything?"

"I'll go with Kelly and get some snacks for the kids. Eric's mom and dad are taking Cassie and Eric and some of their friends to the movies tonight after the game," Jennifer said as she followed after Kelly.

"It's so good that the kids are doing things in a group," Kelly said as she and Jennifer joined the back of the concession stand line.

"Oh, yeah." Jennifer nodded. "We don't want them pairing off too early."

Kelly smiled at her dear friend's parental observation. Ever since Pete's niece Cassie had moved in with Jennifer and Pete two years ago, Kelly and friends had witnessed a fascinating transformation. Pete and Jennifer became parents, in fact. Pete's grandfather Ben had been raising Cassie on his own until his massive heart attack two years ago. Cassie was only a toddler when her mother, Tanya, Pete's music-loving sister, had tired of her brief stint as a mother and went back to her former lifestyle—following one rock band after another as they played all over the Rocky Mountain West. Boyfriends came and went, it seemed to Kelly. Tanya would show up once a year or so for a quick visit and then hit the road again. A wayward spirit.

Kelly glanced at her close friend Jennifer and noticed a different expression on her face. A worried expression. Curious, Kelly asked, "Is something wrong, Jen? You look like you're worrying about something. Either that, or you have a stomachache." She smiled.

Jennifer gave Kelly a half smile in return. "Boy, we know each other so well, we can't hide a thing."

Concerned now, Kelly leaned forward. "What's up? Are you okay? Is Pete okay?"

"We're good. We're good." Jennifer nodded. "It's not us. It's . . . it's Tanya. Pete's had a couple of phone calls from her."

"What kind of phone calls? Does she need money or something?"

Jennifer shook her head. "No, no. She's been asking to see Cassie. Or rather, have Cassie come down and stay with her in Denver for a while."

Kelly didn't like the sound of that at all. "What do you mean, stay with her for a while? Tanya's never in one place long enough for Cassie to stay with her."

Jennifer's big brown eyes looked up at Kelly. "Don't we all know it. But she's telling Pete that she's settled down with one guy, Donnie, in Denver. It's been a year now, which is pretty long for Tanya."

"Oh, I'm really impressed," Kelly said, her voice dripping with sarcasm.

Jennifer gave Kelly a crooked smile. "Those were my thoughts exactly. Anyway, Tanya says she wants to spend more time with Cassie. She wants Cassie to stay with her for a while before school starts again. And before she and Donnie go out on the road again."

Kelly screwed up her face. "She can't be serious. Cassie's in the midst of her softball team's final games. And Megan says she's got tennis matches scheduled, too. It's the last month of summer." She gestured in aggravation. "Cassie's got a life here. She's busy with her friends. Tanya can't pull her away from all that just because she wants to play mother."

Jennifer laughed softly. "I can always count on you for an honest reaction, Kelly. Thank you for that. But whether we like it or not, Tanya is Cassie's mother, so Pete has to take her request seriously."

"Dammit! What's gotten into Tanya?"

Jennifer shrugged. "I don't know. Pete and I figure she's in her late thirties now, so maybe she's having second thoughts about her lifestyle. All those years following the rock bands and musicians around. Maybe she really does want to settle down with this guy. Who knows?"

"Well, she can settle down with What's His Face, but that doesn't mean she can take Cassie with her," Kelly said indignantly as she moved closer to the front of the concession line.

Jennifer reached out and gave Kelly a quick hug. "That's what Pete and I think, too. We haven't said anything to Cassie yet. Pete's still talking to Tanya. We're hoping she'd agree to having Cassie come down to Denver for a weekend. We'll see. Keep your fingers crossed."

"All right. But I think you two should go talk to a lawyer and a family social worker or whatever. Start finding out what your legal rights are. You two have been Cassie's de facto parents for over two years now." Kelly looked Jennifer in the eye and dropped her voice.

Jennifer smiled. "Pete's already called Marty. We're going to see him on Monday. Start the legal proceedings to formally gain custody."

Kelly let out a long-held breath. "Okaaaaay. That makes me feel a whole lot better." The line moved forward again, and Kelly gave the teenager behind the counter a big smile.

"I want a hot dog with chili and ketchup and mustard and relish."

The teenage girl blinked. "You want all of that on one hot dog?"

"Yeah. Why not?" Kelly said with a laugh.

Kelly started across the gravel driveway separating her cottage from the Lambspun knitting shop. Monday afternoon's sun was blazing early-August hot. In another two or three weeks, the temperatures should slowly start to inch downward toward the mid and low eighties. September in Northern Colorado was usually very warm and mild and sunny, sunny, sunny. As usual, the dependability of that Colorado sunshine was one of the things Kelly loved best about living in her old hometown of Fort Connor. "Hey, Kelly," Burt's voice sounded from the café patio garden.

Kelly turned to see her father figure and mentor walk toward her. "Hi, Burt. How was your Saturday in Denver this past weekend?"

"It was great. Mimi and I will definitely get away some other times like that," he said with a big smile.

"I agree. Both you and Mimi work really hard and are always here at the shop, taking care of customers. Connie and Rosa can handle things for a weekend, especially if you have guest instructors coming in to teach Saturday classes."

"You make a very good point, Kelly. And believe me, I've presented the same case to Mimi. She's simply not ready to cut back on the schedule yet."

Kelly fell in step with Burt as he walked down the sidewalk bordering the patio garden, heading toward the shop front entry. "Well, maybe this past weekend will give Mimi an idea of how much fun it would be to take a little break every now and then."

"Let's hope so, Kelly. We went to the Performing Arts Center in Downtown Denver and saw a Broadway musical. And we even visited the art gallery close to downtown." Burt walked up the brick steps and heaved open the wide wooden entry door.

"Well, hello, you two," Lambspun staffer Rosa said when Kelly and Burt entered. Rosa's arms were filled with plump oblong skeins of multicolored yarns. "Mimi wants to talk to you about that Denver supplier, Burt. She just got off the phone with him." Rosa continued to stack the yarn skeins on top of the antique dry sink in the foyer corner.

"Thanks, Rosa. What'd I tell you, Kelly," Burt said with a grin. "That woman doesn't know how to slow down." He walked away through the adjoining loom room toward the front of the shop.

Kelly paused by the antique dry sink cabinet and fingered the colorful new yarn skeins Rosa had placed there. Fall colors. Forest green and purple plum and burnt orange. Mimi and the Lambspun elves always started putting out hints of the autumn to come while it was still August. Letting knitters and crochet folks and all the fiber artists start to think about warm sweaters and scarves and mittens while it was still summer hot outside. Planting seeds, Kelly figured as she headed toward the central yarn room.

At that moment, Lisa and fellow grad student Nancy walked out of the main room. Lisa had her arm around

Nancy's shoulders. Kelly noticed Nancy's red-streaked face and lowered head as she walked with Lisa toward the front door.

"Give me a call after you get out of class, okay?" Lisa said. "And let me know if you talk to your father."

Kelly couldn't hear what Nancy's wet voice mumbled to Lisa in the foyer. But Lisa replied in a lowered tone before Nancy walked out of the shop. Then Lisa turned around and approached Kelly. She had a worried expression on her face.

"What was that all about?" Kelly asked. "Nancy looked all happy and pleased to start a new project the last time I saw her."

Lisa let out a long sigh. "It's complicated. Let's go to the table. Everyone else has left so we'll be alone."

"Sounds serious," Kelly observed as she followed Lisa into the main room, dropping her briefcase bag onto the long library table. A shaft of bright August afternoon sun streaked through the wood-rimmed windows, shining across the floor and table. The table's dark walnut shone under the sunlight, bringing up the faint reddish highlights buried deep in the wood.

Lisa pulled out a chair right beside Kelly at the end of the table. "Nancy is having problems with her boyfriend."

"That sounds pretty typical for young college students. I know you said she's a graduate student, but she looks pretty young to me."

Lisa nodded. "Yeah, she is. Nancy's very smart. Book smart, as she says." Lisa gave a crooked smile. "She's always made good grades and taken advanced courses in school, she told me. But she's kind of awkward and inexperienced on the dating scene apparently. She's gotten into a romantic relationship with this guy in her finance and investments class—"

Kelly perked up. "That sounds like accounting to me. I thought she was a fellow psychology student like you."

"Well, she has taken almost all of the psych courses she needs for her master's degree. But she's also taking some business courses in finance, if you can believe it. I don't know how she handles it all. But as I said, she's supersmart."

"She must be. But what does all that have to do with her boyfriend troubles, if anything?"

"Nothing really. I was simply giving you a little background on Nancy so you can understand what's happening. Anyway, Nancy started dating this guy in her class, and their relationship moved pretty fast. She said she was helping him in their finance class studies, then they started sleeping together."

Kelly leaned back into the wooden chair beside Lisa. "There's nothing new in that story. What happened?"

"Well, apparently Nancy believed all this guy's sweet talk about their being together as a couple and all that. So when she found out last week that she was pregnant, she was really excited. She actually thought this guy, Neil, would be happy, too." Lisa caught Kelly's gaze.

"I have a feeling I know where this is going," Kelly said in a sarcastic tone.

"Ohhhhh, yeah," Lisa said, releasing a tired sigh. "This guy did not take it well—"

"Big surprise."

"And he told Nancy he didn't want to see her anymore.

Maggie Sefton

He's about to get his MBA and start a bright career with this beer manufacturer who's expanding into new territory in Arizona."

"What a sweetheart. Now I know why she was crying."

"Yeah, she's really devastated. I knew she was all excited about this relationship, but I had no idea how much until she started opening up today. Nancy had convinced herself they were going to get married, and she was spinning all sorts of daydreams about their life together."

"Oh, brother . . . that is so sad. I hate stories like that." Kelly screwed up her face. "What's Nancy going to do now?"

"She's moving back in with her father in town and giving up her space in an apartment."

"Oh, boy, that could be a difficult conversation."

"Actually, I know her father. He's an excellent counselor over at the community center and for Larimer County. And he works with recovering alcoholics, too."

"Ohhhhh, good. So at least he'll be understanding. I hope."

Lisa nodded. "Oh, yes. It's not him I'm worried about. It's Nancy. After she explained to me what happened with Neil, she said she hoped that maybe he would 'change' his mind about the baby. Maybe he reacted out of shock at the news."

Kelly looked Lisa in the eye. "That sounds like a lot of false hope to me."

Lisa didn't reply, simply nodded her head in agreement.

28

Three

Kelly grabbed her cell phone after the second ring. Boyfriend Steve's name flashed on the screen as she clicked on.

"How's it going? Does that new client like any of those building sites?" Kelly asked as she emptied the coffeepot into her large mug on the kitchen counter.

"Actually, no. That surprised me, because he sounded like he really wanted to be up here in the mountains. I'd found four different sites in the Summit County area. Great views from all four, so I thought he'd like at least one of them."

"Sounds like he's having second thoughts about living in the more isolated areas." Kelly snapped the lid on her mug as she glanced outside into her cottage backyard.

Rottweiler Carl was stretched out on the grass in one of his favorite sunny spots, sound asleep. Midday nap time calling. Irresistible. Of course, Brazen Squirrel was well aware of Big Dog's nap schedule. Consequently, Brazen and the smaller brown squirrel—Kelly was convinced she was Brazen's mate—were making tracks across the fence and down to the ground. Scampering along the backyard, checking for tasty nuts or other yummy seeds that summer's harvest provided. Kelly noticed brown squirrel kept looking over her squirrelly shoulder in Carl's direction. Clearly making sure Big Dog had not awakened.

"Yeah, I think that's it. Once he was up on the different sites, I was able to explain to him exactly how water and electric power could be obtained. He never seemed interested in hearing those details when I mentioned them in our earlier meetings. But he started asking questions this morning."

"I'll bet he did. Once people understand what's actually involved in living farther out, it starts hitting them. That's what Jennifer always said. Particularly when they hear how much it costs to provide electricity and water. Oh, and maybe there will be a cell tower you can get a signal from."

Steve's chuckle came over the phone. "Ohhhhh, yeah. When I told him it could be thirty thousand dollars or so to drill for water, his eyes popped wide."

Kelly had to laugh. "And that's assuming you find water the first time you drill. The higher up you go, the farther you have to drill. So add another twenty thousand or so to the bill. They don't call these the Rocky Mountains for nothing."

"That's for sure. Anyway, I went over everything with him. Digging and installing a septic system and leach field."

"And the cost."

"Yeah. He had his calculator out by then. That's when I explained the power situation. If he chose a lot that was only a little farther out from the last electric utility pole, then he could attach to that last pole and obtain electricity from the Rural Electric Cooperative. For a price, of course. If he was the first one on a new section, his cost would be higher until more new customers attached after him. That's how an electric cooperative works. All the members cooperate in sharing the costs of providing electric power poles and lines and transmission costs."

"Did his eyes start to glaze over by then?" Kelly teased as she leaned back against the kitchen counter.

"Just about. Once I told him the costs could be over thirty thousand dollars initially, his eyes got even wider. That's when he asked about solar power."

"That's always an option. How large is his family? Oh, yeah, does he have school-age children? That's another consideration."

"No, he and his wife would be the only ones living there. Their older children would come to visit periodically, he said."

"Well, maybe their electric needs will be moderate then. A solar array can be kind of pricey to start with. It will save money down the road, but you have to be able to pay the initial costs."

"I explained all that to him, and that's when he told me both he and his wife were self-employed and had Internet-based businesses. They were both online on their computers every day."

Kelly started to laugh. She'd heard the smile in Steve's

voice. "Oh, brother. They will definitely need two solar arrays to bring in the power they need."

"That's what I told him. He got really quiet after that."

"Has his wife seen any of the places yet?"

"He's sent her the videos showing the landscapes from all four sites. She's flying into Denver tonight from Omaha. So tomorrow morning I'll take both of them out to see whatever is on their short list. He said he'll go over all the details with her tonight at dinner. They're staying in Downtown Denver at that new residence hotel."

"So you'll be staying in Denver again tonight? Darn."

"Yeah, it's easier to get an early start in the morning. That's assuming this couple want to see any of these mountain sites. Once he explains all the costs to his wife, they both may have a change of heart."

"For sure. Those thousands of dollars add up quickly when you're developing virgin mountain property. Pretty soon you're talking about real money."

Steve laughed softly. "Spoken like a CPA. That's why I've been talking with the real estate broker who handles a lot of these mountain sites. She's told me about another development that's closer in and less difficult to build on. Yet the properties are situated so they have that isolated feel with panoramic views. Anyway, we'll see if those sites live up to her salesman's description. I wanted to be able to show this couple something else in case they decide today's sites are a little too isolated."

"Smart. I'll bet you that couple is having that discussion right now. And tomorrow, they'll want to see those other sites." Kelly took a large sip of coffee, strong and black.

"We'll see. They have to decide where they want their house located. My job is to design a house that will fit that location."

"Plus you love the challenge," Kelly teased.

"Yeah, that, too," Steve admitted with another chuckle.

"Okay, I'll let you know how our game goes tonight. Don't forget, we're all getting together at Megan and Marty's tomorrow night."

"Got it on my schedule. Don't worry. I'll be back on time. It'll be fun to see what the little firecracker is up to."

"Cassie will be babysitting, so she'll have Molly under control."

Steve laughed out loud. "You hope."

Kelly had to join his laughter. *Ohhhhh, yes.*

As Kelly strolled through the quiet and empty patio garden, she spotted Megan getting out of her car in the driveway up ahead. "Hey, Megan!" She gave a wave.

Megan looked up and smiled. "Hi, Kelly. I thought I'd bring Molly over now, since it's late Friday afternoon. The shop is quieter."

Kelly watched with interest as Megan released a chubby-cheeked baby with a mop of fiery red curls from a car seat in the back of her automobile. "Come on, Molly. Let's go visit Mimi and Burt." Then Megan lowered the baby into a fabric and metal baby carrier. Molly's sturdy little legs kicked and wiggled as Megan secured straps around Molly.

"Boy, you've really got that down pretty slick. It used to take you a lot longer to get Molly into the carrier."

Maggie Sefton

"Practice, practice," Megan said with a wry smile as she slid her arms through the carrier and lifted baby Molly behind her back, facing forward.

"Hey, hey, Molly," Kelly said with a big smile. "Wanta go see Uncle Burt and Aunt Mimi?" Molly grinned back at Kelly and patted her mother's head.

"Here we go," Megan said, setting off toward the Lambspun front entry at her usual quick pace. Kelly did notice there was a slight slowdown, caused by the extra weight no doubt.

"How much does Molly weigh now? She looks bigger every time I see her. It's been two weeks, I think." Kelly walked alongside the twosome.

"She's ahead of schedule because she's almost tripled her birth weight now. Usually it's at a year. She's gonna be a big girl," Megan said as she climbed the steps to the wooden entry door, then abruptly stopped at the top step. "*Yeow!* Let go, Molly!" she cried out, eyes shut. Molly had a fistful of Megan's dark curls and yanked.

Kelly winced, watching. "Wow, that must hurt."

Megan reached behind her head and pried Molly's tiny fingers away from her hair. "Ohhhh, yeah. *Ow!* Let go, Molly!" Molly merely gurgled and gave one more yank before releasing her mother's curls.

"Here, let me get the door for you two," Kelly said, walking ahead of her friend.

"Let's see who's here," Megan said as she stepped inside. "Look, Molly! There's Mimi!"

Kelly watched Mimi's face light up as she spotted

34

Molly and Megan enter the shop. "Look who's here, Burt!" Mimi cried out. "Megan and Molly!" She dropped the yarn skeins in her hand into a basket and hurried over to greet them.

Molly broke into a big smile and waved her hands. "Kuh-kuh! Kuh-kuh!" She gurgled.

"Oh, my word!" Mimi clapped her hands. "She's talking!"

"Well, kind of," Megan said. "So far, it's mah-mah and da-da. But this week she started with the kuh-kuh. We think it's cookie."

"That makes sense," Kelly said. "Mimi gives her a cookie every time she comes here."

Mimi clapped her hands in front of Molly and made all sorts of cooing noises. Burt appeared from the loom room. "Well, well, if it isn't my favorite redhead! Hey, Molly!"

Kelly watched both Mimi and Burt make all sorts of cooing and funny sounds, all designed to elicit smiles and baby noises from Molly. For her part, Molly gurgled and grinned at the adults' antics. All intended for her amusement. Mimi and Burt were picture-book grandparents, to Kelly's way of thinking.

"Do you want some coffee, Megan? Jennifer always leaves a carafe for me in the café in the afternoon." Kelly said as she walked into the main room and dropped her briefcase bag onto the library table. Megan followed after Kelly and gently lowered the baby carrier behind her to the table.

"Do you want to come to Mimi? Do you?" Mimi beamed as she clapped her hands again.

"Let me slip out of this and I'll pick her up for you,"

Megan said, sliding one arm then another from the baby carrier, which was resting on the table.

"I can get her, Megan," Burt said, reaching over and releasing the straps around Molly and lifting her from the carrier. "My oh my, what a heavy girl you are, Molly."

"Nearly tripled her birth weight early," Megan said.

Mimi wagged her head in appreciative grandmotherly fashion. "Molly is doing everything early. She started walking a couple of weeks ago at nine months, and she's talking."

"More like babbling," Megan observed with a smile.

"That's how it starts," Burt added, holding Molly, who was staring across the room.

It seemed to Kelly like Molly was looking in the direction of the shelves where Mimi had stacks of colorful yarns arranged.

"You have a lot to say, don't you, Molly?" Mimi said, between cooing noises.

"She sure does," Burt chimed in. Molly, however, wasn't paying attention. She began to wiggle and squirm in Burt's arms. "Uh-oh, it looks like she wants to get down, Megan. Is it okay?" He glanced at Megan.

"Yep. But we're gonna have to watch her. She can clear out my bottom kitchen cabinets lightning fast."

"Ohhh, let her crawl, Burt. Molly wants to explore. We'll wash her little hands. I've got a container of wipes here on the table." Mimi leaned over and lifted a round familiar-looking plastic container of wipes.

Molly kept wiggling and making anxious little noises. "Okay, Molly, here you go." Burt lowered her gently to the floor in a sitting position.

Kelly watched as Molly looked around, from left to right, then started crawling—fast. Straight over to the bottom yarn bins, where she proceeded to scoop out every skein of yarn from one bin then reached into the neighboring bin. In a flash, those yarns lay on the floor as well.

Kelly had to laugh, as did Burt and Mimi, as Megan ran over to the bins and scooped up Molly under one arm. "Told you. We have to watch her like a hawk."

Molly protested loudly, sturdy legs kicking, obviously wanting to return to her fiber pursuits. Newly discovered colorful activities.

"Boy, if she's this fast now, she's gonna be a heckuva base runner when she's older," Kelly said, still laughing.

"Ohhhh, let her play, Megan," Mimi pleaded. "She's not hurting anything. They're yarn skeins."

Megan rolled her eyes. "I don't know, Mimi. She'll pull every single yarn skein out. They'll be all mixed up."

"Ohhh, pooh," Mimi said with a dismissive wave of her hand. In full grandmother mode now. "They're easy to sort out. Let her play."

"Yes, go ahead, Megan," Burt said with an indulgent smile. "My grandkids are all in elementary now. It's great to be around a baby again."

Megan wagged her head. "Okay, but don't say I didn't warn you," she said, returning a wiggling Molly back to the floor.

Kelly watched in amusement as Molly took off like a shot, straight to the yarn bins, and proceeded to clear out the remaining lower bins. Then, she stood up on those sturdy little legs and cleared out the four bins above.

• • •

"Hey, folks," Pete said, and he and Jennifer stepped inside Megan and Marty's foyer, Cassie right behind them. "I hope you've got some of those cheesy bites you made last time, Megan."

"We saved some for you guys," Megan said as she walked into her kitchen and pointed to a small tray on the counter. "Cassie, I fixed a separate plate for you with some things to munch on while we're all at dinner."

"Thanks, Megan," Cassie said with a big smile as she walked into the great room, where Kelly and Steve and the rest of the gang relaxed, bottles of craft brews in hand. "Where's Molly?"

Marty popped from around the corner of Molly's small bedroom. "Hey, Molly, look who's here. Cassie!" He hiked Molly up onto his shoulders and held on to her legs as he strode over to join the group.

"Careful, Marty!" Lisa warned, hand reaching up.

"He's not going to drop her," Greg reassured her.

"I don't know," Kelly said, peering at Marty as he bounced into the room. "When he does stuff like this, I remember how clumsy he was when we first met him."

"You mean, when we first met Spot, the Wonder Dog?" Steve joked as he leaned back on the sofa.

Molly, meanwhile, was laughing happily as her father danced around with her, both little fists clasping Marty's red hair.

"Okay, Molly, time to let go," Marty said, and Molly gave several yanks.

"Ooooooo, I remember baby hair yanks from babysitting my cousins' kids when I was in high school," Jennifer said.

"But it's so much fun," Marty said, grimacing once again.

Cassie walked over then and clapped both hands in front of Molly and Marty. "Hey, Molly! I've got a special treat for you! Wanta see it? Wanta see it?"

Molly's attention immediately shifted to Cassie's smiling face. She released her death grip on Marty's hair and reached both arms out for Cassie.

"That's a girl," Cassie said, taking Molly into her arms.

"She's got the magic touch," Kelly said, watching Cassie do a little bounce step while she held Molly.

"Thank goodness," Megan said, coming back into the room, a Fat Tire ale in her hand. "We tried using some of the nursing students at first, then some older babysitters that had recommendations." Megan rolled her eyes. "None of them worked out that well. They all said Molly cried a whole lot while we were gone."

"And that made you guys feel awful, I'm sure," Lisa said, leaning against boyfriend Greg, who was perched on the arm of a huge cushioned chair beside the sofa.

"Oh, yeah," Marty agreed, squatting down on a hassock beside a comfy chair.

"Well, I'm sure glad Kelly told us about that babysitting class early this summer," Jennifer said as she leaned against the kitchen counter. "Cassie loved it, and she learned a lot. Even CPR techniques on babies and children. She was already hoping to start babysitting this summer, so it was perfect timing."

"Look what I've got," Cassie said, reaching into her jeans

pocket and bringing out a small gray elephant. "An elephant! See his trunk."

She held the flexible little toy closer to Molly, who immediately reached for it and brought it straight to her mouth.

"That's her ID check," Marty said, chuckling.

"Don't worry, I washed it off carefully before I brought it over," Cassie reassured him.

"Did you pay for that with your babysitting money?" Pete asked with a grin. "That was thoughtful of you."

"It sure was, sweetie. You didn't need to do that," Megan said.

"Better start saving that money for college, kid," Greg teased. "The university keeps raising tuition, even for Colorado residents."

"Oh, I am saving," Cassie said, swaying side to side with a little bounce in between. "Eric's saving for a car already. He doesn't get paid for chores around his folks' ranch, but Uncle Curt pays him to do chores around his ranch. Eric's got a bank account and everything."

Kelly glanced over at Pete and Jennifer. "I think that's a subtle hint, guys. Better take her to the bank before school starts."

"Sounds like a good plan, Cassie," Pete told his niece. "Let's find an afternoon this next week when we can go over to the bank together and start a savings account for you."

Cassie beamed. "Thanks, Uncle Pete. I've been keeping it in a jewelry box. That'll be great." She glanced around the room, where Kelly and friends were relaxing. "Are you guys gonna try to get dinner before the game or afterwards?"

Steve checked his watch. "We were going to grab something at the concession stand before we have to take the field and start to warm-up. Then we thought we'd stop in Old Town for pizza afterwards. Is that too late for you?" He glanced to Pete and Jennifer. "How late is she allowed to stay up babysitting on a Saturday night?"

"Jen and I talked about it and decided eleven o'clock would be her deadline. Until she's older, that is." He grinned at Cassie.

"Okay, there we have it," Steve said, shifting forward in the chair. "We have our marching orders. Shouldn't be a problem."

"You know, you guys should start leaving now," Cassie said, nodding toward the door. "Molly's playing with the elephant, and we're going over to the corner with the toy box. But first, we can go into her room and grab her favorite teddy bear."

"Smart strategy," Greg said, smiling, then stood up. "Let's do as Cassie says and go while the going's good."

"Sounds good," Pete said with a grin, escorting Jennifer toward the front door. "Cassie, we'll see you later. I'd give you a kiss but I don't want to draw attention to the Group Exit."

"You got it, Uncle Pete," Cassie said with a grin, then bounced and danced toward the enormous toy box in the corner of Megan and Marty's great room. Molly was still gnawing on the elephant.

Megan put her Fat Tire bottle on the counter. "I hope that thing isn't made of something toxic," she said softly as Marty beckoned her toward the door.

"Don't worry, Megan," Cassie's voice called from the corner. "I looked up the manufacturer online and checked reviews."

"Come on, honey," Marty called to Megan, who had hurried over to give Molly a quick kiss on the cheek. Molly gurgled and bopped her mother on the head with the gray elephant.

Kelly laughed quietly as she and Steve placed their empty bottles on the counter and they started toward the door. "This generation is gonna be so wired. I love it."

"Oh, yeah," Steve said with a grin. "See you later, Cassie," Steve said with a wave as he and Kelly walked out the door. Greg and Lisa were already outside getting into their car, as were Pete and Jennifer. Megan and Marty were walking toward their driveway.

Another beautiful summer night in Fort Connor, Kelly thought as she and Steve walked to his truck. Tonight should bring another fat and full moon. She could see it now pale in the still-bright August sky. Steve had been right. He'd told her the gang would still be able to get together once Megan and Marty became parents. They would simply use a babysitter, like their other acquaintances did. And what a perfect babysitting solution they had found in Cassie.

Four

"**Well,** hi there," Kelly said to Lisa as she walked into Lambspun's main room.

Monday afternoon had been busier than usual, so a fiber and knitting break was in order. Kelly plopped her knitting bag onto the library table. She could hear the sounds of voices coming from the adjoining workroom and figured Mimi or someone was teaching a class.

"You must be caught up with your accounts and are taking a break like I am," Lisa said as she looked up from the rose red yarn she was working. Kelly couldn't tell what it was going to be yet, because there were only a few rows of stitches on Lisa's needles.

"Right you are," Kelly said as she settled into a chair across the table from Lisa. "My Denver client has been moving and shaking again. He's remodeling a sports store in one of the larger shopping centers in Northglenn. It's one of the largest in the Denver suburbs, so there're always a lot of customers. But apparently, there have been some customer complaints that a few of the more extreme winter sports didn't have enough equipment carried in that store. So it looks like inventory numbers will be increasing along with the remodeling."

"I just love it when you talk accounting," Lisa teased. "Inventory sounds so sexy."

"I guess it depends on what's in the inventory," Kelly played along. "If it was a lingerie store like some of those we see in the malls, then the inventory could be described as sexy."

Kelly pulled out the scarf she was knitting for Mimi's charity project. Royal blue yarn dangled from the needles. Another row and Kelly could start to bind off. Almost finished. She picked up the stitches where she'd left off. "How's your friend Nancy doing? Have you spoken to her? I have to admit I've thought about her and the situation with her pregnancy."

Lisa's expression sobered. "Yes, I saw her at the university yesterday. And she said she finally got her things out of the other apartment and was moving back home with her dad."

"How did he react when she told him about the coming baby?" Kelly glanced up briefly from her stitches. The familiar rhythm was settling in now. Sliding the needle under the stitch. Wrapping the yarn. Sliding the stitch off one needle onto the other. *Slip, wrap, slide. Slip, wrap, slide.* Another yarn row forming on her needles.

"She was going to tell him last night. I was hoping to see her today after I'd finished my classes, but she wasn't around. Maybe tomorrow."

The tinkling doorbell sounded around the corner from the foyer. In a minute Nancy Marsted walked into the main room. Propitious timing, Kelly thought, as she watched Nancy give her a quick smile then hurry over to the other side of the table next to Lisa.

"Hey there, Nancy," Lisa said with a welcoming smile. "I've been thinking about you. Are you all settled in at your dad's house?"

Nancy nodded, medium brown hair falling across her forehead. She brushed it back. "Yes, I brought all my stuff over last night and moved in."

"Did you have a chance to talk with him?" Lisa asked in a quieter voice.

Nancy glanced briefly at Kelly, and Kelly stopped knitting, ready to get up and move into the workroom with the current class.

"Kelly was worried that you looked so upset the other day, so I shared your news with her. Kelly is very discreet and she also gives good advice. So we can speak freely."

A little surprised by Lisa's compliment, Kelly spoke up. "I hope you're feeling okay, Nancy. Are you seeing a doctor yet? I remember how Megan was those first few months when she was pregnant with Molly."

"Not yet," Nancy said, looking down a trifle bashfully.

"Don't worry. I know about all the good doctors here in Fort Connor," Lisa said with an authoritative nod.

"And our friend Megan is a great reference, too. She is mega-detail-oriented and she's got recommendations for everything," Kelly added.

"Now, how did your talk with your father go?"

"Oh, my dad was really understanding, like always," Nancy said earnestly. "In fact, he's kind of excited about the baby. He's been lonely ever since my mom died three years ago. That's not what I'm worried about."

"Oh?" Lisa put her needles down in her lap. "What's bothering you?"

"My dad said he was going to have a talk with Neil . . . my boyfriend." Nancy glanced down briefly. "And I have a bad feeling about that. Neil is still refusing to talk to me. I tried to talk with him after a class yesterday, and he just ignored me and walked away." This time Nancy stared at her hands in her lap, her fingers clasped tightly together.

"Nancy, your father is an experienced counselor. I know him," Lisa said and leaned forward toward Nancy. "I've seen him work with others. He's in charge of counseling newcomers to an Alcoholics Anonymous group in town. He's used to handling all sorts of situations. I don't think you should worry. In fact, he may be able to meet with your boyfriend and get through to him."

Yeah, and let Neil know he's a jerk, Kelly thought to herself. But she didn't say anything. She didn't want to interrupt the quiet counseling Lisa was engaged in with Nancy. Kelly could tell how anxious Nancy was when she noticed her bitten fingernails. The first time Kelly met Nancy a few days ago, she'd noticed how nicely manicured Nancy's nails were. No more. Nancy's understandable stress had taken a toll on her hands.

"I hope so. But . . . but my dad is always optimistic about things. Even years ago when he was still drinking, I remember he would always encourage me and convince me I could solve any problem." A little smile flirted with the corners of Nancy's mouth. "He'd say, 'You can do it, Sunshine. You can do anything you set your mind to.'"

Kelly let her needles rest in her lap, watching Nancy's face. The anxious expression had vanished for a moment and she'd brightened visibly. But only for a moment, then the worry returned.

"He calls you Sunshine?" Kelly asked, smiling at Nancy. "That brings back memories of my father. He used to call me 'Tiger' when I was growing up."

"Boy, was your dad psychic or what?" Lisa teased. "If we have a problem with someone, we sic Kelly on them. She'll go toe-to-toe with them. In your face." Lisa laughed, eyes dancing.

"Lies, all lies," Kelly said with a dismissive wave of her hand, joining Lisa's playfulness. Nancy looked like she could do with a few moments of lighthearted conversation.

Nancy's little smile returned. "Your father sounds a lot like mine. Does he live here?"

"He used to years ago. In fact, I grew up here until I was twelve, then we had to move. But my dad is dead now. Smoking."

Kelly picked up her knitting needles again. "Did you grow up here in Fort Connor? Lots of the university students are local."

"No, my dad and I moved here six years ago after my mom died. We lived in Wisconsin, where my dad and mom grew up. But I finished high school here. We both fell in love with Fort Connor and Colorado when we got here. The mountains and the Cache La Poudre River running through town."

"That sounds like most of us," Lisa said, picking up her needles again, too.

"Boy, how many times have I heard that story?" Kelly asked with a smile. "I wish I had a dollar for every time I've heard that a university student decided to stay here once they came."

Lisa leaned over and placed her hand on Nancy's arm. "Don't worry, Nancy. Your father is just being your dad. He wants to talk to your boyfriend Neil. And I'm sure it will go well. Let's think positive, okay? Maybe your dad can get through Neil's attitude."

Kelly had to bite her lip to keep from adding "Neil's bad attitude" to the end of Lisa's sentence. Nancy didn't say anything, simply gave a little nod. But Kelly noticed her momentarily relaxed fingers had clenched each other tightly once more.

Just then, a cheerful voice came into the room. "Well, hello, girls!" Mimi chirped, giving them a bright smile. "I don't believe I know your friend, Lisa."

"Mimi, this is Nancy Marsted. She's a graduate student at the university, too. We met in one of our classes together, and I convinced her to start knitting."

Mimi's pretty face lit up. "That's wonderful! I'm so glad you stopped by to visit us, Nancy. What are you working on?"

Nancy gave Mimi a small smile. "I've started a baby sweater but I haven't gotten very far. I'm not really very good at knitting."

"Well, we can certainly help with that," Mimi said, walking around to that side of the table. "Do you have it with you, dear? I'd be glad to help you if you'd like." Mimi pulled out the chair next to Nancy.

"Well, yes . . . it's down in the bottom of my shoulder bag," Nancy said with a sheepish look as she lifted her large fabric bag from the floor. She dug into the bag and pulled out a tangled mass of yarn and two dangling needles. "Uh-oh, I'm afraid I've ruined it."

Mimi gave a little wave of her hand. "Nonsense, we specialize in rescuing knitting projects, don't we, girls?" She gently took the tangled mess from Nancy's hands.

Lisa and Kelly exchanged a glance and nodded dutifully as they answered in unison, "Absolutely." Mother Mimi to the rescue. Perfect timing.

Kelly pulled her car into a parking space in the driveway between the knitting shop and her cottage. Being inside her car with the air-conditioning, Kelly felt the shock of the August heat the moment she stepped from her car. Thank goodness August usually marked the time when the hotter temperatures of the summer gradually moderated week by week into the lower eighties by the end of the month or early September.

Slipping her briefcase bag over her shoulder, Kelly grabbed her travel mug and walked into the green shade of the café's garden patio. It was time for a refill after spending the morning with client Arthur Housemann debating which rental property would be a better purchase.

Her cell phone jangled then and Kelly deliberately stepped sideways along the flagstone path so as not to disturb the customers enjoying lunch at the outside tables dotted among the flowering bushes and decorative trees. Steve's name appeared on the phone screen.

"Hey there. Are you going to be down from that mountain property in time to make it to the game tonight?"

"I should be. I'm actually on the edge of Denver now at a coffee shop off the interstate," Steve's voice came over the phone. "After I get some things done at the office, I can head home. Of course, there's rush hour, but what else is new?"

"Sounds like a plan. I'll already be at Rolland Moore field since our game starts early at six. So don't rush heading over there. You'll have time to stop by a fast food place or a deli and grab something better than concession fare. Cassie's team doesn't start playing until seven thirty."

"That's a good idea. By the end of the season, concession park franks are getting a little tired." He chuckled.

"I hear you. Drive safely, and look out for the crazies, okay?"

"Always. See you later." Steve's phone clicked off.

Kelly dropped her cell phone back into her bag and started to move away from the shady corner of the garden when Jennifer walked over to her. "Do you have a minute, Kelly?"

"Sure, what's up?"

Jennifer gestured to a nearby empty table. "Why don't we sit down. Lunchtime is winding down so Julie can handle it. If she needs my help, she'll give me a wave."

"Sounds like a good idea. You probably need to get off your feet by now anyway," Kelly said as she settled into a black wrought iron chair.

Jennifer sat across the circular table and momentarily closed her eyes. "Wow, it does feel good to sit down."

Kelly smiled and waved at passing waitress Julie. "Jen will never ask for it, but could you snag her an iced tea while you fill up my mug, please?"

"Sure, no problem," Julie said with a bright smile. "I'm glad you got her to take a break. Jen usually refuses."

"I've got the magic touch," Kelly said with a laugh. Watching Julie walk away, Kelly glanced at her longtime friend. "So what's going on? Everything okay?"

"Yeah, the café's going great. I just thought I'd give you an update. Pete spoke with Cassie last night after ball practice and told her that her mother, Tanya, wants her to come down to Denver for a weekend before school starts to spend some time with her."

Kelly stared at her friend's face. She noticed some of the worry lines she'd seen the other day. "What did Cassie say to that idea? I mean, how did she respond? Were you there when they talked?"

Jennifer nodded. "Yes, I was there while they talked. Cassie was confused, understandably. I could tell from the expression on her face. She asked Pete why. 'Why does my mom want to see me now?'"

"Good question. That would be the first thing I'd ask, too. Why, after all those years of ignoring her, would Tanya suddenly become interested?"

Jennifer caught Kelly's gaze. "That was my first thought, too. But I kept it to myself."

"What did Pete say? Cassie's a smart girl. He'd have to give her a believable reason."

"Yeah. And I think he did. Pete explained that it was really important to Tanya. And she wanted to get to know Cassie better before she was all grown up."

Kelly felt that resonate inside, and she nodded. "That is a good reason. What did Cassie say?"

"I could tell it made sense to her, watching her face," Jennifer said as she glanced toward the green bushes. Thickened by summer's heat and regular watering, their leaves had grown wide and fat, spreading like waiting fans in the quiet and still shade.

Another thought surfaced in the back of Kelly's mind. "There's only one thing which could complicate that. Softball season is coming to a close. The league championship games have started already. They're playing tonight in the second round. And the final games won't be until next weekend. Cassie probably won't want to miss those games, I'm guessing."

Jennifer smiled. "You guess right. Cassie brought that up first thing. She said she couldn't go to Denver until those games were over. And that leaves the last weekend in August as the only one available. The following weekend is Labor Day, and Pete and I have already promised we'd join Mimi and Burt and Cassie on a camping trip up in Cache La Poudre Canyon."

"Oh, yes, I remember Mimi saying something about that." Kelly grinned. "Apparently Mimi and Burt and Cassie will be doing all the cooking so you two can sit back and relax."

"That's exactly how they explained it," Jennifer said with a smile. "Of course, I'm not big on camping outdoors, but Burt has assured me they have special tents with comfy air mattresses and all that." She wagged her head. "But I don't know. The idea of trying to walk out in the dark to the outdoor privy, well, that's not exactly my idea of a good time. I'm afraid there would be a bear waiting for me behind some tree."

Kelly sank back in the chair and laughed out loud. "I don't think you'd have to worry about bears waiting for you in the dark. Those are small black bears up in the canyon anyway. About a hundred pounds."

"That's big enough to do some damage."

"Shoot. Carl almost weighs that. He's over ninety pounds."

"Even so, a hundred pounds is big enough to be scary."

"Actually, the only one who'd be hunting at night would be puma. Mountain lions. Cats hunt at night," Kelly said with a deliberately wicked smile.

Jennifer's eyes popped wide. "Thank you *so* much, Kelly! Now I'm really scared. I'll probably cower in the tent next to Pete all night."

"You can always take Carl up in the canyon with you. Of course, he'll be barking during the night whenever he hears all the different creatures moving around." She grinned.

Jennifer gave her an exasperated look. "You are impossible, you know that. I'm going to tell Julie to substitute hot tea for your coffee," Jennifer teased as she pushed back her chair.

"So it's decided then? Cassie will go down to Denver weekend after next."

Jennifer nodded as she gave a little stretch. Julie was walking their way with a glass of iced tea and Kelly's coffee mug. "Yes. Pete called Tanya last night and told her that was the only weekend Cassie had free before school began. And after the school year started, the fall sports season had games scheduled every weekend. So it's that weekend or wait until holiday vacation days."

"Well, I hope Tanya understands. Cassie has made a life for herself here, and her mother will simply have to accommodate herself to it if she wants to see her daughter." Kelly reached out to accept her coffee mug from Julie's outstretched hand.

"Here you go, Kelly," Julie said, then handed the iced tea to Jennifer. "Sit down, Jen. You can talk to Kelly longer. Three couples have already left and the other two tables are still talking. No rush."

"Thanks, Julie. I appreciate that. I have to take this new client out to some of the new housing developments in Fort Connor. So we'll be climbing lots of bare staircases and scrambling over dirt all afternoon."

"Be careful in those new houses," Kelly warned. "I've been to several that my client Housemann is building. And those new-built staircases are just wooden planks nailed together in some places. No sides, no backs even. Empty spaces to fall through all over the place. Dangerous."

"Don't worry," Jennifer said, returning to her chair. "I'm very careful in those new houses. They can be hazardous to a real estate agent's health."

"For sure," Julie said with a vigorous nod. "And for the record, I agree with you guys. Cassie's absentee mom will simply have to change her schedule to fit in with Cassie's. Tanya can't just show up and expect Cassie to drop everything and go see her. Not after her mom has practically ignored her all these years." Julie's pretty face had puckered with a frown. "That's just my two cents. So there." And with a nod, Julie turned and hurried back to the grill counter. Back to work.

Kelly looked over at her friend, who was smiling after Julie. Kelly waited until Jennifer turned back to her then said, "So *there*." And gave a definitive nod of her own.

Five

Kelly's cell phone sounded from inside her cottage as she poured fresh water into Carl's large doggy bowl on the backyard patio. Carl immediately began to slurp, long pink tongue splashing water from the bowl.

Kelly slid the patio screen door closed and snatched her ringing phone from the kitchen counter. Lisa's name flashed on the screen. "Hey there. Are you coming to Cassie's game tonight? League games have already started."

"You bet. I love watching the kids play. Greg will have to miss it because a student friend has a thesis party. I just heard from Megan, too. She was not able to schedule an earlier babysitter so Marty will be coming to the game alone. She hates to miss it, but we'll see her afterwards at your house."

"It's hard to believe that the school year will start in a couple of weeks. Cassie will be a freshman in high school."

"I know what you mean. Watching Cassie and Eric grow like weeds these last two years, it's really amazing."

"Yeah, I know. It seems like only a few months ago Cassie came to live with Jennifer and Pete." Kelly took a sip from her everyday mug on the counter. The last of her morning coffee. "I've got to start on my client accounts now, but I haven't decided if I'll go on over to the patio garden or inside the shop to work. It's gorgeous outside and will be in the eighties all day."

"I know. I wish I could be outside but I've got physical therapy patients all this morning, and then I'll be going over my research notes for this psych paper I'm writing. So I'll be working this afternoon."

"Hey, why don't you come over to the garden patio and study your notes there? No need to close yourself up in some building. I work outside in that patio all the time. Even with customers at the tables. Believe me, it doesn't disturb my concentration at all."

"Hmmmmm, that is tempting."

"C'mon. Do yourself a favor. It's the middle of August, and September will be here, and the regular university school year will start. Then you'll be taking another psych class. Enjoy summer while you can."

"Boy, you are one heckuva salesman, Kelly. I think you're wasted doing accounting."

Kelly had to laugh. "Ohhhh, no. My dad was a salesman for a national auto parts manufacturer. And I remember how much work he had to put into getting sales. Regularly. Every day. That's a hard job. Accounting is easy compared to that."

"Easy? Ha! Easy for you maybe," Lisa teased. "Listen, I've got to get to the sports medicine clinic. My patient will be there in half an hour. I'll see you tonight at the ball field."

"No, you can see me this afternoon in the café patio garden like I suggested," Kelly countered.

Lisa's soft laughter sounded over the phone before she clicked off.

Kelly shoved her phone into her white summer pants pocket, then grabbed her empty travel mug and her briefcase bag and headed for the cottage front door. She might as well take her own advice and find a comfy small outdoor table in the café patio garden and start on her client accounts. Besides, one of Eduardo's yummy cinnamon rolls would easily serve as breakfast.

Stepping outside in the beautiful sunny August morning, Kelly checked the cars in the driveway. Breakfast customers. Carl barked once behind her and she turned to see her rottweiler behind the chain-link fence. It was made secure years ago by an addition to the top of the fence to make sure Carl the Explorer didn't go roaming again.

"Keep those squirrels in line, Carl," Kelly called to her dog. Carl woofed once in reply then trotted back into the yard to do as he was bade.

Kelly walked slowly over to the garden patio, glancing around her and savoring the view of the Rockies in the distance behind the outlines of Old Town Fort Connor. Once more, she was glad that years ago she'd decided to leave the East Coast and stay in Fort Connor and make it her home. Even though that decision meant Kelly had to walk away from her corporate CPA career in Washington, DC, to create an entirely new accounting career in Fort Connor. And she had done so.

Now, Kelly's high-level accounting expertise was completely focused on two clients. Both of them extremely successful businessmen in entirely different areas. Both of them more than satisfied with the corporate-level accounting that Kelly provided. One of them, Arthur Housemann, older and wiser, called Kelly's level of service "concierge accounting." Something available to just a privileged few. Kelly had laughed at that description and wished her father were still alive to share her success. But then she looked around her world and her life in Fort Connor, and she knew she had more than enough "family" to share success and struggles with. Kelly counted herself lucky.

As she strolled into the patio garden itself, Kelly spotted a table beside the small outdoor classroom building in the corner of the garden. Kelly promptly claimed it, setting her briefcase bag on the table, and pulled out a chair.

"Hey, Kelly, can I get you some coffee?" Julie asked as she walked along the flagstone path, tray in one hand.

"You're reading my mind again, Julie," Kelly said and handed over her oversized mug.

"I'll be right back," Julie promised.

Kelly settled in at the table and pulled out her laptop and client files. The sound of traffic along the busy street was muffled by the tall stucco walls that surrounded the back and side walls of the garden and café.

"Hey there, Kelly," another familiar voice called.

Kelly looked up to see Father Figure Burt walking

through the garden, heading her way. "Hey, Burt. Want to join me for a cinnamon roll?"

"Don't tempt me, Kelly," Burt said as he walked up. "I'm trying to stay on my diet. Mimi and I both. We slipped a few times when we were in Denver. Found some new restaurants."

"You and Mimi deserve to 'slip' every now and then, if you ask me," Kelly decreed in her best executive tone. "Both of you are far too good." Kelly gave Burt an enigmatic smile as she pushed her files and computer across the table. Julie was headed her way with a newly filled coffee mug.

"Here you go, Kelly. Can I get you anything else?" Julie slipped her waitress pad from the pocket of her summer pants.

"Matter of fact, you can bring me one of those yummy cinnamon rolls," Kelly said. "And bring two forks, would you, please? I'm trying to corrupt Burt."

"Oh, Lord," Burt said with a sigh and shook his head. "Believe me, Kelly, neither Mimi nor I need any encouragement to corrupt our diet plans. We're quite capable of doing that ourselves."

Julie gave a little laugh. "All right. One cinnamon roll and two forks coming up. Can I get you some coffee to go with that, Burt?"

"Oh, why not? It looks like I'm going to need it. Kelly's in a rare mood. I'll need the extra caffeine."

"One bite won't hurt," Kelly tempted again.

Burt eyed her over the table. "That's the problem, Kelly. One bite easily leads to another and another."

"Have you and Mimi been doing your cardio workouts on the treadmills? That's the best way to compensate for a sudden caloric intake," Kelly said then took a deep drink of Eduardo's dark brew. Black Gold.

"Mostly every day. So we are being pretty good with that. But at our ages, we have to watch the food *and* do the exercise. Can't do one without the other, or the pounds stay on." He eyed Kelly with a devilish smile. "You and your friends are getting a free ride now because you're in your thirties. You work out regularly, and you can eat all the pizza you want as well as French fries and ballpark desserts. But wait a few years, and you'll notice the pounds take longer to come off. And you have to work harder, too."

Kelly pondered Burt's advice. "Sage words. I'll store them away for future reference," she said, suddenly remembering something she wanted to ask Burt. "Changing the subject, has Jennifer talked to you and Mimi about Cassie's mother, Tanya?"

Burt's amused smile disappeared. His entire visage changed. Frown and worry lines that were obscured by a smile only moments ago were plainly visible now. "Yes, she and Pete spoke with us early this morning before the café opened."

"What do you think about it?" Kelly deliberately held back more of her response. She was more interested in Burt's reaction.

"I have to say I wasn't entirely surprised. It's not unusual for a young woman in Tanya's situation to suddenly decide she wants to get to know the child she'd placed in a relative's care years ago. Usually it happens when the child becomes a teenager, and the mother realizes that the baby they'd walked away from is nearly grown up. I'm sure it's a shock to Tanya."

Burt's thoughtful response gave Kelly pause. She realized her first reactions had been entirely emotional, based on what she assumed were Tanya's selfish motives.

"You're kinder in your comments than I was when Jen told me," Kelly admitted. "I confess I haven't had many good thoughts about Tanya's announcement. Cassie's created a life here, and she's surrounded by people who love her and care about what happens to her. I guess that's what upsets me. Tanya thinking she can simply walk in and yank Cassie away from all that on a whim."

Burt gave Kelly a fatherly smile she recognized. "That's understandable, Kelly. I feel like that, too. But Pete and Jennifer have to be fair to Tanya and honor her wishes. Especially now that they're going to file for custody. After all, she is Cassie's birth mother."

"You're right, of course," Kelly said begrudgingly. "I'm only thinking of Cassie and Pete and Jennifer."

"And us," Burt added as Julie walked up to them.

"Here you go, Kelly. One cinnamon roll and two forks." Julie placed the yummy-looking homemade pastry on the table and two bundles of napkin-wrapped silverware.

"Thanks, Julie. This looks delicious as usual. And smells divine," Kelly said, sniffing the cinnamon-and-cloves aroma that wafted up from the warm pastry.

"Ohhhh, Lord," Burt said with a sigh. "I feel my resistance crumbling by the second."

"Go on, Burt. One bite won't hurt," Julie tempted before she left to check on other breakfast customers.

Kelly unwrapped the knife and fork and gently sliced into the tender glaze-topped cinnamon roll. She lifted a scrumptious-looking bite to her mouth and savored. "Ummmmmmmmm."

Burt laughed softly and picked up his silverware.

Kelly tabbed through the spreadsheet columns that filled her laptop screen. Don Warner's newest Denver development project was already generating expenses. Revenues would not appear for many more months. Kelly was glad she'd been able to convince Warner to establish an extra account to ensure there were enough funds to cover these early developmental costs on new projects.

Her cell phone jangled, jarring Kelly out of her numbers-induced trance. She picked up the phone sitting beside her laptop. Lisa's name flashed. "Hey there. Are you coming over here to enjoy the summer greenery outside? It's after one o'clock."

"No, I won't get there, Kelly. I'm over here at the university in the outdoor café at the student center plaza. Nancy came up to me after our class, and she was really concerned about her father. Last night he went to see Nancy's old boyfriend, Neil, and, well . . . apparently their meeting didn't go well."

"Really? I thought you said her father was a counselor for AA and for some other local agencies."

"Yes, he is. But Nancy says her dad must have lost his temper because he came back to their house all upset. He'd gone into Neil's favorite bar over in Old Town to talk to him. And apparently instead of talking reasonably, they had an argument. I'm trying to get the rest of the details from Nancy. She's really upset. Crying about Neil, and crying about her dad. She's in the restroom now, wiping the smeared makeup off her face from all the crying."

"Crying about her dad? Why? Just because he lost his temper? I'd lose my temper at that sleazeball Neil, too." Kelly took a deep drink of coffee.

"Not just that. Nancy thinks her dad started drinking again. She says he got home really late. And he was talking differently, the way he did before he quit drinking. And she could smell it on his breath."

"Uh-oh. Not good, not good at all."

"That's for sure."

"It sounds like you're trying to counsel Nancy."

"I'm doing my best. I told her I'd be glad to take her to the women's health center next to the university. That way she can register and start educating herself on prenatal care and make an appointment to see a nurse practitioner. She should have a checkup to make sure there are no health problems that could worsen with pregnancy. Like early-onset diabetes."

"Oh, boy, that's excellent advice. It sounds like she's definitely keeping the baby."

"Yes, and she's very serious about nutrition. So that's good."

"Oh, yeah. I remember everything that Megan was doing when she was pregnant with Molly. All the vitamins and minerals and healthy foods. I swear, I don't think she had a slice of pizza until after Molly was born," Kelly said with a laugh.

"You're right. Listen, I see Nancy coming back to the table. I'll see you tonight at the game. Six o'clock."

"You got it. See you then. Give Nancy my best."

"Will do," Lisa said before her phone clicked off.

Kelly looked around at the lunch diners, eating, talking, and relaxing in the balmy August afternoon. Checking her mug, Kelly decided to work inside for a little while. Her previously shady table was now fully in the sun, and sun glare on her laptop screen was annoying. Gathering up her laptop and client files, Kelly headed for the back door of the café. She might as well put in an order for iced coffee while she was passing through.

Climbing the wooden steps to the original front door of the café, Kelly paused to notice again the forgotten cement pathway that wound around the side of the sprawling beige stucco red-tile-roofed farmhouse turned knitting shop. Back when her aunt and uncle owned the farmhouse decades ago, there were only two long wooden tables nestled in the greenery. And only her uncle's truck and her aunt's car parked outside the stucco walls surrounding the patio garden. Now several cars were parked along the back and the sides of the café and the Lambspun shop. Customers.

Spotting Jennifer, Kelly waved her mug and placed it on a nearby tray stand. "When you get a chance, can I have an iced coffee fill-up, please?"

"We'll take care of it," Jennifer said as she balanced a loaded tray on her hip. "Cassie's in the main room putting away a new yarn order that just came in."

"Oh, good. I haven't seen her in a couple of days," Kelly said as she walked toward the corridor that led to the center of the shop and the main room with its long library table. She saw Cassie as soon as she entered. A large pile of multicolored yarns were stacked at the end of the library table. "Hey, Cassie, you're helping Mimi with the latest yarn shipment, I hear."

Cassie turned quickly and gave Kelly a big smile. Kelly noticed again how the young fourteen-year-old girl's face was slowly changing. Subtle changes, moving from childhood to adulthood. Childish plump cheeks slimming down.

"Hey, Kelly. I'm adding this new shipment to the last ones left in these yarn bins. It'll be a little tight, but there's nowhere else to put them." She picked up two more slender oval-shaped skeins and wedged them into the top of one of the yarn bins.

Kelly settled into a chair nearby and took out her laptop and client files. She intended to finish the almost-completed expense worksheet, but first she wanted to grab this quiet moment when she and Cassie had the main knitting room all to themselves.

Julie appeared then with Kelly's mug. "Iced coffee, Kelly. We'll leave a pitcher for you up front if you like," she said, placing the mug on the table.

"That'll be great, thank you, Julie."

"No problem," the waitress said as she sped from the room. Back to the customers.

Kelly relaxed into the chair and took a long cooling sip of iced coffee. Black and strong. Just the way she liked it, either hot or cold. She waited until Cassie had finished with the entire pile of yarns before she spoke. "Are you ready for tonight's game? Most of us will be there. Lisa said Greg will be at a student friend's thesis party, so he'll have to miss it."

"Yeah, we're ready. I think we can beat Arvada this time," Cassie said as she plopped herself into the chair not far from Kelly's. She dangled one long leg over the side of the chair.

Teenage sprawl. Kelly recognized it from all the years she'd coached teenage girls' sports teams. And from her own memories of herself growing up. Gangliness gradually gave way to coordination. Arms and legs moving together smoothly. Or would be. Everyone matured differently.

"I think you guys can do it," Kelly agreed, then paused for a moment. "Jennifer told me that your mom, Tanya, wants you to come down to Denver with her for a weekend." She watched Cassie's face for a reaction.

Cassie glanced down and picked up some yarn fibers from the table. "Yeah. Pete says my mom really wants to see me before the school year starts."

"Well, the championship games are this weekend, but the following weekend is free. So I guess you'll go then, right?"

Cassie gave one of those inscrutable teenaged girl shrugs. Inscrutable to all except those who remembered their own teenaged years. "Yeah," she said, fingering the bright red fibers of a silk scarf another knitter had left on the table. Halfway finished, it was still luscious.

"It sounds like your mom wants to have a chance to spend some time with you. You're growing up so fast."

A partial shrug this time. "I guess," Cassie said, picking up the red yarn and running her fingers across the stitches.

Kelly paused, then said quietly, "Were you kind of surprised she asked?"

This time Cassie's voice changed. Still examining the red yarn, she said simply, "Yeah." One word. But Kelly could distinctly hear the unspoken message in her tone. *Well, yeah! It's about time.*

Kelly took a sip of iced coffee while she chose her next words. She set the mug on the table and leaned back into the chair. "I don't think I ever told you this, Cassie, but my mother walked out on my father and me when I was five months old."

Cassie's head jerked up, and her big blue eyes stared at Kelly. "*What!* Are you serious?"

Kelly nodded. "Absolutely. My dad said my mom left a note saying that she didn't think she could handle taking care of a baby anymore. She was afraid of being a bad mother, so she left."

Cassie stared, then finally said, "That's . . . that's awful."

Kelly gave an inscrutable shrug of her own. "You know, I didn't think about it much when I was growing up. My dad was great and adored me. And Aunt Helen and Uncle Jim did, too, so I never felt a lack of love. And when I looked around at other friends' families, I saw a lot of divorced moms and dads. So it was okay."

"Did you ever hear from her?"

Kelly shook her head. "Never. My dad didn't mention her again, and neither did Aunt Helen nor Uncle Jim. There weren't any other relatives around, so they were my entire family as I grew up."

Cassie glanced out into the room. "Kind of like Grandpa Ben and me."

"Exactly. That's why I'm telling you. Not everyone grows up in a family that has a mom and dad and the kids. There are all sorts of families out there. Different shapes and sizes." Kelly smiled. "You had Grandpa Ben as your parent for many years, and now you have your uncle Pete and Jennifer as your parents."

Cassie looked back at Kelly. "And you had your dad."

Kelly nodded. "Yeah. And you also have your mom. She may not be there all the time, but at least she cares enough to want to see you."

Cassie looked out into the room again. "Yeah, I guess."

"My mother never showed up at all. So you really are lucky, Cassie." Kelly gave her a grin.

Cassie eyed Kelly. "I wonder if she ever regretted leaving you guys."

Kelly shrugged again. "We'll never know. Hey, who knows? Maybe I was a really ugly baby," she teased.

Cassie's eyes popped wide. "Are you *kidding*? You're beautiful, Kelly!"

Kelly threw back her head and laughed. "Ohhhh, such flattery!"

Cassie shook her head. "You couldn't have been an ugly baby. Impossible."

"Well, maybe I had too many stinky diapers."

Cassie laughed out loud at that.

"I'm glad you're able to babysit Molly later tonight.

When is your team getting together? You guys need to celebrate your wins."

"We're going to wait until Saturday night." Cassie placed the luscious red scarf back on the table.

"Hey, if you guys win against Arvada tonight and then win the Saturday game, you'll be unbeatable going into Sunday," Kelly said with a grin.

Cassie laughed softly, long leg dangling over the chair arm. "Ohhhhh, yeah. That would be sweet."

Six

"**Great** game, Cassie," Marty said as he stepped down from the bleachers. "That was a sharp double to left field. Brought in two runs."

Cassie smiled over a spoonful of chocolate ice cream that was dripping into the plastic cup in her hand. "Thanks, Marty. Are you ready to head back to your house? Megan will be looking for us." The spoonful disappeared into Cassie's mouth.

Kelly stepped down from the bleachers and glanced around the darkening sky. The bright lights illuminating City Park ball field had already turned on as the summer sun slid behind the mountains. "Knowing Megan, she's probably pacing the floor right now."

"Yeah, you're right," Marty said with a chuckle. "Okay, Cassie, grab your gear and we'll go to the car. Luckily I found a parking space right across from the swimming pool." He jangled his car keys.

"Don't worry about her gear," Pete said, standing behind Cassie. "We'll take it back to our house. We'll be picking Cassie up from your house after we leave Kelly and Steve's tonight."

"How's your dad doing, Pete? I've been meaning to ask," Lisa said as she rose from the bleacher row and stretched.

"He's doing about the same, which is always good news. The nurses tell me he's getting physical therapy every week, but we don't really see any improvement. At least I don't see it. What about you, Cassie?" Pete turned to his niece.

Cassie swallowed another bite of chocolate before answering. "Grandpa Ben looks just about the same as he always does when we go down to see him. He sits in his wheelchair and watches television and reads magazines." She looked away. "It's kind of sad."

Pete patted her on the shoulder. "Yeah, I know it is, honey. But at least he's still with us. We can be grateful for that."

"For sure," Jennifer said from the side of the bleachers, which were rapidly clearing out.

Parents and families and friends of the two local girls' softball teams had spread across Fort Connor's City Park grounds, heading for parking lots or picnic tables where other friends had cookouts going. Kelly could detect the scent of cooking hamburgers floating on the twilight air.

"Okay, guys, Kelly and I are heading back to our place. We've got chips and beer and I think I saw a pastry box from the bakery on our kitchen counter," Steve said as he draped his arm around Kelly's shoulders.

"Okay, Cassie, let's move it. The sooner we get you to our house, the sooner Megan and I can find out what's in that pastry box," Marty said with a big grin as he beckoned Cassie away from the bleachers.

"See you later, guys," Cassie said with a wave as she caught up with Marty's long-legged stride. Her own long legs were getting longer, growing.

"What's in the box, Kelly? Inquiring minds want to know," Jennifer teased.

"It's that bakery's specialty. German chocolate cake with a to-die-for frosting. And believe me, they slather it on thick between every layer. And on top, of course."

"Really?" Steve said, eyebrows shooting up. "Well, let's get a move on, then. I want to get home before Marty arrives. That way, I can snitch some frosting." Steve headed away from the bleachers, jingling the car keys in front of Kelly.

"Oh, brother. I'm in big trouble," Jennifer said as she and Pete strolled across the grass.

"We all will be. I'll be running five miles farther tomorrow morning," Kelly said with a laugh, joining her friends as they walked across the grassy sections beside the fields.

"When's Greg coming?" Megan asked after she licked some frosting from her fork. A half-eaten slice of German chocolate cake sat on her plate. Not for long.

"I texted him when we were leaving the ball field and told him about Kelly's dessert. I figured that would bring him back right away." Lisa scraped the last of the cake frosting from her plate as she sank back into the sofa cushions.

"Where is he again?" Pete asked, taking another bite of the rich cake.

"He's at a thesis acceptance party for one of his graduate student friends at the university," Lisa replied.

Kelly glanced around the great room. Her friends were sitting or sprawled on the comfy chairs, sofa, and love seat that she and Steve had combined from her cottage and his Denver apartment. She and Steve had moved into one of the last houses in Steve's housing development on the northeast side of Fort Connor. The same development where Lisa and Greg had bought a home several years ago. Megan and Marty had followed suit a couple of years later, as had Kelly and Steve. Jennifer and Pete had joined them the following year. Now, whenever the gang wanted to get together, all they had to do was walk around a few corners.

Kelly checked her watch. "Yeah. I'm surprised Greg isn't here already. He's usually the first one to line up whenever food is mentioned."

"Don't worry. Greg will show up any minute and immediately accuse Marty of having two slices and leaving him only one," Steve joked, his plate already scraped clean. Not a fleck of cake or frosting visible.

"Well, then, I should get another slice now. I don't want to make a liar out of him," Marty said with a grin and jumped up from the love seat he was sharing with Megan.

"Mar-*teeeeee!* Take a teeny slice. Everyone else will want another taste," Megan warned her husband.

"I'll text Greg and tell him what kind of cake it is. Better yet, I'll send a photo," Pete said, slipping his cell phone from his pocket as he rose from his chair beside Jennifer's.

"And tell him that Marty's circling it right now," Jennifer added with a laugh.

Pete walked over to the kitchen counter and snapped a photo with his phone. He scrolled through different phone screens, then clicked. "Okay. There it goes. Now, Marty, come over here and lean over the cake." Pete beckoned.

"Absolutely," Marty said obligingly. He leaned over the cake, holding his plate in one hand and his fork hovering directly over the scrumptious dessert.

"Perfect," Pete said with a grin as he clicked his mail program again. Electronic messages traveling through the ether faster than a single breath.

The chorus of an old bluesy jazz song sounded. "That's mine," Lisa said as she reached beside the sofa for her purse.

"Did Molly go to sleep okay?" Kelly asked Megan as she perched on the edge of Steve's favorite overstuffed armchair.

"Pretty much. She plays so hard during the day that she usually falls right to sleep at night," Megan said, sinking back into the love seat.

"Most of the time," Marty added as he returned to the love seat with only a small slice of cake. "Other times, she cries. It's hard to figure out."

Kelly glanced over at Lisa, who was talking on the phone.

"I'm Greg Carruthers's wife. Who is this again?" Lisa was sitting up straight now.

"I've heard that babies do that—" Jennifer started to say until Kelly waved her quiet.

Kelly was watching Lisa, whose face had gone white in seconds. All color drained away.

"What? But . . . but how—" Lisa blurted out, her voice higher.

"Something's up," Steve whispered to Kelly as he put his plate on a nearby end table.

Kelly just nodded as she and all her friends had their attention riveted on Lisa.

"Oh, my God . . ." Lisa said, her voice breaking. "Where is he?"

Kelly and Steve both stood up at the same time, as did their friends, one by one. Standing silently.

"I'll be right there. Fifth floor. I'm coming." She snapped her phone closed and looked up at her friends with a blank expression. "Greg's been in an accident. A car hit him while he was cycling home," she said, voice wavering. "I've gotta go now. They're getting ready to take him in for surgery at the hospital." Her hand clutched at her chest. "Oh, God."

"Come with us, Lisa." Pete went to her immediately, lifting her up from the chair by the arms. "Jen, take Lisa in the backseat with you."

"We'll follow you," Steve said, striding toward the front door. He held it open for Pete and Jen and Lisa as they passed through.

Kelly grabbed her shoulder bag and snapped off a couple of lights. "We'll all be right behind you, Lisa," she called out as she watched the rest of her friends file silently out the door.

Kelly moved her folding chair closer to Lisa, who was sitting in the midst of her friends who had clustered around her in a semicircle. Kelly reached out and placed her hand on Lisa's arm. It felt cold. The hospital air-conditioning was quite efficient, and cold air was pouring out of a nearby vent in the ceiling above.

"It's going to be all right, Lisa," Kelly reassured her friend, repeating the same words others in the group had said. She had nothing else to offer. Simply words.

"They've got fantastic doctors and surgeons here, Lisa," Megan offered. "Marty's cousin in Loveland was in an awful car wreck last year, and these doctors were able to repair everything. Even facial surgery. They're wonderful."

Lisa didn't answer. She just sat hunched, her arms clasped around herself, staring at the door from the waiting room into the hospital. She gave a little shiver.

Kelly looked over at Steve. "Steve, why don't you bring that old jacket in from your truck. Lisa's cold as ice. She needs to warm up."

"You got it. Be right back." Steve turned from his pacing the floor and headed for the waiting room door.

"They sure have their air-conditioning cranked up," Jennifer said, rubbing her arms. "I know it's August, but temperatures drop at night. Don't they adjust those thermostats?"

"I think part of it is we're all worrying," Pete said beside her.

Marty popped up from the folding chair for the fourth time in fifteen minutes. Seemingly unable to sit still. He started to pace. "I'm going to call Cassie. See if everything's okay and Molly's still asleep. Then I can tell her we'll be back later tonight."

"Good idea," Megan said. "Don't tell her anything else. We don't want to worry her."

"Yeah." Pete nodded. "Jen and I will explain everything to her when we pick her up tonight."

"Be back in a minute," Marty said, pulling his cell phone from his pocket as he hurried toward the door.

"You guys don't have to stay," Lisa said in a quiet voice.

"We want to," Kelly said, giving her friend's arm a Mother-Mimi-reassuring squeeze before withdrawing her hand.

Lisa looked around anxiously. "It's been an hour already. The doctor said it would be an hour. How come they're not finished?"

This time Jennifer reached over and placed her hand on Lisa's arm. "The doctor said about an hour, Lisa. Don't worry. You don't want them to hurry."

Kelly decided a little humor couldn't hurt. "You don't want them to leave anything undone. That would be like leaving dangling yarn tails on a scarf. They've got to tie off everything. Make sure everything looks pretty."

"Dangling yarn tails," Megan repeated with a smile. "Yeah, Lisa. We want Greg looking good when they finish."

Jennifer kept her hand on Lisa's arm. "It'll be all right, Lisa. Like Megan said. These are wonderful doctors and surgeons. They'll take care of Greg."

Lisa's face puckered. "He looked awful when they took him in. I didn't even recognize him. He was all beat up. His face was black and blue . . ." Her voice choked.

Marty walked back into the waiting room. He glanced at the far end of the room, where an older man sat in a chair reading a magazine. Clearly waiting to hear on some other patient's progress. He leaned over toward the group and spoke in a lowered voice. "I told Cassie we'd be home a little later than usual. She said everything was fine. Molly hasn't made a peep. She's checked on her a couple of times already, and Molly's just snoozing away." Marty glanced above. "Thank gawd."

"Amen," Megan said, nodding. "Some nights, Molly will wake up and start to scream. I think it's indigestion or something. Mimi told me they used to call that 'colic' when babies did that. They'd cry and cry and all you could do was to walk them back and forth. Then after a while, they'd just simply stop crying and fall asleep again."

"We've worn a path through the living room carpet," Marty said with a rueful smile.

Steve strode into the waiting room then, a Colorado State University jacket in his hand. "Here you go, Lisa," he said, walking up behind her chair. He draped the jacket around Lisa's shoulders.

"Thanks, Steve," Lisa mumbled, pulling the jacket around herself.

"No problem," Steve said, settling among his friends again.

Just then the waiting room doors swung open and an older man in green hospital scrubs walked into the room, glanced around, then headed toward the group.

Lisa sprang from her chair. "Doctor! Did you operate on Greg Carruthers?"

"Yes. I'm Dr. Manchion. Are you his wife?" the doctor replied as he approached.

"Yes. Well, we've been together for years," she blurted out. "I'm the family contact."

The doctor glanced down at the paper-filled clipboard in his hand. "Yes, you're Lisa Gerrard, then?"

"Yes, yes!" Lisa bobbed her head. "How is he? How's Greg?"

"He came through surgery just fine. He's a healthy man in really good shape." Dr. Manchion shoved the clipboard under his arm. "His left leg was broken, but it was a clean break and was easily set. The same is true for his left arm. No problems there. Of course, he was bruised all over. It looks like he was first hit by the car on the left side, and the force of that threw him on top of the car. Then when the car braked suddenly, he slid off onto the ground."

Kelly cringed inwardly hearing the doctor's description. Steve came up beside her and put his arm around her shoulders.

"It was lucky he was wearing one of those high-impact helmets. Otherwise there would have been brain injury as well. Because of the helmet, he'll probably only have a slight concussion, if that."

"Oh, thank God," Lisa breathed, eyes closed. "How will we know if he has a concussion?"

"He'll complain of headaches, of course, but Greg will be under a doctor's care. So you won't have to worry about it. With these injuries, a broken left leg and a broken left arm, he will need skilled care for at least four weeks or more before he can go home."

"Really?" Lisa's eyes blinked wide.

"Yes, definitely. Unless, of course, you are home all day and could help him move around and take care of basic needs, then you could have in-home nursing care come in regularly to check on him. And physical therapists, too. And occupational therapists." Dr. Manchion looked at Lisa.

"Oh, goodness, no," Lisa admitted. "I work all morning Monday through Friday at the sports clinic. I'm a physical therapist. And I'm at the university every afternoon taking classes or monitoring graduate students in psychology."

Dr. Manchion gave a wry smile. "That's why I suggested skilled care. We have two excellent rehabilitation centers in town where most of my patients go immediately upon being discharged from the hospital. Their stays vary from two weeks to two months, depending on the injuries."

"That makes a lot of sense, Lisa," Steve said in a quiet voice. "I've had a lot of friends tell me the rehab center over on Centre Avenue is excellent. They recommend it highly."

"Of course, you'll have to see how much your health insurance would pay for that level of care. If it pays anything at all," Dr. Manchion said, raising an eyebrow. "Everyone's situation is different."

Kelly considered what the doctor just said, and she wondered again at how much her health insurance paid for rehabilitation from serious injuries and surgery. She made a mental note to check into it.

"Wow, that's another thing. Neither of us has ever had a serious injury before, so I have no idea how much my university health insurance pays for grad students. Greg is with a private technology company here in town and supposedly they have good insurance. At least, that's what Greg told me." Lisa shrugged. "But I admit, I am clueless as to the details."

"Don't feel bad," Dr. Manchion said. "Most people are in exactly the same situation as you two. Only after a serious injury occurs do people realize they need to check into the details." He glanced again at his clipboard. "Oh, yes, Greg was lightly sedated when he was being prepped for surgery, so the staff couldn't ask him any questions about choice of doctors. Do you know who Greg's orthopedic doctor is? Or if he has one?"

"Yes, I do know that," Lisa said with a half smile. "Dr. Madan. He's with the orthopedic center out east on Prospect Drive."

Dr. Manchion scribbled on the pages on his clipboard. "Excellent. I'll make sure copies of all x-rays and hospital records are sent to him. And you'll want to contact the orthopedic center and find out what their procedures are for postsurgical care. I imagine Dr. Madan will want to visit Greg either tomorrow or the next day. By that time, the anesthesia will be out of Greg's system so Dr. Madan can discuss with him the level of postoperative care and procedures."

Lisa nodded. "I'll make sure to call their office tomorrow."

Dr. Manchion clicked his pen closed and slipped it into the chest pocket of his green scrubs. "Don't forget to let their office know where Greg will be located. Either your home or one of the rehab centers in town." He smiled at Lisa. "You're going to have a lot of phone calls tomorrow."

"Oh, yes," Lisa said with a firm nod. "I certainly will. And thank you, Dr. Manchion, for going through all those different procedures and protocols for me. I appreciate it."

Dr. Manchion smiled. "You're welcome, Lisa. Rehab is a challenge, but I imagine you're well aware of that, considering you are in the business yourself."

"Thanks again, Doctor," Lisa said as he turned to walk away. More patients to see. More patients to put back together again.

"Wow," Kelly said softly, catching her friends' gaze.

The rest of Lisa's friends echoed similar sentiments as the realization of what Greg's rehabilitation would be like settled in. A lot of work for Greg and for Lisa.

Seven

Cassie raced over to Kelly the moment Kelly stepped into the Lambspun foyer. "I've been waiting for you ever since we got in early this morning," Cassie declared, her blue eyes wide with worry. "Jennifer and Pete told me what happened to Greg last night. That's *awful*!"

Kelly could feel Cassie's anxiety radiating off her. Not unlike Kelly's own. Neither she nor Steve had slept well last night because of their worry for Greg. She'd touched base with Megan when Steve drove off for Denver, and Megan shared that she and Marty had been awake a lot during the night, too. And, of course, Molly was awake at 6 A.M. Early morning feeding.

"Well, I don't know anything more than Jennifer and Pete," Kelly said as she walked toward the main knitting room. "No one's been able to see Greg except Lisa. She saw him as he was being wheeled into surgery and briefly when he was in the recovery room. But Greg was still under anesthesia and wasn't fully awake. So Lisa's camped out at the hospital." Kelly plopped her briefcase bag onto the table and pulled out her empty coffee mug.

Cassie followed Kelly into the central yarn room. "Does Lisa need any help? I'd be glad to go over to the hospital this afternoon and sit with her."

Kelly smiled at the young teenager. "Don't you have batting practice with me and the other girls early this afternoon? This is tournament weekend, remember? You've got games this afternoon and evening."

Cassie glanced away. "I know. I figured it would be better to do something to help Greg or Lisa rather than playing softball."

Kelly put her hand on Cassie's shoulder. "Actually, the best thing you could do for both of them is to hit some doubles tonight. Once Greg's anesthesia wears off and he's able to talk to Lisa, she can tell him about your games. I'm sure it'll help Greg get better. And both he and Lisa will be proud of you. Besides, they only allow family members into the hospital rooms of patients who've had surgery. None of us can go in and see Greg except Lisa."

Cassie gave Kelly a quizzical look. "Lisa's not related to Greg. And they're not married. Lisa told me. So how does she get to see Greg?"

"Smart question," Kelly said, laughing softly. "Marty would be proud. It sounds like a lawyer question. Actually, Lisa and Greg have been living together for over seven years, so legally Lisa is considered to be Greg's 'common law' wife. That gives her certain rights under the law."

"Wow. That's interesting. I'd never heard of that," Cassie said with a surprised look.

"A lot of people don't know about that part of the law, but it's true. Now, I'm going to get a fill-up of coffee before I start on those accounts this morning." Kelly moved toward the central yarn room.

"I'd better stay here and finish up these magazines," Cassie said, returning to the other end of the library table. "New editions have come out."

"Plus, I hear the scraping of chairs, so Mimi's knitting class must be over," Kelly said, looking back over her shoulder. "Lots of new knitters will be filling the shop." Kelly continued toward the hallway leading to the café and spotted her friend Jennifer beside the grill counter loading breakfast dishes onto her tray. "Hey there. I hope you and Pete got a decent night's sleep because Steve and I didn't. Neither did Megan or Marty." She walked over to the grill counter. Grill cook Eduardo was grilling sausage patties on one side of the grill and French toast on the other side.

"Are you kidding?" Jennifer asked, raising a brow. "Pete and I slept for a little while early in the night. Then we both woke up and started tossing and turning. Neither of us could sleep after that." She lifted the tray filled with scrumptious-looking breakfast selections to her shoulder.

Kelly set her empty mug on the counter. "I texted Lisa this morning about six o'clock, and she was already at the hospital. She said Greg was half asleep from all the medications he's being given. Painkillers mostly."

"That's understandable. Can you imagine how much pain Greg's in now? A broken leg and a broken arm, plus he's been operated on." Jennifer rolled her eyes. "I don't even want to think about it."

"Lisa says he's black and blue all over. Even his face is scratched and bruised. Thank God Greg was wearing his helmet." Kelly glanced over at the steaming grill and watched as Eduardo cracked two eggs. The eggs spread perfectly on the hot surface, the translucent egg white rapidly changing to white. A bright yellow yolk in the middle. Perfect sunny-side up.

Eduardo glanced over his shoulder at Kelly and Jennifer. "Greg's lucky to be alive. My cousin Carlos in Denver was killed when he was riding his bike along Colorado Boulevard on the way to a class he was taking at Denver University. This guy had been drinking and sideswiped Carlos. Knocked him off his bike and into traffic." Eduardo shook his head and turned back to the grill.

Kelly quickly pictured the horrible scene. She couldn't help it. Her mind instantly translated Eduardo's words into a vivid image. "That's awful, Eduardo! I'm so sorry your cousin was killed. How old was he?"

"He was just twenty-nine," Eduardo answered, attention focused on the grill as he effortlessly flipped the two eggs over for a couple of seconds, then flipped them onto a plate.

"He left his wife, Alicia, and two young children, didn't he? I remember your telling me about the accident a couple of years ago." Jennifer shifted the tray.

"Yeah, he did. Luisa was five and Tomas was three. They live with my folks over in Arvada now. Alicia wasn't able to pay all the bills herself." Eduardo glanced back over his shoulder. "Get rid of that heavy tray, Jen," he fussed.

"Yes, sir," Jennifer said with a smile as she turned toward the main part of the café. "Let me know if you hear any more from Lisa at the hospital, okay?"

"Will do."

"Here, let me refill that for you, Kelly," Eduardo said, reaching over the counter for Kelly's oversized mug.

"Don't interrupt your cooking, Eduardo. I can wait for Jen. I think Julie's outside on the patio."

Eduardo grinned, revealing his gold front tooth. "That's okay, Kelly. We all know what you're like without plenty of coffee."

Kelly chuckled. "Oh, boy, my reputation as a caffeine addict is set in stone, I guess," she said as she accepted the mug. "I suppose I'd better find a quiet spot and get to work. And stop bothering you guys."

"You never bother us, Kelly," Eduardo said as he placed more sausages on the grill. "You make us laugh."

This time Kelly laughed out loud as she walked back to the hallway leading into the knitting shop once again. At least she had entertainment value.

"Oh my, oh my," Mimi said softly as she sat in the chair beside Kelly at the knitting table. Two women were browsing the magazines on the shelves and talking to each other. "This is just *awful* news! Poor Greg. I wish Burt and I could go over to see him. But I know only family is allowed. Besides Greg's in no shape to have outside visitors now. Have you heard any more from Lisa since this morning?"

"She texted me after lunch that Greg was gradually coming out of the grogginess, which is a good thing." Kelly picked up one of the yarn skeins that lay on the table nearby. Soft pink mohair mixed with silk, the label read.

"It's a good thing this is Saturday. Lisa doesn't have to go to the university to work or take classes." Mimi toyed with another mohair and silk yarn skein scattered on the table. "Has she been at the hospital ever since Greg was brought in last night?"

Kelly took a sip of coffee. "No, Pete and Jen took her home, but she returned to the hospital early this morning. I texted her at six A.M., and she was already there."

"Oh, my."

"Lisa texted she wanted to be there when Greg regained consciousness. I wonder if he recognized her?" Kelly mused aloud. "I mean, if you're that groggy, maybe you can't recognize people you know. Part of your brain is either drugged or asleep."

"Ohhh, I think there's another part of our brain that stays awake during everything," Mimi said, giving a definitive nod. "And it recognizes things and people, but we can't talk about it." She shrugged. "I don't know if that makes any sense or not."

"I think it makes as much sense as anything else I've heard about people being unconscious."

A familiar voice came from the central yarn room. "Oh, good. The two of you are together. Now I don't have to repeat myself," retired Fort Connor police detective Burt Parker said as he strode into the main room.

"Hey, Burt." Kelly lifted her mug to him in greeting as her mentor and father figure pulled out a chair beside his wife.

"Oh, I'm so glad you came while Kelly is still here," Mimi said, turning to him. "Did you learn anything from your old friends at the department?"

Burt leaned forward and folded his arms on the table in familiar fashion. "Well, there's not much to learn so far. I spoke to Dan on the phone, and he said police are searching for clues on the hit-and-run driver, all right. They haven't found any yet. But what's interesting is it turns out Greg was the second victim of a hit-and-run driver last night."

"*What!*" Kelly stared at Burt.

"*Merciful heavens!*" Mimi said, her hand to her chest.

The two women perusing magazines at the other end of the library table glanced at Mimi briefly, then returned to their magazines.

Burt noticed and lowered his voice. "Apparently there was a fatal hit-and-run around that same time. The fatality was a man who might have been walking toward his car, which was parked along the street that runs behind several of the craft breweries. That's the very same street where Greg was hit. But it was farther ahead near the corner stop sign."

"Oh, my word!" Mimi repeated, softer now, her right hand clutching at her chest in a familiar reaction Kelly had witnessed for years. Mimi's shocked response to any bad news.

Kelly leaned toward Burt and kept her voice down.

"That's got to be the same driver, don't you think? What was the time frame?"

"It's very probably around the same time, because a driver who turned from a cross street is the one who spotted Greg lying in the street at the corner. And he called 911 and emergency services. Apparently the EMS ambulance and fire department rescue noticed this other guy lying along the road when they drove up in response to Greg." Burt looked at both of them. "I have to tell you, in all those years working for the department, I've never seen an accident scene like this one is turning out to be. I've been called to multiple fatalities but they involved automobile crashes. This is a double hit-and-run."

"Do they know who the victim is? Was he young or old?"

"Dan said they're in the process of establishing his identity now. But he's a younger guy. Ambulance crew said his driver's license revealed he was twenty-five years old."

"Oh, no, that's so young!" Mimi exclaimed.

Burt nodded. "It sure is. Of course, he may have been drinking and staggered into the path of this car, we don't know."

Kelly frowned. "But then, why would the driver go and hit Greg then? Do they think the driver might have been drunk?"

Burt shrugged. "Police have no idea what caused both hit-and-runs. Who knows? Maybe the driver accidentally hit the young guy who walked in front of his car. Then maybe the driver drove off in a panic and hit Greg at the corner."

"He had to have been panicked to run into two people like that," Kelly said.

"Police will come up with more information when they start interviewing people, I'm sure. There don't seem to be any witnesses on that dark street, but time will tell. People have a way of turning up."

Kelly remembered that from some of the past murder cases she had involved herself in. People did indeed turn up. Some of them from the unlikeliest places.

"On which street was the second guy found?" Kelly asked.

"He was found lying on Taylor Street, and Greg was hit at the corner of Taylor and Abercrombie. Both of them are adjacent to Old Town and have a brewpub on each one. The Halftime Bar is on Taylor, and the Lager House is on Abercrombie."

"I'll bet that young man who died was a student, a graduate student," Mimi said sorrowfully. "The parents are going to be heartbroken, simply heartbroken."

Kelly exchanged a brief glance with Burt but neither said a word. Kelly remembered that Steve had told her years ago about the tragic death of Mimi's only child, her son, Jeffrey. He had taken some unknown drugs at a party up in Cache La Poudre Canyon and had wandered off from the party. Friends found him later that evening, lying on the rocks below in a cliffside ravine. Dead. There was never any more information on the tragic accident. Friends had noticed him walk out the door of the mountainside home but no one followed him. And no one witnessed what was undoubtedly an awful accident. All that Mimi was ever told was that her son was "pretty high" the last time anyone spoke to him at the party.

The Fort Connor medical examiner told her that they found a mixture of amphetamines and other stimulants all mixed together in her son's system. Jennifer and Lisa had said that Mimi was shocked by the report. Her son had never experimented with drugs in high school apparently. At least, not that his mother ever knew. Unfortunately, if this occasion was an experiment, it turned out to be fatal. And Mimi was "devastated," in Lisa's words. She also told Kelly that she suspected the son's death played a role in Mimi's divorce from her husband.

"I'm sure they will be grief-stricken, Mimi," Kelly said, wanting to say something reassuring but at a sudden loss for words.

"Whenever a young person dies in an accident, it's always traumatic. And tragic for their loved ones," Burt said as he placed his hand over Mimi's in a comforting way.

"I've heard of the Halftime Bar," Kelly said, trying to gently turn the subject away from the sad memories this incident had brought back from the past. "Apparently it's a pickup bar. Lots of college students there, from what I've heard."

"That's for sure," Burt agreed. "The Lager House has a more diverse or mixed crowd. But none of that matters if the customers don't exercise some good judgment and watch how much they're drinking."

Kelly had to smile. "Boy, Burt. You are an optimist. Even after all these years of being in a university town. Good judgment is not usually associated with college student behavior, especially freshmen students."

Burt chuckled. "You're right, Kelly. I remain an optimist, even after all these years."

"That's one of the things I love about him," Mimi said with a smile and leaned over to kiss Burt's cheek.

Kelly stroked Carl's silky black ears as she finished her morning coffee. Carl crooned his contentment with the ecstatic ear rub even if it was one-handed. The sound of Kelly's cell phone ringing interrupted Carl's doggie song. "Okay, Carl. Time for me to return some business calls before the day is over. You return to doggie patrol."

Kelly had noticed that Brazen Squirrel had used Carl's pleasure break for a fast scamper across the chain-link fence. Carl, however, was oblivious. Kelly decided she wouldn't squeal on the little creature. There would be countless more encounters between these two adversaries.

Carl bounded out into the afternoon sunshine as Kelly slid open the cottage screen door and retrieved her ringing phone. Lisa's name flashed on the screen. "Hey there," Kelly greeted her friend. "How's Greg doing?"

"He's slowly getting more awake. Meanwhile, I'm trying to catch up on some reading. One of my friends e-mailed me the class assignments. Lord knows when I'll return to class."

"Don't even worry about it, Lisa," Kelly counseled. "You're doing great in your classes. And you're doing the right thing by staying there with Greg. That way when he wakes up, he'll see you there."

"I actually hope the poor guy stays asleep for a while longer. He's bound to be in a lot of pain when he does wake up. Hey, before I forget, another friend e-mailed me that there was a fatal hit-and-run in Old Town that same night. She saw it on an online website that has local Colorado news. Did you hear anything about that?"

Kelly leaned against the kitchen counter. "As a matter of fact, I heard about it from Burt yesterday afternoon. Apparently some guy who was turning the corner onto the street where Greg was hit called 911. And Burt said the ambulance crew found the second guy lying dead on the street as they drove to treat Greg."

"Good Lord! Two hit-and-runs in one night? I can't believe it."

"In the same area, too. And one of them fatal. Burt said the fatality was a young guy about twenty-five. He was hit farther down that street closer to the brewpubs. So he was probably walking back to his car after being out with friends or something."

"People park all around there for the Old Town cafés. Boy, I hope the newspaper and TV stations put that message out there. Be sober when you're walking and driving at night. Do you think there's a chance the two accidents are connected somehow?"

"Burt seems to think they are, and I agree. Who knows? Maybe someone hit the young guy first, and then drove off in a panic. And didn't even notice Greg at the corner."

"Well, the police will find out. Oh, I think I see Greg's orthopedist in the hallway. Talk to you later." Her phone clicked off.

Kelly ran water into a pitcher and refilled Carl's large water dishes on the outside patio. Carl was busy snuffling and sniffing squirrel feet in the bushes. Brazen was safe on a cottonwood limb high above. All was right with the world . . . at least the small part comprising Kelly's cottage and doggie and squirrel soap operas.

Eight

"That is awful news, Kelly," her client Arthur Housemann said. "And who could imagine a double hit-and-run. How could anyone do such a thing?" He gazed out the window of his top-floor office, which looked out over the city of Fort Connor to the east.

Kelly followed his lead and looked out Housemann's large office window at how far the city of Fort Connor had spread since she first returned to her childhood home several years ago. When she was a child in elementary school, the population of Fort Connor was less than eighty thousand people. In the thirty years since, the city had spread beyond its original boundaries and the population had nearly doubled. The latest census numbers showed Fort Connor to be close to one hundred and fifty thousand people. And that did not count the college students who attended the state university. Since the Front Range of the Rocky Mountains bordered the city on the west, and the small town of Wellesley was to the north, Fort Connor's growth spilled to the east and the south. Kelly was always surprised at the new housing developments that kept appearing.

"Some of us think the driver either was drunk or scared. Maybe he accidentally hit the first guy and then panicked and ran into Greg at the corner," Kelly said.

"I still find it hard to believe. He must have been driving fast because of Greg's injuries. A broken leg and a broken shoulder, too?"

"A broken arm. Broken left leg and broken left arm. Plus sprained all over. Lisa says Greg's black and blue everywhere." Kelly made a face.

Arthur wagged his head slightly. "Poor boy."

Kelly smiled at another of her mentors. Housemann was also a father figure to Kelly and had many of her late father's mannerisms and ways of speaking. That was another reason Kelly enjoyed visiting the first of her two exclusive clients. It was like visiting and talking with her father again. Arthur always gave good advice. In addition, Kelly enjoyed learning more about her successful real estate investor and developer client's strategies. Arthur Housemann had weathered all the real estate booms and busts of the last thirty years. In a volatile business like real estate, that record was phenomenal.

"Well, Greg is healthier than most people and is . . . uh, was in great physical shape, so I expect his rehabilitation to be quicker than most."

Arthur smiled for the first time. "From what you've told

me over the years, Greg is a real outdoors guy, always biking and rock climbing. So I imagine Greg will take it as a personal challenge to regain his 'fighting shape.'"

"Oh, yes. And he's lucky that Lisa is a physical therapist. She'll probably have Greg working extra," Kelly added, laughing softly.

Arthur laughed along with her. "I think that's a good bet, if ever there was one. In fact, if I was a betting man, I'd put cash money on Greg."

Kelly eyed her successful client. "What do you mean, you're 'not a betting man'? You've taken risks on developing homes in entirely new areas of Fort Connor for years. And you've succeeded greatly. And financially, I might add."

Arthur chuckled. "Thank you, Kelly. Coming from you that is a high compliment, indeed. As you know, I never enter into an investment without doing the proper research. Area demography, location of retail and shopping in vicinity. All that."

Kelly grinned. "You're thorough, that's for sure, Arthur. That's why it's a piece of cake doing your financial statements."

This time, Arthur Housemann threw back his head and laughed out loud. Kelly joined in, celebrating her client's success.

"**Hey,** Lisa, how's Greg doing?" Kelly asked over the phone as she opened her car door and stepped outside into the Lambspun parking area.

"He's still groggy. Anesthesia is slowly wearing off."

Kelly could hear hospital noise in the background. "I wanted to check another news site before giving you a call. But I finally saw an online site that mentioned the name of the victim of that Old Town hit-and-run."

"Oh, thanks, Kelly. Who was it?"

"Apparently the victim was identified as a graduate student at the university. Neil Smith." Kelly waited for Lisa's reaction.

"What? That's Nancy's boyfriend!"

"I thought the name sounded vaguely familiar when I read it. Of course, Smith is a common name, but the fact that he's a graduate student at the university also narrows it down."

"Good Lord! Have you seen Nancy? I wonder how she's taking it?"

"I haven't been in the shop yet today, I've been with a client. But you're right. This is bound to be a shock to her. Even though this Neil sounded like a prime bastard for turning his back on Nancy. *And* her baby. His baby, too."

"My thoughts exactly," Lisa said. "Listen, I see one of the nurses turning into Greg's room. I'll talk to you later." Her phone clicked off quickly.

Kelly dropped her cell phone into her shoulder bag, locked her car, and headed toward the Lambspun front entry. As Kelly walked into the shop, she nearly ran into Cassie, who was on her way out the door. "Whoa! Sorry. I didn't know a tornado was coming through the door." Kelly stepped aside.

Cassie giggled as she held open the door. Halfway in,

halfway out. "Didn't mean to run you over, Kelly. But Jen is waiting for me outside in the car. She's finished with her real estate work early and wants to take me school shopping."

"Ooooo, school shopping. New clothes. That's always fun. Have a great time and buy some cute stuff. Oh, and say 'hi' to Jen. Remind her we're getting together tonight after Steve and Marty's game."

"Will do," Cassie said, releasing the door. "See you later." The heavy wooden entry door closed slowly.

Kelly continued into the central yarn room, where another woman was browsing the bins of colorful yarns. Kelly paused by the round table in the middle of the room. It was stacked with short stubby skeins of multicolored wools. All the skeins looked to be in the same spectrum of colors. Blues and greens with some touches of brown. Forest green joined with bright turquoise blue and a muted sable brown.

Next to those skeins sat skeins of burnt sienna mixed with a festive pumpkin orange and a cinnamon brown. Kelly squeezed both fat little skeins. The gauge of the wool was exactly like the one Kelly used for her first knitting project years ago. A sturdy wool that could be transformed into a scarf or a placemat. Versatile.

Kelly walked over to the bins that lined three walls. They were stacked with different-sized skeins and balls of bamboo and silk, wool and mohair, and a wondrous variety of alpaca. Kelly reached out and stroked a large fat skein of creamy white baby alpaca. Soft, unbelievably soft. She'd finished knitting the scarf for Mimi's charity project. Did she need another scarf for next winter? Probably not. She'd made several scarves of wool, mohair, alpaca, and silk, even ribbons over the years since she first came to Lambspun and learned to knit while she sat around the library table. Just like countless other beginning knitters.

Her fingers toyed with a skein of soft gray baby alpaca. *How about mittens?* Did she need more mittens for the upcoming winter? she wondered. *Hmmmmmmm. Decisions, decisions.* Just then, Mimi's voice cut into her quandary.

"Isn't that a luscious wool, Kelly?" Mimi said as she walked into the central yarn room. "It would make a wonderful winter sweater."

A little bell in the back of Kelly's mind went off. *A sweater. Of course.* "You're right, Mimi. This would be perfect for a winter sweater. And it's so soft." Kelly stroked the fat gray alpaca again.

"And gray is so versatile, too. You could wear it anywhere next winter," Mimi said with a smile. "Around the shop. Skiing, whatever."

Kelly picked up one of the fat skeins and looked at the label. "Size eight needles. Three stitches to an inch. That will look nice."

"If you started now, you'd be finished in time for winter weather," Mimi tempted her.

Kelly laughed softly. "You're incorrigible, Mimi. You're the very best encourager of knitting projects I've ever met." She held out the skein. "How many of these would I need to make a winter sweater? A rough guess."

"Well, a winter sweater would need long sleeves—"

"Oooops. I've never made long sleeves," Kelly demurred.

Mimi gave one of her dismissive little waves of her hand.

"It's only a few inches more than you've done before for a short-sleeve sweater. It'll be a piece of cake."

"If you say so." Kelly smiled. "Well, it's time I learned how to do a long-sleeved one anyway. Might as well do it now."

"I agree. You'd probably need five skeins of that wool. Why don't we pick out a pattern?" Mimi walked toward the hallway and beckoned Kelly to follow her.

Skein in hand, Kelly dutifully traipsed after Mimi, down the hallway heading toward the workroom and the office beyond.

There sat the two gray metal file cabinets stuffed full of patterns—knitting, crocheting, weaving, and more.

Mimi pulled out the middle drawer of one of the file cabinets and began to finger through the header index tabs of the folders. She removed five different file folders. "Here are five really nice winter sweater patterns I think you'll like, Kelly. Why don't you take these to the table and go over them. See which one you like the best." She held out the folders.

"Which ones are the easiest?" Kelly said as she accepted them.

"They are all easy, Kelly," Mimi said.

Kelly smiled. "That's what you always says, Mimi. Remember, what's easy for you is usually harder for me."

Mimi made a little tsking sound with her tongue. "Nonsense, Kelly. You're a good knitter now."

"Maybe so, but I still get confused, especially when reading instructions." Kelly stared at the five folders. "Okay, I'll go see which one survives the cut." She walked to the doorway.

"There you go," Mimi encouraged her. "Pick the best one."
Kelly waved the folders overhead as she headed toward the main knitting room again. "The easiest is the winner."

Kelly read over the instructions for the long-sleeved sweater and stared at the drawing at the top of the pattern. It was very pretty. And the instructions sounded a bit easier than the other two sweaters. She'd definitely found the winner.

Nancy Marsted walked into the main room and glanced around. "Hi, Kelly."

"Hey, Nancy. How're you doing?" Kelly dropped her pen on the notepad. She wondered how best to approach the subject of Neil Smith.

"I'm okay, I guess." She glanced behind her toward the central yarn room. "Is Lisa here?"

"No, Lisa is at Poudre Valley Hospital," Kelly said, noticing Nancy's anxious expression and deciding that Nancy clearly thought of Lisa as her personal counselor. That was understandable, especially when Nancy was going through a stressful period. Unfortunately, Lisa had enough stress of her own to handle right now, and her concentration was entirely focused on Greg.

Nancy hurried over to the chair beside Kelly at the table, her eyes wide as saucers. Two women were browsing the instruction books at the other end of the table and commenting to themselves. "Is Lisa all right? Did she get sick? Or have an accident?"

"No, no," Kelly reassured with a smile. "Lisa's fine. She went to the hospital to see her boyfriend, Greg."

"Ohhh, I'm glad to hear that," Nancy said, visibly relaxing. Then she gave a little wave of her hand. "I don't mean I'm glad her boyfriend is in the hospital."

"I know what you meant." Kelly smiled at Nancy's anxious behavior. Eager to please, not wanting to offend.

"Is he sick? Lisa's boyfriend, I mean."

Kelly settled back into the chair and took a drink of still-warm coffee from her travel mug. "No, Greg's not sick. He's been injured. He's got a broken leg and a broken arm. And he's a mass of bruises all over."

"Oh, no. What happened to him?"

Kelly leaned closer to Nancy and lowered her voice. "He was hit by a car Friday night over in Old Town."

Nancy's eyes went wide again. "Really?"

Kelly nodded. "Yeah. He was riding his bike home when he was hit by a car. A hit-and-run."

Nancy continued to stare at Kelly. "Oh, no!" she whispered.

"Oh, yes," Kelly whispered back. "Whoever did it was probably drinking at one of the bars. If they were drunk, they may not have even noticed him."

"That's . . . that's awful," Nancy said, leaning closer to Kelly. "Is there anything I can do to help? I mean . . . is there anything Lisa needs?"

"I don't think so. We're all checking in with her over at the hospital by phone. No one but family members are allowed up there with surgery patients."

Nancy's eyes went wide again. "He had surgery?"

"Oh, yeah." Kelly nodded again. "The doctors had to carefully set that broken leg and make sure everything was all right. And they took care of his broken arm, too. He's got pulled muscles, tendons, and ligaments all over his shoulders and back. He's going to need physical therapy for weeks and weeks. Months probably."

"That's so . . . so awful," Nancy said sorrowfully.

"I know. At least Lisa is a PT. So he'll have an 'in-house' therapist, which is good." Kelly gave a wry smile.

Mimi walked into the main room and glanced over at Kelly and Nancy. "Hello, Nancy. It's good to see you. Kelly, how's that pattern search coming?"

"I narrowed it down to three, Mimi. And I've finally eliminated two of them." She looked over at Mimi. "I chickened out as usual and want to try the easiest one."

Mimi laughed her little musical laugh. "You're so funny, Kelly." Then she walked toward the two women at the other end of the table. "Can I help you ladies with anything? Are you trying to decide on which knitting instruction book is better?"

The younger woman spoke up. "Yes, as a matter of fact, you can. You're the owner of the shop, right?"

"Yes, I am," Mimi said with her bright smile. "How can I help?"

"Well, I'm trying to choose a basic beginner's knitting instruction book for my mom," the younger woman said, pointing to the woman beside her. "I've shown her the beginning stitches but she wants to have a book with pictures of the stitches because it helps her to learn them better."

"Oh, it certainly does," Mimi agreed with a nod, addressing the older woman. "I used an excellent instruction book with pictures when I first started out years and years ago."

Mimi walked over to the bookshelves. "Now, let's see, we should have a copy of it here. I always try to keep a copy in stock," she said, her finger trailing over the spines of the books on the shelves. "Ah, yes! Here it is." She removed the book from between the others and spread it open on the table between the two women.

Kelly decided to use the busy conversation at the other end of the table as background noise, and she leaned forward toward Nancy. "Nancy, I read on a local online news site about the fatal hit-and-run in Old Town the same night Greg was hit. And the news site today had the name of the victim. Neil Smith. That sounded familiar. Was that your boyfriend, Nancy?"

Nancy lowered her head, her eyes seeking her lap where her hands were clasped. "Yes . . . yes, that was him. My Neil," she said in a soft voice.

"I'm so very sorry to hear that, Nancy. I know you still cared for him." Kelly paused. She hated to speak ill of the dead, even though she wanted to. So she changed the subject. "Tell me, have you checked into doctors yet? I think I mentioned our friend Megan Harrington. She did a thorough search on all the obstetricians in the city when she was pregnant. So let me give you her phone number. She'll be happy to tell you about her top five list." Kelly deliberately gave Nancy a smile. She needed to focus on the future.

"Thank you, Kelly." Nancy looked up, gratitude in her eyes. "I really appreciate that. I was hoping Lisa would be able to give me recommendations."

Kelly decided to steer Nancy away from her dependence on Lisa, and this was a good time to start. "Lisa's got her hands full with her boyfriend Greg's recovery and his eventual rehabilitation. Since she's a physical therapist, she'll be heavily involved in his rehab. Plus she's still working."

"Oh, I was hoping she could talk, even on the phone," Nancy said, clearly disappointed.

Kelly gave a dismissive wave. "She's not even taking our calls right now, Nancy," Kelly deliberately fudged. "Besides, Lisa has never had a baby. She doesn't know about obstetricians. Megan's your girl. Believe me, Megan is thorough to a fault. Plus, she can give you advice about prenatal care. In fact, you should call her today and find out about obstetricians. You'll need to make an appointment. Here's Megan's phone number." She scrolled down her directory then scribbled the number on a notepad at the table.

"I guess," Nancy said, looking unsure.

"Oh, definitely," Kelly said, resorting to an imitation of Megan in full advice-giving form. Then she relaxed into the chair and proceeded to repeat everything she remembered Megan saying about prenatal health. In detail.

Nine

Kelly pulled out a wrought iron chair in the café's garden patio. A beautiful August morning that was more balmy than hot simply begged to be enjoyed. What better place to sort through complex client accounts? Her cell phone started to ring as she was about to settle into the chair.

Lisa's name flashed on her phone screen. Kelly quickly clicked on. "Hey there. Are you at the hospital? How's Greg doing today?"

"Yeah, I'm here. And Greg's fully awake now. All effects of anesthesia and the first heavy-duty painkillers have worn off. He's still getting some painkillers, but now he can really feel the extent of his injuries. Poor thing," she added in a sad voice.

"Oh, brother. I hope they give Greg some of the same goofy drugs they gave me when my ankle was broken. I was loopy for a while."

Lisa gave a little laugh. "Yeah, you sure were. I'm sure they'll be using some different painkillers for Greg. I noticed he would grimace when the nurses and orderlies came to put him on the gurney. They're transferring him to the rehab center this morning."

"Oh, that's great! Now we can visit him, right? Or should we wait a little?"

"I'll check with his doctor when he comes in this morning. He should be here pretty soon. Dr. Madan always makes morning rounds for his hospital patients. He may limit Greg's visitors until he's comfortably settled in at the rehab center."

"That makes sense." Kelly waved at waitress Julie as she approached and handed over her empty coffee mug. Julie smiled and snagged the mug from Kelly's outstretched fingers then sped off to check on the other breakfast customers who were enjoying the beautiful summer morning. "Does Greg even feel like talking?"

"Not really. He mumbles a few words to me and his voice is scratchy and hard to hear. So I have to lean close to him to make sure I hear everything he's saying."

"Oh, boy. It sounds like none of us should be visiting Greg anytime soon. We wouldn't want to put any stress on him when he's trying to heal from those injuries. It's too soon."

"Yeah, I think he'll be doing better in another few days. Once he's transferred to the rehab center, he can get settled in. And the physical therapists are going to start working with him tomorrow."

"Wow. That soon?" Kelly was surprised.

"Oh, yes. That's the usual routine after surgery, especially when the patient is strong and healthy and normally physically fit. Greg will have PT in the morning and occupational therapy in the afternoon. Every day. Seven days a week."

"Wow. What's occupational therapy? I thought everything was physical therapy."

"Occupational therapy helps patients learn how to do the ordinary daily routines like brushing their hair, brushing teeth, moving around, getting dressed. Stuff like that."

Kelly pictured all the daily routines and movements and motions that she did as a part of getting showered and dressed every morning. "How in the world can Greg do any of that? He's got a broken arm and a leg in a cast!"

"Well, they won't start on getting dressed right away. Both physical therapist and occupational therapist will probably start with simple movements with his good arm. Nothing strenuous, of course. They'll be careful, don't worry."

"Okay. I'll take your word for it. Boy, I forgot about all that routine stuff. Good thing Greg is a guy."

Lisa gave a short laugh. "Why's that?"

"He won't have to put on makeup," Kelly said as she accepted the refilled coffee mug from Julie. The sound of her friend's laughter drifted over the phone.

"Saying good-bye to summer, Kelly?" Mimi called as she walked through the patio garden to the small classroom cottage.

Kelly looked up. "Bite your tongue, Mimi," she called, then beckoned Mimi over to her outdoor table in the shade.

"This is a great place to work on your accounts," Mimi said, glancing about the garden as she joined Kelly. "Even I wouldn't mind paying the shop's bills out here in the summer shade."

"Pull up a chair, and I'll update you on Lisa's phone call a few minutes ago."

"Oh, yes, please do," Mimi said, her smile vanishing as she settled into a wrought iron chair across the table from Kelly.

"Lisa said Greg's fully awake now. All effects of anesthesia and the first heavy-duty painkillers have worn off. Unfortunately, she said that also means he can really feel all of his injuries." Kelly made a face.

"Ohhhhh, poor dear," Mimi said sorrowfully, her face reflecting her concern.

"I know. I feel the same. Lisa also said that Greg will be transferred from the hospital to the rehab center over there on the west side of town."

"So soon after surgery?" Mimi's eyes went wide in surprise.

"Apparently patients don't stay in hospitals as long as they used to years ago. Doctors get the severely injured ones like Greg transferred to rehab centers. I remember Steve and I went to see a friend of his over in one of the assisted-living facilities in town. That guy only had a broken arm and shoulder, but he lived alone so he couldn't really do a lot for himself at first. He was over at assisted living for about three weeks as I recall."

"You're right," Mimi said, glancing off into the garden. "I've heard others speak about the shorter hospital stays. Even new mothers are sent home the next day."

Kelly had to smile. "Well, if they're not sick, they're probably anxious to return home, especially with a new baby. Anyway, physical therapists are going to start working with Greg tomorrow."

"Goodness. So soon?"

"That's exactly what I said, Mimi." Kelly smiled. "Lisa reassured me that's the usual routine after surgery, especially when the patient is strong and healthy and normally physically fit. Greg will have PT in the morning and occupational therapy in the afternoon. Every day. Seven days a week."

"Oh, yes. Occupational therapy. That's the normal everyday things we do without thinking."

"Well, you're smarter than I am, Mimi. I had to ask Lisa. Things like brushing your hair, brushing teeth, moving around, getting dressed. Things like that."

"Oh, my, it sounds like Greg will be there a long time. Several weeks. Over a month."

Just then, Lisa's voice floated out into the garden. "Hey there, you two. Mind if I join you?"

Kelly swiveled in her chair and smiled at her friend standing in the driveway beside her car. "Absolutely," Kelly called, beckoning her over. "I was just updating Mimi with what little I knew about Greg. You can give her all the details."

Lisa hastened through the café garden patio without a glance to the surrounding greenery. "I'm so glad I found the two of you together," she said, depositing her tapestry bag on the table.

Julie approached them. "Hey, Lisa, do you want something cold to drink? It's starting to get hot outside."

"Actually, I do. Bring me a huge iced tea, would you please? Thanks."

"Sure thing," Julie replied as she continued walking through the garden, ever-present coffeepot in hand.

Lisa sank into a chair across from Kelly and Mimi. "Boy, I can really use that iced tea about now."

"You do look frazzled, dear," Mimi said in a solicitous voice.

Lisa gave a short laugh. "Frazzled, huh? That just about sums it up, Mimi."

"Has Greg been transferred to the rehab center yet?" Kelly asked, taking a sip of her iced coffee. Thankfully, their table was still nicely shaded by the overarching cottonwood trees and smaller maple trees. The August sun may not have been as intense as July's, but it was pretty close. Kelly figured her dermatologist would be pleased she was in the shade.

"He's being transferred now. That's why I thought this would be the perfect time to come over here and see you guys." Lisa released a long sigh. "And catch a breath. I've missed classes for two days, but my friends have e-mailed me their notes and stuff. So I've been studying while I've been sitting in chairs at the hospital. Most of the time, Greg is sleeping. Thankfully. That way he can't feel how uncomfortable he is."

"You poor thing. Have you had anything to eat? You

look more than frazzled to me." Mimi reached over and placed her hand on Lisa's forearm.

"I agree, Lisa. I'll bet you can't remember the last time you ate something," Kelly commented.

Lisa gave a wan little smile. "I had some soup at the hospital cafeteria last night. Ohhhh, and I had a doughnut this morning as I drove over to the hospital."

"That's it?" Kelly stared, astounded. Lisa was always so sensible.

Lisa shrugged. "That and coffee."

"Oh, my goodness, Lisa. That's not enough—" Mimi said before her cell phone's ring cut her short. She slipped the phone from her pocket and glanced at the screen. "Oh, my, this is another vendor I've been trying to contact." She swiftly rose from the chair. "Kelly, you make sure Lisa gets some real food, will you? She needs sustenance with all the stress that she's under right now."

"Consider it done, Mimi," Kelly said as Mimi hastened from the table. Catching Julie's eye, Kelly beckoned her over to the table. "You need nourishment. And not just the eighth food group, coffee."

At that, Lisa gave a short laugh. "Spoken by the queen of caffeine."

"Believe me, I know whereof I speak," Kelly lectured with a raised brow. "I'm ordering you one of Eduardo's Wicked Burgers, and you're going to eat it right now. There's no way you can continue going back and forth to the hospital and keeping up with your grad courses without food."

"There's no way I could eat one of those!" Lisa stared at Kelly, clearly astonished by the suggestion.

"Then you'll eat what you can. And I'm going to sit right here with you while you do," Kelly declared, deliberately using her best schoolmarm voice. Glancing at the ground beside Lisa's chair, Kelly reached over and snatched Lisa's tapestry bag and dropped it on the other side of her own chair. Out of Lisa's reach.

"Hey, I need that," Lisa protested mildly, waving her hand.

"Not right now. Right now, you're going to eat," Kelly ordered. Julie walked up then with a tall glass of iced tea. "Julie, Lisa needs food immediately. Tell Eduardo to look out the window into the patio and see how weak and puny Lisa looks and ask him to serve up one of his Wicked Burgers, please. The faster the better. Lisa's wasting away even as we speak."

Julie grinned. "Oh, we can't have that. She is looking tired and pale." Julie peered at Lisa as she handed her the glass. "Yep. You need some of Eduardo's good food to revive you. I'll tell him to get on that burger right away." With that, she sped off.

Lisa wagged her head. "You two are impossible, you know that? You also know how I hate to waste food."

"Believe me, it won't be wasted. Frankly, I think your innate good sense brought you over here so you could obtain nourishment." Kelly gave her a big grin.

"Ahhh, the queen of justification strikes again," Lisa said with a chuckle.

"I thought you said I was the queen of caffeine. Do I get two crowns?"

"Neither of those queens has a crown. Caffeine girl has a

coffee cup. And justification . . . well, I'll have to think on that." Lisa leaned back in the chair with a sigh. "You know, now that I'm sitting down, I realize that I really am tired."

Kelly took another deep drink of iced coffee and noticed Jennifer heading their way with a plate totally filled with a large burger.

"I heard there was a starving physical therapist outside who was in desperate need of sustenance," Jennifer said with a smile. "And you're in luck. Eduardo had just finished grilling some burgers. So voilà! Eduardo's famous Wicked Burger." She set the plate in front of Lisa with a flourish.

"Oh, my Lord," Lisa exclaimed. "I forgot how big they are. I can't eat this."

"Don't worry about it. Eat what you can," Jennifer said, placing the empty tray under her arm. "We don't want you fainting over a PT client in the midst of a session."

Lisa gave a little snort. "I gave all my appointments to one of the other therapists. So I won't be falling over anyone."

"Except yourself if you don't eat," Kelly admonished. "Now, take a bite. Those things are beyond yummy. Eduardo puts grilled onions on there, too."

"Enjoy!" Jennifer said as she headed toward other customer tables.

"Okaaaaaay," Lisa said, carefully lifting the huge burger with both hands. Juice dripped down onto the plate. She took a bite. Then closed her eyes. "Ummmmmm," she hummed in obvious enjoyment.

"Told you," Kelly teased. "Take a bigger bite next time because those grilled onions are in the middle."

Lisa did as instructed, and this bite elicited a louder hum of enjoyment. Kelly sipped her iced coffee and smiled as Lisa continued to savor the Wicked Burger. After several minutes, she heard a voice call from the driveway.

"Hey, Lisa, do you have a moment?"

Kelly recognized Lisa's classmate fellow grad student Nancy Marsted waving at them from the sidewalk leading to the shop.

Lisa glanced over. "Oh, my. There's Nancy. She's left several messages on my cell phone and I just haven't had time to call her back."

"You've been kind of preoccupied, Lisa. I already told Nancy you were at the hospital and what happened to Greg." Nancy started walking toward the gate that led into the café patio garden.

"Oh, Lord, I don't have the energy to counsel her now," Lisa said with a worried expression.

"Counsel her? I thought she was a fellow psychology student."

"She is, but I've become like a big sister to her. Nancy's kind of needy. And she comes to me with all the dramas in her life. I've heard everything about that boyfriend of hers in great detail. The one who was hit by a car."

Kelly couldn't miss her friend's dejected look. "You want me to steer her away? I already did that when Greg was first in the hospital. Nancy came looking for you, and I told her you weren't going to be around for a while because of Greg's accident. You were at the hospital and then you were going to supervise his rehab. So let me run interference for you again so you can finish. I'll ask her lots of questions and distract her until you've eaten every bit of that burger."

Lisa gave a crooked smile. "Thanks, Kelly. I'm amazed I've eaten so much already."

"Leave it to me," Kelly said, waving Nancy over to their table as she approached. "Hey, Nancy, have a seat. Lisa's taking a lunch break because she hasn't eaten in two days, so we won't interrupt her until she's finished."

Nancy's eyes flew wide. "Two days! That's awful, Lisa."

"That's exactly what I told her," Kelly said, leaning over the table and focusing her brightest client smile on Nancy. "So how are your classes going?"

"Uhhhhh . . . fine. They're fine," Nancy said, glancing from Kelly to Lisa and back.

Kelly switched to a more fertile subject, sure to capture Nancy's attention. "By the way, I mentioned to Lisa that your boyfriend was the victim of the hit-and-run accident. You were very lucky you weren't with him that night. You could have been killed, too. Or severely injured."

Nancy looked up, startled. "I . . . I hadn't thought of that."

"Well, I bet your father was happy you were no longer seeing that guy anymore. Your dad's a counselor, right?"

"Yes, yes, he is." Nancy glanced away. "And that's what I came to talk to Lisa about."

"Something about your father? What was it?" Kelly continued to try and deflect Nancy's laser beam focus on Lisa. She'd noticed Lisa had almost completely finished the burger.

"I went to the Halftime Bar and tried to talk to Neil, but he turned his back on me. Said he didn't want to have anything to do with me or the baby. He even said he wasn't the father! Right there in front of all those people! I called my dad right afterwards and told him everything. I was crying, and Dad got real upset. He said he was going to talk with Neil again." Nancy glanced anxiously from Kelly to Lisa.

Kelly paused, wondering what to say. Then Lisa dabbed a napkin to her mouth and focused on Nancy. "Forgive me, Nancy, but Greg's accident has totally wiped a lot of stuff out of my head. I can't remember what you told me about your father's encounter with your boyfriend. Are you sure your father actually talked to Neil at the bar?" Then she popped the last bite of burger into her mouth.

Clearly grateful that she'd gotten Lisa's attention, Nancy blurted out. "I *know* he did! Dad told me he found Neil at the bar that night and tried to talk to him. But Neil didn't want to listen. He even turned his back on my father." Nancy's worried expression intensified. "And that's when my dad got mad. He told me he accused Neil of abandoning me. And . . . and our baby. And Dad said he kind of lost it then."

Nancy's eyes started to tear up, Kelly noticed. "Well, that's really understandable, Nancy. You're his daughter and he's worried about you. What do you think your father meant when he said he 'lost it'?"

"He said he yelled at Neil . . . and got really mad at him. Dad didn't say anything more. But he looked really, really sad." Nancy started chewing her bottom lip.

Curious, Kelly asked, "Do you think your dad got in a fight with Neil?"

"I don't know. I'm not sure if he stayed at the bar longer or what. That's what's worrying me. And I'm pretty sure he's started drinking again. That really worries me, too." She looked away.

"I forgot you told me about your father drinking again. Was his speech slurred or something?" Lisa asked after she took a sip of water.

Nancy looked back at Lisa then Kelly. "No, his speech was okay. But I think I smelled it. I could always smell liquor on Dad's breath when he was drinking before."

Alcohol and anger, Kelly mused. A dangerous combination. "That's too bad. Lisa told me your dad was a recovering alcoholic."

"Yes, and he's been sober five years," Nancy said, her face clearly revealing her worry.

An idea popped into Kelly's head. "Didn't you tell us that your father was a counselor over at Alcoholics Anonymous?"

"Yes, but I don't know if they'll let him continue now that he's started drinking again."

"I have a good friend who also works with AA here in town, and she's a recovering alcoholic, too. Let me ask her what the procedure is when someone falls off the wagon, as they say. Surely, that's happened to others. Let me see what she says."

Nancy's big blue eyes widened. "Ohhhh, would you? Thank you so much, Kelly. I really appreciate that. My dad has gotten kind of quiet lately, too. That's another thing that's bothered me. Usually my dad is outgoing and wants to talk, but not now." She glanced out into the garden.

"It sounds like your father is feeling bad about slipping back into the old habits," Lisa said quietly. "He's probably feeling guilty, too, because he can tell he's disappointed you. Just give him time. I'm sure with AA's help, he'll get back on track."

"I hope so," Nancy said.

Kelly could hear a tiredness in Lisa's voice, so she decided to run interference once again. "I'll make sure I talk with my AA friend, Nancy, and I'll let you know. You can usually see me here at the shop or the café, working on my accounts outside in this beautiful weather." She gave Nancy a big smile. "Meanwhile, I'm going to the hospital to check on Greg while Lisa goes home and takes a nap. She's exhausted." It was a blatant lie, but Kelly figured it was the easiest way to rescue therapist Lisa from needy Nancy. She closed her laptop and started gathering her files from the table.

Thankfully, Nancy got the message, Kelly noticed. "Well, I've got to get back to the university. I have a class in an hour. Are you coming, Lisa?"

Lisa shook her head, tiredness showing clearly. "No, a friend is bringing me her notes and I'm doing the reading at night. I probably won't return to class until next week. I'll be spending most of the day with Greg in rehab."

"Don't worry, Nancy," Kelly interrupted in a cheerful voice as she stood up and slipped her briefcase bag over her shoulder. "I'll keep you updated with Greg's progress. Or Mimi will. Mimi is wonderful at looking after all of us. We call her Mother Mimi. If you don't see me here, don't hesitate to ask Mimi how things are going. Lisa will be missing in action for a while." Glancing to her tired friend, Kelly offered, "Do you want me to carry your bag, Lisa?" Then she added for emphasis, "You look really beat."

It must have worked because Nancy rose from the table as well. Lisa gathered her things and stood. She gave Nancy a tired smile as she and Kelly started to walk away. "Take care, Nancy. I'll see you back in class sometime next week, okay?"

Nancy nodded. "Okay, see you then. I hope Greg's recovery goes well."

"We're all keeping our fingers crossed," Kelly added, pointing Lisa to the opposite part of the garden. "Take care, Nancy." She gave a little wave.

"Thanks, Kelly," Lisa whispered. "I didn't know how tired I was until she started telling me about her father, and I swear, my brain just froze up. I had nothing to offer."

"That's what friends are for, Lisa," Kelly said as they wound their way through the greenery on the way to the back of Pete's Café. "We all need rescuing sometimes. And rescue comes in many forms."

"Amen," was all Lisa said.

Ten

Kelly tabbed between spreadsheet columns as she sat at Lambspun's knitting table. Checking the small plate beside her elbow, she speared the last bite of Pete's cinnamon roll. *Yum.* Her cell phone rang then, and Kelly chased the delicious taste of cinnamon and brown sugar with still-hot coffee. Burt's name flashed on the screen.

"Hey, Burt. I take it you're out doing shop errands, right?"

"You got it, Kelly," Burt's deep voice sounded over the phone. "I'm hungry for one of Eduardo's salads, so I'm heading back now."

"Hungering for a salad?" Kelly teased. "I haven't heard that before. Those salads are good, but those burgers are what strike my fancy."

"Well, you're right about that, Kelly," Burt said with a

little laugh. "But those Wicked Burgers are not on my diet, I'm afraid."

"I don't think they're on anybody's diet, Burt. But they are definitely to die for. So whenever I want to forget about healthy eating, I indulge in one of those." She tabbed to another column on the spreadsheet. "I'd better get back to this spreadsheet, Burt. That way I can relax and chat with you when you're back at the shop."

"Sounds good. I'll tell you about my phone call with Dan when I get there. See you soon." Burt clicked off.

Kelly checked the list of expenses and quickly entered the remaining items. As she did, three women entered from the adjoining workroom, all talking rapidly. Kelly had heard the babble of voices in the next room and recognized the familiar sound that indicated one of Mimi's classes had ended and the students were excited about their new projects. The women settled at the other end of the table and returned to their various knitting projects. Finished working, Kelly saved the spreadsheet and closed her laptop. Then she glanced at the women. "I'll bet you three have just finished one of Mimi's classes, right?"

The middle-aged women all looked Kelly's way. "Yes, we have. Mimi's intermediate knitting class."

"Oh, that's excellent. What are you all working on?" Kelly asked.

All three obligingly held up their knitting needles with their current projects dangling from them. Kelly spotted a sock, a beginning sweater, and something that could be either a sock or a hat. On the circular needles, it was hard to tell.

"Oh, wow, you're all doing very well," she praised them.

"The sweater looks halfway done, and so is the sock." She pointed at the questionable one. "And that looks like it could be a sock but maybe a hat. Which is it?"

"It's a sock," the blond woman said, laughing a little. "It looks a little different because several of my early stitches are . . . well, they're definitely not up to Mimi's standard."

Kelly joined her laughter. "Boy, do I know what that's like. I still don't think my knitting is up to snuff, but Mimi is so kind, she always encourages me no matter how ugly my projects look."

The brunette woman countered, "Now you're exaggerating, Kelly. I've seen several of your knitting projects and they look perfect."

"Whoa!" Kelly let out a loud laugh. "The word 'perfect' and my knitting do not belong in the same sentence."

The brunette gave a dismissive wave of her hand, similar to Mimi's gesture. "Now you're just being silly."

Kelly relaxed against her chair and took a sip from her coffee. "Do all of you live here in Fort Connor?"

All three women nodded. The gray-haired one spoke first. "Yes, our family has been here for a couple of decades. My father was a university professor, so my two sisters and I grew up here. We all went to the university and married fellows we went to school with." She smiled at the other two women. "I'm Lucy, and this is my sister Leann." She pointed to the blond woman to her right.

The brunette glanced over at Kelly. "And I'm their cousin Geraldine. My husband and I own a bar downtown. Since we're new at this business, we do everything. We work at the bar, wait tables. Whatever the customers need."

"Wow," Kelly said, looking at the woman in awe. "That is one huge endeavor from what I've heard. Doing all the work, cleaning up, handling the customers."

The woman nodded, concentrating on her knitting. "I told my husband I had to take a break for this class. Knitting helps me keep my sanity. Plus it's midday, so the bar's not open now. Besides, we don't have an early crowd. They show up later." She gave a short laugh.

"Don't they ever," Leann said over the sock.

"You should talk to Jennifer in the café. She waitresses here in the mornings and does real estate in the afternoons. She's been in that business for a lifetime. Which bar is it?"

Geraldine looked up briefly before concentrating on the strange sock. "Oh, I did speak with her. Jennifer was a great source of advice. We own the Halftime, right around the corner from Taylor Street and Abercrombie."

Kelly recognized the name of the bar. The same one where Nancy had met that sleazy guy Neil. "I confess I've heard of it. A friend called it a pickup bar."

Geraldine nodded. "Yeah, I'm afraid it does have that reputation."

Lucy gave a snort. "Lots of sleazy lowlifes hanging around."

"I'll say. And that scum who preyed on Mary," Leann said in a sharp voice.

"Well, yes. Jennifer said the bar crowd is a mixed bag," Geraldine offered.

Kelly leaned forward over her coffee mug. "That sounds like a story."

"A sad one, I'm afraid," Lucy said.

Leann spoke in a quiet voice, fingers still working the yarn. "We all have another cousin, Sarah, who has a daughter named Mary. Mary was born with a developmental problem that resulted in a slight limp.

"Mary had worked hard to get over her motor skills disability. By the time she entered university, her slight limp was barely noticeable after several years of physical therapy and hard work. Mary was a good student and worked steadily toward her graduate degree in business, specializing in advertising. She was a gifted writer and enjoyed writing ad copy for various products. Mary assured her mother and her protective older brother, Reggie, that an office job in advertising would be perfect for her.

"Unfortunately, Mary was out with friends one night, and they decided to go to the Halftime Bar. And while she was there, Mary met a guy from one of her graduate classes. He acted really interested in her and very solicitous toward Mary. So Mary, who had only dated a little, started going out with this guy. Reggie was naturally protective and wanted to meet him."

Leann took a breath before continuing. "This guy acted the perfect gentleman with Reggie, and Mary said he was always polite every time they went out. But apparently he wanted more from his dates with Mary. They went out one night, and this scumbag must have used one of those date rape drugs in Mary's wine."

Lucy interjected, "No doubt he got it from some other scumbag college friend. I've heard those students can buy anything they want. Someone will be selling it. That's the problem with a college town."

Leann took another breath. "Anyway, poor Mary woke up naked in his bed the next morning. She didn't remember anything that happened after they were having dinner together at an Old Town pub. Apparently he wanted to continue their amorous activities, but Mary said she was confused and ashamed. She'd never been with a man before, and she had wanted the first time to be special. Now she couldn't remember a thing. Mary said she quickly dressed and ran from his apartment, then took a taxi to Reggie's office. He works as a sales rep for a building supply store. Reggie told our cousin that Mary ran into his office, threw herself into his arms, and broke down in tears."

Kelly screwed up her face. "That is an awful story. Poor Mary. She sounds like an innocent lamb who literally ran into the bad wolf at the bar."

"And it gets worse," Lucy said in a bitter voice. The sweater she was knitting had added several rows of stitches—angry stitches, no doubt—onto her needles.

"Oh, no," Kelly said in a dejected voice. "What happened?"

"Reggie was furious at what happened to his innocent younger sister. So the next night, Reggie charged into the Halftime Bar. The bartender pointed out this guy, and Reggie confronted him in front of everybody at the bar. He accused him of deliberately attacking his sister. Reggie said other guys at the bar had to restrain him, and the bartenders escorted him out."

"I remember one of our bartenders told us what happened. That was a couple of years ago, I think," Geraldine said, glancing up at Lucy.

Lucy nodded. "Well, the tragic thing is that in the weeks

following all of this, Mary's physical disability returned in a more pronounced form, giving her walking problems. Reggie was convinced it was because of that memory drug the guy used on her that night. Reggie confronted him again at the university this time and accused him loudly in front of other students. Then he pushed Smith so hard he fell to the ground. I heard from a student friend of Mary's that Reggie stood over him and threatened him. She said that the guy was so scared, he turned white."

"I'm glad he was scared. I wish Reggie had given him a thrashing like our father used to say," Leann said angrily.

"It sounds like that guy certainly deserved it," Kelly commented. She sipped her coffee, watching Lucy and Leann add more stitches to their projects. Meanwhile, her little buzzer went off inside. Curious, Kelly decided to follow up and toyed with the idea of mentioning Nancy's story without using her name. "You know, a friend has told me about someone she knows. A graduate student at the university, like your cousin's daughter. Her friend met this really charming guy at the university. They started dating and getting serious," Kelly deliberately fudged as she continued a modified version of Nancy's story.

"Anyway, she said this grad student had not dated very much but was very impressed with how great this guy seemed to be. Really polite and intelligent. So the relationship escalated. The grad student said this guy kept talking like they were a couple and all that. Well, once the grad student learned she was pregnant, she told the guy, expecting him to be happy. Instead, the guy rejected her. Told her the baby wasn't his and accused her of sleeping around.

Right in front of all these people at the Halftime Bar. The grad student ran away in tears."

Geraldine rolled her eyes. "Oh, brother," she said in a dejected tone.

Lucy and Leann both turned toward Kelly. "Oh, no!" Leann said.

"This is depressing," Geraldine said, shaking her head sadly.

Lucy frowned. "I wish I could say I'm surprised, but I'm not. Some guys are definitely predators. Did your friend make mention of this guy's name by any chance?"

Kelly paused, knowing she could not be completely forthright with the women. "I think she mentioned the name 'Neil' if I remember correctly."

Lucy's eyebrows shot up and she exchanged a glance with her sister Leann, who nodded. "That's got to be the same guy," Leann replied. "Neil Smith."

"It certainly sounds like it," Lucy concurred.

"You know, wasn't 'Smith' the name of the person who was killed by a hit-and-run driver last week in Old Town?" Geraldine asked, looking around at Kelly and the others.

"Now that you mention it, I think you're right." Kelly pretended surprise.

Once again, Lucy and Leann exchanged glances. Then Lucy spoke in a solemn voice. "If it was really this guy, I have to say I believe that was a fitting punishment."

"Amen," said Leann.

Kelly sipped her coffee. She wasn't about to add anything to the pronouncements of the two sisters. Judgment had already been rendered.

• • •

Burt walked into the café alcove just as Kelly rose to refill her iced coffee glass from the pitcher Jennifer left on the café counter. "Hey, Burt. I was hoping to see you this afternoon."

"Not surprised you're over here in the empty café," Burt said, standing at the counter while Kelly filled her glass. "It's peaceful and quiet here. By the way, I wanted to update you on the police search for the hit-and-run driver."

Kelly quickly finished pouring into her cup. "Yes, please do. You know I've been curious. Here, let me fill yours." She started pouring the black liquid into Burt's coffee mug.

"Thanks, Kelly. Dan says they've canvassed that entire street and the nearby streets. Asking everybody if they saw or heard anything that night. Any squealing of tires or crashing sounds. Anything at all." Burt dumped some powdered creamer into his coffee mug and stirred. "Unfortunately, no one can remember seeing or hearing anything unusual." He took a deep drink of coffee.

"Really? It's Old Town on a Saturday night. You'd think someone would have been wandering around."

"Don't forget, that area is really on the edge of Old Town. It borders the cafés, and the businesses are closed up at night. Not many houses or apartments with people living there, either. So there really isn't much happening along that dark street leading to the corner like there is on the closer streets of Old Town."

Kelly frowned. "Well, damn."

Burt chuckled. "I can't tell you how many times I've thought the same thing, Kelly. About other cases usually."

"So there's no way to catch the hit-and-run driver?"

"Not as long as the perpetrator who committed the crime has the vehicle locked away in a garage where no one can see it. Unless the driver decides to bring out that vehicle and an officer spots it, there's absolutely no way to learn who the driver was. Apparently no one was walking around to see it. At least, no one has come forward to the police and said they were in the area and saw something. And until someone does, the cops are stopped dead in the investigation. It goes nowhere."

"Are police still investigating Neil Smith to see if there's anyone from his past who might have decided to seek revenge on this guy?" Kelly queried. "I just heard another sad story of an unsuspecting university student who went out with Neil Smith and woke up in his bed the next morning. Couldn't remember a thing."

Burt scowled. "As I've said before, predators are out there. And it looks like Neil Smith was one of the worst. I have to confess, I have absolutely no sympathy for him."

"Well, I just listened to three knitters, sisters Leann and Lucy and their cousin Geraldine, who told the tale of their other cousin's daughter who was used and abused by Neil Smith a couple of years ago. A really sad case. And that girl's older brother actually accosted Smith in an Old Town bar. It sounds like he had reason to wish Neil Smith ill, to say the least."

Burt's brow shot up in the way it did when he heard something intriguing. Kelly had learned to recognize the signs. "Oh, really? I think I'll have a conversation with them the next time they're in the shop."

"Do that. They were mesmerizing, for sure. And they make no bones about the animosity they hold for Smith. They particularly mentioned how angry their cousin's son, Reggie, was about what happened to his sister."

Burt's crooked smile appeared. "You've been sleuthing around again, Sherlock. I can see. I will make sure to follow up on that and get back to you."

"Thanks, Burt." Remembering something, Kelly added, "Oh, and while you're at it, you might want to have a talk with Lisa. She and I had a conversation earlier with a college student friend of hers, Nancy Marsted. She told Lisa and me that she was worried about her father. Apparently he was so upset when she told him what happened to her with Neil Smith, he fell off the wagon and started drinking again. He told Nancy he went out looking for Smith one night and actually confronted him in one of the Old Town bars."

Burt's smile vanished. "That's definitely not good. Were the police called?"

"Apparently not. He told Nancy the bartenders escorted him out and he left. But Nancy says her father's been acting really quiet ever since then. She's clearly worried. And Lisa and I couldn't help wondering if her father might have done something he regretted."

Burt exchanged a look with Kelly. "I am really sorry to hear that. It's a sad story. I think I will definitely give Dan a call this afternoon."

Kelly took another drink of coffee. "I figured Dan should know."

"You figured right, Kelly."

"Who knows? Maybe Nancy's father waited in his car for Neil Smith to leave the bar then ran him down that night. If he started drinking again, maybe he can't even remember."

Burt looked at her sadly. "Who knows, Kelly."

Eleven

Light raindrops sprinkled on Kelly as she quick-stepped across the driveway from her cottage. A couple of hours ago when she and Steve were taking their early morning run, the skies had been clear and sunny. But it was summer, which meant dark clouds could suddenly roll across the mountains and bring a summer rain shower, complete with rumbles of thunder and a flash of lightning or two. Then just as quickly as they'd come, the clouds would blow away to the east and out of town. And bright sunshine would blaze in the sky once more. Summer storms.

A car horn beeped as Kelly reached the sidewalk bordering the café patio garden, and she turned to see Megan pull into a parking spot. Several couples still sat outside under the large café table umbrellas enjoying breakfast. Kelly paused on the sidewalk and waited for her friend.

"Hey there," Kelly greeted her as Megan scooted around the car. "Are you taking a break from clients?"

"Sort of. I also wanted to check on some yarn I'd ordered. A special order from Chile. Mimi said it might be in this week."

"Oooo, that sounds interesting," Kelly said as she turned toward the shop entrance. "Where's Molly?"

"She's with a new sitter. I'm trying out a nursing student who also babysits. Cassie has been a lifesaver this summer, but she'll go back to school next week. Hey, why don't we grab one of those tables out here?" Megan suggested, pointing toward the garden patio. "This little shower won't last long. You know they never do in the summer. Besides, I love the smell of the rain."

"Sure," Kelly said, following Megan as she sped down one of the stone pathways leading into the garden. "I love that smell, too. Especially if it hasn't rained in a while." She sniffed the damp air. "Wet plants."

Megan headed toward a table that had recently been vacated by more timid customers, who probably weren't as comfortable sitting outside as light rain sprinkled around them. Kelly had watched them scurry inside the café earlier. Now she could barely feel the raindrops.

"Have you heard from Lisa this morning?" Megan asked as she pulled out a chair.

Kelly settled into a wrought iron chair across from Megan and set her sturdy briefcase bag beneath the table. Laptops didn't like rain in any form, showers or storms. "I got a brief call from her saying that Greg was looking a lot more alert. He likes the physical therapist and doesn't mind the occupational therapist, even though he can't manage those activities yet."

"That's good news. I wonder when we can go over and visit. We've sent a bunch of flowers, but Greg's not a big flower guy."

Kelly laughed softly. "That's true, but even Greg will appreciate the thoughts behind the flowers. We all care about him, and that's the only way we can show it now."

"Marty's dying to give Greg a book he found at an antique store. You know how Greg loves history. Well, Marty found a book with original engravings in it from the eighteen hundreds."

"Greg will love that," Kelly said, gesturing to Jennifer, who was walking their way.

"What are you two silly things doing sitting here in the rain?" Jennifer said, grinning at them.

"It's barely sprinkling," Megan said. "I was going to see if Cassie wanted to go practice at the tennis courts with me then I remembered she's going down to Denver, isn't she?"

"Yes, she left with Pete just a little while ago. Tanya is meeting them at the shopping center which is down the street from her apartment."

"Well, at least she was able to finish up the final softball season with her teammates. I know that meant a lot to her," Kelly said, noticing the light sprinkle had picked up slightly. More raindrops splashed down on the broad-leafed plants beside their table.

Jennifer nodded. "Yes, she also didn't want to leave until she heard that Greg was doing better. So Lisa called last night and told Cassie that Greg was settling in at the rehab center and actually starting his physical therapy exercises. That helped."

Kelly could see the slightly worried expression on Jennifer's face. "I bet we'll be able to visit Greg at the rehab center soon. So that will be something for Cassie to look forward to when she returns."

"We'll all look forward to that," Megan added. "Is Tanya bringing Cassie back or Pete?"

"Pete will get her. In fact, we'll probably both go down to Denver Sunday afternoon and poke around in LoDo and some of the shops. Maybe try a new café. Then we'll get Cassie."

"Why don't you and Pete come out to the game tomorrow night," Megan suggested. "Otherwise you two will be rattling around in the house by yourselves and you're not used to that."

"That's a good idea. I'm missing Cassie already, and I know Pete is." Jennifer glanced around. "You know, it's not really a light sprinkle anymore. So I'm putting up this umbrella." She pushed the fabric umbrella open with a practiced hand. "And I'll return with the coffeepot." With that, Jennifer scurried off through the glistening wet plants, leaving her slightly damp friends laughing.

Kelly tabbed through the columns of client Don Warner's accounting spreadsheet, entering revenues and expenses, watching the totals change at the bottoms of the columns. Her eye caught the red-colored type appearing in one column, indicating a negative amount. Kelly zeroed in on it like a hawk spotting a field mouse.

The light rain sprinkle had turned into a light shower. And Kelly actually enjoyed working outside beneath the umbrella in the sweet-smelling rain. Especially now that she had a full mug of hot coffee. She took a deep sip, enjoying the heat on her throat while she eyed the disobedient numbers in that one column.

"Hey there, Kelly girl!" Jayleen Swinson's voice called out behind her.

Kelly swiveled around in the chair and spied Jayleen waving at her from the parking lot. "Hey, Jayleen. Come and join me. It's nice underneath the umbrella here in the rain."

"I reckon I will," Jayleen said as she walked into the garden patio. Colorado cowgirl Jayleen always had a Stetson over her graying blondish curls, so clearly a rain shower didn't bother her. She still didn't look her sixtyish years.

"I bet Julie will be out with her coffeepot as soon as she spots you," Kelly said, pushing her laptop aside. Spreadsheets could wait.

"Well, now, that will really hit the spot," Jayleen said, settling into a wrought iron chair across the table from Kelly. Glancing above at the umbrella and around the garden, she smiled. "You've got yourself a nice little nest here, Kelly. Perfect for your kind of work. Staring at columns of numbers and all that."

Kelly chuckled. "Well, I confess I do a lot of staring and thinking, before I try to make those numbers behave."

"Has Greg been transferred to that rehab center yet? Mimi's been keeping me updated every couple of days. Then I tell Curt. We've both been worried about that boy." Her normally cheerful countenance clouded.

"He was transferred yesterday, and Lisa says he's settling in and has started with his physical therapy."

Jayleen found her smile again. "Well, now, that sounds more like the Greg we know. I predict that boy will make a quick recovery. Any idea when he'll be allowed visitors?"

Kelly shook her head. "Nope. Lisa hasn't gotten the word yet. We'll probably go over in shifts because there's a lot of us."

"You can make up a schedule on one of those spread-sheets. Put all those columns to good use." Jayleen's expression changed and a worried look appeared. "By the way, I was wondering if Burt's told you how the police hunt for that hit-and-run driver who ran into Greg is going?"

"I actually talked to Burt earlier today, and the cops haven't found anyone who was around on the streets to provide information. So they have no clues as to who it could be. I thought maybe someone in town would come out of the woodwork when the newspaper story came out. Whoever hit Greg is probably the very same person who ran into and killed that graduate student farther up that street."

"I reckon you're right." Jayleen nodded. "Lord a mercy, who in the world could run their car into one person and then drive just a little ways down the street and hit someone else?" She shook her head, clearly amazed.

"Since that street is just outside Old Town, I'm still hoping that someone who was walking back from the bars in that area of Old Town will call the cops with information. Or maybe someone driving by."

Jayleen stared toward the wet garden, raindrops plopping on the varieties of foliage plants and annuals scattered around the edges of the garden along the fence. "I was really hoping the police would have found someone by now. Or that person would have turned himself in. Mainly because I'm feeling guilty about something I heard from a fellow AA member the other night."

That comment immediately caught Kelly's attention. "Did one of your AA friends know something about the hit-and-run? Or did one of your members say something in the group sharing time?"

Jayleen shook her head. "No. But one of the members I've known for years told me something a while ago that's stayed with me ever since. It's been tugging at me."

"What was it?"

Jayleen released a long sigh. "This fellow straightened himself up five years ago. I was his AA mentor, and I was real proud of him. He stopped drinking and has been clean and sober ever since. Did it for his daughter, he said. Well, at one of the meetings, I noticed him acting different. Pre-occupied. So I came up to him afterwards and asked if something was going on in his life. He motioned me over to the side and said he was worried about his daughter. She'd been dating this guy and had gotten real serious. She thought he was serious about her, too. The guy talked about their being a couple and even making plans for the future. When the girl became pregnant, she told the guy. And that no-good so-and-so rejected her right in front of all these

147

guys in a bar! Accused her of sleeping around and all that trash. My friend Felix said his daughter came running home in tears." Jayleen's face screwed up.

"Oh, brother," was all Kelly said, even though her instinct was buzzing like mad.

"Anyway, I could tell how upset Felix was, watching him tell me about it. Thunderclouds were storming across his face. And that was the last time I saw him at our AA meetings. He hasn't been back since. I confess, I'm worried that he started drinking again. And . . . and he might have done something when he was drunk that he can't live with." Jayleen looked over at Kelly. "I'm afraid that he might have gone over to those bars when he was all liquored up, and . . . I don't know. Maybe he saw that lowlife come out of the bar and deliberately ran him down." She wagged her head sadly. "Lordy, Lordy."

Kelly took a deep drink of coffee and savored the burn at the back of her throat. Meanwhile, she pondered whether she should reveal what she had learned from Nancy Marsted. Clearly, Jayleen's friend Felix from the local Alcoholics Anonymous had to be the same person. Nancy's father.

"You know, Jayleen. I'm going to share something Lisa and I both learned from one of Lisa's graduate student friends. Her name is Nancy and she, too, has a father who is a counselor at Alcoholics Anonymous. But I'm going to ask that you keep this information to yourself."

Jayleen's big blue eyes popped wide. "Lord have mercy, girl! You've got my word on it. I won't tell anyone, even Curt."

"Apparently Nancy's father told her that he did find her

boyfriend, Neil Smith, at the bar one night, and he threatened him."

"Oh, Lord."

"Nancy doesn't know what happened after that, but she was worried because she smelled liquor on her father's breath and she knew he'd started drinking again."

Jayleen closed her eyes. "Oh, no," she said, her voice revealing her sorrow.

"And now that her boyfriend is dead, Nancy told Lisa and me she's worried her father may be the driver that ran Smith down the other night. Apparently Felix had been frequenting the bars again and was out that night."

"Lord, Lord," Jayleen said softly, shaking her head. "No wonder we haven't seen Felix lately."

Kelly watched Jayleen as the sadness of losing a brave survivor to addiction's strong pull once again registered on her friend's face. "It's sad."

Jayleen released a long, heavy sigh. "That it is, Kelly girl. And so is what I have to do next. I've gotta tell Burt."

"You won't have to, Jayleen. I've already shared Nancy's story with Burt, and he's alerting his former partner at the Fort Connor Police Department. No doubt they will visit Nancy's father, Felix, pretty soon."

Jayleen shook her head again. "Lordy, Lordy."

Kelly decided to change the subject so Jayleen wouldn't dwell on what happened to Felix. "By the way, you and Curt should come out to the ball field on Saturday evening. Our team is playing in the finals against Greeley West, our main rival. So we could use some more cheering for our side."

Jayleen's smile returned. "I'm sure I can talk Curt into it.

Maggie Sefton

Besides, I think Eric's team may be playing his last game. Cassie's team is already finished." Then Jayleen looked at Kelly directly, straight into her eyes. "Mimi told me Cassie is spending the weekend with her mom down in Denver. I understand why. Sounds like Tanya's finally trying to be a mother."

Kelly glanced out into the garden. The rain spattered rhythmically on the broad plant leaves. Deep forest green, with gently curving dips, like a widespread hand. Her umbrella-shaded table was one of two that were still occupied. "I guess so. Both Pete and Jennifer think Tanya suddenly took a good look at Cassie and realized how fast she was growing up. Before we all know it, she'll be in high school, then gone off to college."

"Lord, don't we know it," Jayleen said.

"So if Tanya is going to try to develop a relationship with her daughter, now's the time." Kelly leaned back in the chair and took a deep drink of coffee.

Jayleen grinned at her. "Pretty good advice coming from someone who's never had kids."

Kelly shrugged. "I've been coaching kids in softball for years now, and that's given me a bird's-eye view of a lot of parents and how they act around their kids. Some parents are relaxed and comfortable with their kids and other kids. Other parents are kind of standoffish and don't really interact. They're more like chauffeurs. They come right at the time the kids are finished, pick up their kids, and drive off. Other parents come earlier and watch the kids practice. Some stay for the entire session. Now, I have no idea if any of that gives a clue as to the parents' relationship with their kids or not, but it's always made me curious."

"You know, it's interesting to hear you say that. I've watched parents and their kids and wondered the same thing. Of course, I totally screwed up any chance of having a relationship with my kids years ago. So I certainly have no right to pass judgment on others." She stared out into the garden.

Kelly watched her older friend's face, saw the trace of sadness flash across her features briefly. Jayleen had confessed that her years of being an alcoholic had totally ruined any chance she had of having a relationship with her son and daughter. Jayleen's second husband had legally adopted both kids when they were elementary age, and they grew up thinking of him as their real parent. Their mother was never there. Bars and liquor provided a much stronger hold on Jayleen than family ties ever could.

By the time Jayleen joined Alcoholics Anonymous and totally rebuilt her life, her attempts at reconnecting with her children failed miserably. Both her son and her daughter were in college by then and wanted nothing to do with her. She wasn't there when they needed her, and there was no place in their lives for her now. She was a stranger. Neither of them had any good memories of their mother. Only drunken scenes. When Jayleen recounted those stories to her, Kelly's heart had given a little squeeze of pain for her friend.

"I think you've done a lot to redeem yourself, Jayleen," Kelly said. "You're great around kids. You've given riding and alpaca care lessons to 4-H groups for years. And you're an excellent grandmother to Curt's grandkids, and Cassie adores you."

"I do love those kids," Jayleen said with a smile. "And I confess that I think of Cassie as the granddaughter I never had."

"I kind of sensed that, Jayleen. Both you and Mimi had tragic events occur in your lives that took away the chances to have grandchildren. Mimi's only child, her son, died while still in college. And yours, well, your ex-husband became their parent, it sounds like."

"Ralph was a good man. Is a good man, I'll say that. And he took over when I dropped all my responsibilities in his lap." She wagged her head again. "He's a jewel in my eyes. I've told him that, too. Actually wrote him a letter apologizing for everything I'd put him through years ago. And my kids. I wrote them letters, too, but I'm not sure they ever read them."

Kelly stared at her friend. "Wow, Jayleen. That was a big step. Huge."

Jayleen gave her a wry smile. "It's all part of Alcoholics Anonymous. The twelve steps. One of the biggest steps is Forgiveness. Forgiving other people. And then, forgiving yourself. That's even harder."

Kelly had nothing to say that could possibly add to that profound concept. So she simply raised her mug of coffee to her friend in salute. Jayleen simply smiled.

Twelve

"**What** do you want on your hot dog?" Steve asked Kelly as he climbed down from the Rolland Moore Park ball field blcachers.

"The works, without onions. Thanks," Kelly replied from her place mid-bleachers.

Megan jumped up from her spot on the bleacher row above Kelly. "Marty, get me one, too. Loaded, of course."

Marty gave her a thumbs-up as he and Steve headed toward the concession stand behind the bleachers.

"Didn't you just finish two slices of pizza?" Jennifer asked. She spooned some chocolate frozen custard from a cup as she and Pete sat beside Kelly.

"Yeah, but I'm still hungry." Megan grinned.

Mimi laughed lightly from her place beside Jennifer.

"You amaze me, Megan. You look exactly the same as you did before the baby."

"That's Megan Metabolism," Kelly said with a laugh as she leaned against the wooden row behind her.

"Amazing, that's me," Megan said as she sat down beside Kelly.

Burt approached the bleachers, two large take-out cups in his hands. "Here you go, Mimi," he said, offering her one. "Chocolate shake. I got strawberry." He grinned. "Childhood favorite."

"Ooooo, that looks good," Megan said, eyeing Mimi's large cup. "I'll have to get one. After the hot dog."

Kelly laughed at her friend, then remembered something. She slid to the end of the row and jumped down from the bleachers, then beckoned to Burt. "You got a minute?" She walked away from the bleachers a few feet.

"Sure, Kelly," he said, following her. "What's up?"

"I wondered if you'd had a chance to talk to Dan at the department today?"

"I left him a message before Mimi and I drove over here to the game, but I haven't heard anything yet."

"Well, I thought I'd share with you something Jayleen told me yesterday. It turns out she knows Nancy Marsted's father, Felix, over at AA. She'd been his mentor and helped him a few years ago when he was trying to stop drinking. She says Felix has been sober for several years now. Anyway, he told Jayleen all about his daughter's experience with that graduate student—"

"Neil Smith." Burt nodded.

"Jayleen told me Felix looked like he was simmering

with rage when he told her. She did her best to try to calm him down, but he walked out of the meeting. And he didn't come back. He hasn't been to AA for over a week now. He hasn't called in. Nothing. No contact. She's called him on his cell phone but he doesn't answer, and he doesn't return her calls. Jayleen's really worried. I didn't tell her that I'd already heard about Nancy Marsted's father and had told you about it." She met Burt's inquisitive gaze. "I wondered if you'd had a call from Jayleen. I know she was feeling conflicted because she's not supposed to reveal anything that one of their partners tell them. They take their confidentiality promise seriously."

"I understand, Kelly. But no, I haven't heard a word from Jayleen. But I will definitely share that information with Dan."

Kelly looked out onto the ball field. The sounds of players cheering caught her attention. Eric was running off the field with a baseball held tight in his glove high above his head. That had to be the opponent's third out. Eric's team won. Eric and his teammates let out jubilant shouts and yells of celebration, while their parents cheered from the bleachers.

"I have a feeling Jayleen confided in me because she knew I would tell you. That way she doesn't have to be the one who squeals on Felix to the police."

Burt gave her a little smile. "I think you're right. And you know that I will leave another message for Dan tonight. If Felix Marsted fell off the wagon and tried to punish the guy who hurt his daughter, Dan will find out."

Cheers sounded from the bleachers again, and Kelly

turned to see Eric striding up to the stands. Jayleen and Curt appeared at the front of the bleachers.

"Way to go, Eric!" Megan called in a loud voice.

"Great catch!" Pete shouted from the bleachers.

"Atta boy, Eric!" Jayleen said as she stood beside Curt.

Kelly spotted a slight flush creep over Eric's face. "Thanks, guys."

Curt reached out and clapped his grandson on the shoulder in a gesture Kelly recognized. "Good job, son," Curt congratulated.

"Thanks, Grandpa," Eric said with a grin as he removed his baseball cap and wiped his dripping forehead against his uniform sleeve.

Kelly and Burt both walked toward the front of the bleachers. Kelly waited until she caught Eric's eye, then gave him a big grin and a thumbs-up sign. "Good job, Eric. That was the winning catch."

Eric grinned. "I couldn't believe it was coming down in front of me."

"You were in the right place at the right time," Jayleen said, giving him one of her encouraging back slaps.

"Hey, good job, Eric!" Steve called out as he approached the bleachers, two hot dogs in one hand and a drink in the other. "Marty and I saw that catch from the concession stand."

"I bought an extra dog with the works," Marty announced, holding out a loaded hot dog as he approached.

"Really?" Eric's eyes popped wide, accepting the ballpark treat.

"Yep, it's yours. I already ate one at the stand, and this other one's for Megan." Marty's grin spread wide.

"Gee, thanks," Eric said then took a huge bite.

Kelly laughed. "Eric's going through another growth spurt. What's your excuse for that giant appetite, Marty?"

"Cranked-up metabolism," Marty answered. "You should have seen me when I was Eric's age."

"Oh, Lord, that must have been a scary sight," Jennifer joked. "I remember my younger brother going through two large pizzas at a time when he was Eric's age. There were no such things as leftovers in our house."

"You got that right," Curt agreed. "I remember Ruthie always made an extra turkey on Thanksgiving so Marty would have enough to eat."

Everyone laughed at that, even Eric right before he consumed the last bite of hot dog. "Boy, your family's grocery bill must be huge," Kelly teased.

Jayleen said, "I've gone shopping with Megan and she fills up two entire grocery carts."

Kelly laughed out loud along with the rest of the group. She thought she heard a cell phone's ring and noticed Pete reach into his pocket. "Well, you've earned an ice cream treat, Eric. After you finish the hot dog. What flavor?"

Eric swallowed down the last bite. "Gee, thanks, Kelly. How about strawberry?"

"Strawberry it is." Kelly was about to walk toward the concession stand when she watched Pete and Jennifer climbing down the bleachers. She couldn't miss their worried expressions. They both beckoned to the group as they approached.

"What's up, guys?" Steve asked as he stood beside Kelly.

"I just had a call from Cassie," Pete said. "She's over at a grocery store coffee bar in the shopping center down the street from Tanya's apartment. Tanya was out buying ice cream, and Cassie stayed behind in the apartment with Tanya's boyfriend, Donnie. Cassie said Donnie started acting funny. She said it made her really uncomfortable, and she left. That's when she walked down to the drugstore and called me."

Suddenly, all laughter and good humor that surrounded them evaporated. Kelly felt a cold fist inside her stomach.

"Did he touch her?" Burt demanded in a low voice.

Pete's face had an angry expression that Kelly had never seen before. Good-natured Pete never got angry. Kelly glanced at her dear friend. Jennifer looked more than worried. Kelly detected a touch of fear in Jennifer's expression.

"She said he put his hands on her shoulders and started rubbing her neck as he talked about playing music. Cassie said it gave her the creeps, as she called it, and she told him to stop." Storm clouds darkened Pete's face now.

"Son of a bitch," Steve muttered beneath his breath.

"That's when she left and walked to the shopping center. She's at the coffee bar in the corner Sooper Dooper grocery store."

"Atta girl," Jayleen said. "You get on the road now, Pete. You need to bring that girl back home!"

"I'll drive, Pete," Steve offered, putting his hand on Pete's shoulder. "That way you and Cassie can talk in the backseat as we drive home."

"Good idea, Pete," Kelly said. "We don't want you getting a distracted driving ticket."

"I'm going along, too, guys," Marty declared. "Just in

case Tanya starts to protest. I can inform her that you have already filed for guardianship of Cassie."

"I'll drive along with you folks," Curt said. "Jayleen, you wait for me with Megan. Marty, you can ride with me."

Pete reached over and gave Jennifer's arm a squeeze. "You wait for me there, too, Jen. I'll call as soon as we get Cassie."

Eric grabbed his grandfather's arm. "I want to go, too, Grandpa," he said, his brown eyes intense.

"Sure, son. You can join the menfolk," Curt said, clapping his grandson on the shoulder again. "Now, let's go and bring our girl home." Curt strode off, Eric beside him, joining up with Pete and Steve and Marty as they strode toward the parking lot.

Burt followed after them, glancing over his shoulder at Mimi. "I'm going to join them. Let him think I'm still with the department. The more of us, the better. We can throw some fear into that bastard."

"Guys!" Kelly yelled. "Give us a call on the way back, okay?"

Steve turned and gave her a quick nod before his long legs took him farther away.

Kelly looked over at Jennifer, who was chewing her lower lip, her face devoid of color. Kelly slipped her arm around her friend's shoulders. "Don't worry, Jen. Cassie was smart enough to get away from there."

"Low-life scum," Jayleen said, her tone making it sound like a swear word.

"You got that right," Megan said in a low voice.

• • •

159

"How far are you from Fort Connor?" Kelly asked her boy-friend over the cell phone.

"Less than half an hour. We're kind of pushing the speed limit."

"Be careful. You said Cassie is okay, right?"

"Yeah. She got out of there as soon as that creep made a move." Steve's voice was tight with anger, which Kelly could hear over the phone. "Thank God. Listen, I'll hand the phone to Pete. He can talk while I'm driving."

Kelly handed her phone to Jennifer. "It's Pete. Steve's driving back. He thinks they're less than a half hour from here."

Jennifer grabbed the phone. "Pete? Cassie's really all right?" The phone pressed to her ear, Jennifer nodded to her friends, who stood around her.

"Thank God," Mimi said from her perch on the sofa. No one sat.

Kelly felt a muscle let go inside her chest. She wouldn't completely relax until she saw Cassie. She glanced at her friends and saw her worry reflected on all their faces.

Megan's front door opened and Pete walked into the foyer, his arm around Cassie's shoulders. Steve, Marty, Curt, Eric, and Burt followed after them.

"At last!" Mimi cried and jumped up from the sofa.

Cassie glanced around the room and made a beeline straight to Jennifer, who held out her arms and enveloped Cassie in a big hug. "We were all so worried," Jennifer said.

Cassie gave her a squeeze then leaned back and stared

into Jennifer's face. "I'm not going back there. Ever. If my mom wants to see me, she can come to Fort Connor."

Pete joined her and slipped one arm around Jennifer's shoulders and the other around Cassie. "I told Cassie there was no way I was going to let her go to Denver alone again. Tanya can damn well come here."

Jennifer glanced from Pete to Cassie. "You won't have to, Cassie. I promise."

Kelly felt the last tight muscles inside her chest let go at last. *Thank God.* "We're all proud of you, Cassie, for getting out of there when you did. Good girl! You listened to your instinct."

"Was that guy drinking?" Megan asked.

Cassie stepped out of Jennifer's embrace. "He was drinking a lot of beer. I don't know if he had anything else." She gave a little shiver. "He stared at me a lot when we were all together in the apartment last night having pizza. It kind of made me feel funny then. Every time I looked over at him, he was staring at me. He'd give me a wink or something." She made a face.

"Smart girl for getting away from there. You did good, Cassie," Kelly said then opened her arms. "We all need a hug." Cassie didn't hesitate. She sped over to Kelly's embrace, and Kelly enveloped her in a big hug.

"Me, too," Megan said, coming closer, arms spread. Cassie smiled and sped over to Megan then a waiting Mimi.

"Oh, my girl, my girl," Mimi crooned over Cassie's ear. Jayleen stood behind Mimi, waiting her turn.

"Hey, thanks for putting these out," Marty said as he walked toward the granite counter between the kitchen and the great room. Several plates of cheese and crackers and chips and dip were spread over the countertop.

Burt, Steve, Curt, and Eric headed toward the kitchen. Kelly hurried over to Steve and gave him a big hug, squeezing hard. "What did that guy do when all of you showed up?"

"The bastard was too scared to come near us," Steve said, releasing Kelly. "Eric, c'mon and help us out with these snacks." Steve beckoned Eric over.

Eric walked to the counter and scooped up a handful of chips, hanging back a little, Kelly noticed. She gestured toward the plates of food. "Eat up, Eric. You haven't had anything since that hot dog. You must be starving."

"I saw a guy peering at us from an apartment window above," Curt said. "I figure that was him."

"Low-life scum," Jayleen said once more, scowling. "If it weren't for the kids here, I'd be cussing a blue streak."

Cassie smiled at Jayleen as she went to her embrace. "I'm okay, Jayleen." Jayleen clasped Cassie tightly.

"What did Tanya do when you guys showed up?" Kelly asked. Steve was draining a can of soda.

"She was shaking like a leaf," Burt answered as he walked over to Mimi, slipping his arm over her shoulders. "I made it a point to remind Tanya that Pete has filed for custody of Cassie. And any judge would be taking Cassie's well-being into consideration. This past weekend will speak loudly as to Cassie's safety."

Pete and Jennifer walked over to the counter, where everyone had gathered. "Marty, let's aim to get those papers filed in the next couple of weeks."

Cassie approached Eric, who had tossed a dip-filled potato chip into his mouth. Cassie scooped up several cheese cubes. "How was your game?" she asked Eric between munching the cheese.

"It was good," Eric said with a nod.

"He did better than good," Kelly said, grinning at Eric as she reached for some cheese cubes. "He caught the winning out for his team."

"Awesome!" Cassie said, giving Eric a smile. "I wish I could have seen it."

Eric swallowed his mouthful of chips and dip. "I'll catch another one." Then he grinned at her.

"Did Tanya act upset when you told her you were taking Cassie back to Fort Connor?" Jennifer asked, her expression still anxious.

Pete shook his head as he popped open a soda can. "No. She looked scared, just like Burt said. I don't think she had any idea of what a scumbag her boyfriend really was."

Kelly reached for a handful of potato chips. "And maybe she did. But was hoping he'd be okay."

"I think that's more like it," Steve added after he drained his soda.

"How's the little one?" Marty asked Megan.

"She went to sleep right away. The sitter said Molly was busy the whole time we were gone. She carried those big blocks around to different rooms and built things. Houses, I guess."

"Good sign. Maybe she'll be an architect," Steve said with a grin before tossing a cheese cube into his mouth.

"No way. She's gonna be an attorney," Marty said, leaning over the tray and scooping dip onto his corn chip.

Kelly laughed softly. They could all use a laugh right now. "Wow, Molly's only nine months old and you're planning her future already."

Megan leaned back into her favorite chair and grinned. "I have a feeling Molly will choose her own career."

Marty glanced back to his wife. "Yeah, you're probably right. Molly's not one to take suggestions. Like it's time to go to bed, or it's time for a bath," he said with a laugh.

Kelly and her friends joined Marty's laughter.

Thirteen

"**Well,** I've gotta say I've seen you looking better," Steve teased lightly as he and Kelly stood around Greg's hospital bed.

Kelly watched Greg's bruised face twist with a smile. "Yeah, I saw myself in a mirror as they were wheeling me in here. Scary."

"He's actually starting to heal," Lisa said, her hand on Greg's arm, the one that didn't have a cast. "The bruising on his face is not as blue. It's purple now."

"Well, this is a really nice place to recuperate, I'll say that," Kelly commented, glancing around the single bedroom. "They've got lots of nurses and nurses' aides scurrying around, and they must have all the newest equipment. This place is only a couple of years old."

"Yes. All the doctors at the sports clinic sing its praises,"

Lisa said. "It's perfect for people to recuperate after orthopedic surgeries and before they go home. Greg needs more physical therapy before he can come home."

Kelly looked at Greg's right leg, which was encased from above the knee to his toes in a cast. And it was elevated from an apparatus attached to the side of his bed. "How is he going to get around on crutches? He's got a broken arm, too."

"He'll have to work his way up to crutches," Lisa said with a wry smile.

"I want one of those electric chairs," Greg said, voice still sounding a little hoarse. "You know. Stick my leg on it and ride around. Terrorize the nurses."

"I can see that," Steve said, chuckling.

Kelly had to laugh. "I'll make sure to warn the nurses before I leave."

"Knock, knock," Jennifer's voice came from the doorway. "We wanted to come in for a minute then let Cassie and Eric visit. Will that be too many people?"

"Steve and I will step out," Kelly volunteered. "We want to let Greg see everybody."

"We'll come by this weekend," Steve said to Greg as he and Kelly headed toward the doorway. "Meanwhile, you just rest up and keep healing, okay?"

Greg held up the thumb on his uninjured arm.

"And leave those nurses alone," Kelly teased in a light-hearted attempt at humor.

However, the seriousness of Greg's injuries had really shaken her when she first saw him. Greg's face was splotched all over with now-purple bruises and so were most parts of his body that were not in a cast. Long red scratches on his arms were healing. Since it was summer, Greg had been wearing short pants when he was biking that night. So even his unbroken leg was bandaged in several places from cuts and abrasions.

Jennifer and Pete were waiting outside the doorway. "Is it as bad as it looks from here?" Pete asked quietly.

"It's scary looking," Steve said, nodding. "But Lisa swears he's improving. And she would know."

"She says he's purple now, instead of blue," Kelly answered, noticing Cassie and Eric hovering nearby. "It's kind of a shock to see big strong Greg lying helpless in a hospital bed."

"Thanks for the warning," Jennifer said, beckoning Pete to follow her into Greg's room.

Cassie and Eric quickly walked over to Kelly and Steve. "He looks awful from out here," Eric said, gazing through the doorway.

"Well, it is a shock to see someone you care about covered in bandages and casts on his arm and leg," Kelly admitted. "So I'll warn you guys. It's gonna be a shock when you first look at him. So be prepared."

Cassie's blue eyes went wide. "Can he talk?"

"Oh, yes. Not much yet. But he's starting to make jokes, which is a good sign," Steve said with a smile.

"That sounds like Greg." Eric nodded with a little smile.

"Yeah, he said he wants an electric wheelchair so he can race around and terrorize the nurses," Kelly joked.

At that, both Cassie and Eric laughed out loud. That was a good sign, too.

• • •

Kelly walked across the driveway toward the garden patio. Café breakfast and brunch customers still filled the tables dotted among the greenery, trees, and plants. Kelly always hated for August to end.

Finishing her client accounts earlier than she expected, Kelly headed toward the Lambspun shop. Skipping up the steps, she yanked open the wooden entry door.

Mimi looked up from the antique dry sink, where she was draping a loose-weave shawl. "Hello, Kelly. It's good to see you while it's midmorning. Often you're too busy to make it over here until later."

"Well, my Denver client kept me on the phone for a couple of hours yesterday with a conference call," Kelly said as she walked into the foyer. "So it's nice today to be able to finish early and come over here and relax." She glanced around the central yarn room ahead and into the loom room, then leaned closer to Mimi. "Is Cassie here or is she out at a tennis lesson or something?"

Mimi smiled into Kelly's eyes and said in a quiet voice, "She's in the main room at the knitting table, and she's doing fine." She gave Kelly a knowing smile.

"Oh, good. I'll sit and chat with her for a few minutes. See if she wants to help us plan a late summer picnic."

"I'm sure she'd love it, Kelly," Mimi added as she walked toward the front of the shop.

Kelly headed straight for Pete's Café. Now, for a tall mug of coffee. Caffeine first. Spying Jennifer standing beside the grill, Kelly got her attention. "Caffeine alert! Zombie status can only be avoided by Eduardo's coffee," she called out as she approached.

Jennifer laughed and reached for the mug dangling from Kelly's fingers. "Goodness, we can't have that, can we, Eduardo?"

Eduardo chuckled as he reached for the ever-present coffeepot and poured a black stream of steaming hot coffee into Kelly's mug. "Nope. We can't have zombies walking around, scaring customers."

"Thanks, Eduardo," Kelly said before sniffing the rich dark aroma. Then she took a big drink.

Jennifer shook her head. "I still can't understand how you can drink that scalding hot coffee like that. In winter it's one thing. But it's summer now."

"I don't know," Kelly said with a little shrug. "Maybe my throat grew asbestos cells inside or something."

"Maybe you are turning into a zombie, Kelly," Eduardo said with a grin as he turned back to the grill.

Two pancakes looked ready to flip. Kelly watched Eduardo effortlessly toss them in a spiraling motion so they both landed on their opposite sides. A perfect light brown.

"Maybe. I'd better watch to see if I develop that scaly zombie skin," Kelly joked.

"Oh, please." Jennifer waved her hand and made a face as she loaded her tray with the plates of pancakes on the counter. "People are eating around here. No more zombie discussions."

"If you insist," Kelly said as Jennifer walked toward the café tables. "Talk to you later, Eduardo." Kelly was about to head back to the knitting shop when Eduardo spoke again.

"Hey, Kelly, tell Steve and the other guys 'thanks' for showing up in Denver over the weekend. Jennifer told me what the guys did. I hope it scared that no-good."

Eduardo then uttered some words in Spanish that Kelly had heard from other people over the years. Eduardo was definitely not wishing Tanya's boyfriend continuing good health. Not at all. "I think they scared the daylights out of him, Eduardo," Kelly said with a wicked smile. "Serves him right. But Cassie took care of herself first. I'm so proud of her. She told him off and got the heck out of that apartment."

Eduardo nodded. "Cassie's a smart girl. And she belongs here with Jennifer and Pete."

"And us," Kelly added with a wink.

Eduardo grinned wide. "You bet." Then he returned to the grill, and Kelly walked back into the knitting shop.

As she rounded the corner from the hallway into the shop, Kelly noticed some bright colors that caught her eye. Summer colors. Fire-engine red and bright turquoise blue, sunshine yellow and shamrock green. Pausing to touch the colorful fibers, Kelly felt the familiar texture of cotton but also something else. Something different. What was it? She burrowed two fingers farther into the yarn skein—summer corn yellow—and stroked the fibers. Maybe . . . bamboo? She checked the label. Bamboo. She'd guessed right. Amazed again at how versatile a fiber bamboo was. It could be turned into sturdy fibers for floor mats or softer fibers suitable for sweaters, even baby clothes. And it was completely natural, not synthetic.

Kelly gave the sunny skein one more stroke then continued toward the main room. She spotted Cassie at the far end

KNIT TO BE TIED

of the room, putting magazines in one of the two racks in the corner.

"Hey, Cassie. I see Mimi has you hard at work as usual," she said as she placed her shoulder bag on the long library table.

Cassie gave her a quick smile. "This is easy, Kelly. Your batting practice early this morning was hard work. My arms are still sore."

"That will only last a couple of days," Kelly said as she settled into a chair. "I worked you girls pretty hard. You'll all be trying out for your high school's junior varsity softball teams soon. So I wanted to make sure you girls were finely tuned, you might say." Kelly grinned then took a large drink of coffee.

"I hope you're right. Usually freshmen play on the freshman team. They don't make JV." Cassie slipped the last magazine on the table into its appropriate slot on the turnstile.

"Unless they're very good," Kelly hinted with a sly smile. "And you and the other five freshmen are really good. I predict you guys will make JV. Unless some heavy-duty talent has moved into town during the summer."

Cassie laughed as she pulled out a chair on the opposite side of the table. "Heavy-duty. That sounds like a truck."

"Yeah, it does, doesn't it? Okay, let's switch adjectives. How about supercharged talent?"

"Supercharged. I like that." Cassie nodded. "That was great of you to schedule a special clinic, Kelly. The other girls and I really appreciate it. If we make the JV, it will be because of all your help."

Touched by Cassie's compliment, Kelly acknowledged the praise with a nod of her head as she raised her coffee mug. "Thank you, Cassie. But it will really be the result of all of you girls working hard this entire summer. Hard work pays off, especially in sports."

"Megan says we have to practice four hours for every hour of lessons in tennis."

"She's right. And that's another reason you in particular have improved so much in batting. You're out there on the tennis court as well, practicing shots. All of that builds up your muscles as well as sharpens your instincts. Tennis is a fast game. You've gotta think fast and move to the ball."

"Boy, is it ever." Cassie picked up a blue and green ribbon yarn knitted piece from the table. "I should finish this belt if I want to be able to wear it next week when school starts."

Kelly pulled the white alpaca sweater from her large shoulder bag. Not quite half finished. Clearly, she needed more knitting time. "And speaking of instinct, I wanted to tell you again how proud I am . . . we all are . . . that you listened to your instinct last weekend and got the heck out of that Denver apartment and away from that creepy guy."

Cassie made a face. "Creep is right. I swear, I can't understand why my mom stays with that guy. He's gross. And he's a total *loser!*"

Kelly pondered how to phrase her reply. Cassie had touched on a sensitive topic. "I don't know why some women stay with guys like that, Cassie. Maybe they're simply afraid of being alone. Living alone can be scary for some people. I lived alone for years before Steve and I got together. But I never really felt like I was alone. I mean . . . I had all my friends that I saw every week. And I came over here and visited with Mimi and lots of knitters at the shop almost every day."

"And you had Carl," Cassie said, glancing up from her knitting needles. Her hands moved quickly through the movements. Row after row of blue and green ribbon yarn formed.

"You're right. I had Carl. Dogs are great company. Cats can be, too. But don't say that in front of Carl."

"My friend Marsha has a great kitty. Black-and-white face, so she calls her Panda. She jumps up on your lap and starts purring right away. She's so sweet."

Kelly slipped a knitted stitch from one needle to the other, joining the others already collected there. Row after row appeared on her needles. She'd relaxed into the "knitting mode" and enjoyed several moments of quiet at the knitting table.

"You know Lisa's friend Nancy?" Cassie spoke into the quiet. "I heard her talking to Mimi a couple of times when Lisa was over at the hospital and rehab center with Greg. She's going to have a baby, isn't she?"

Kelly blinked out of her quiet knitting mode. "Uhhhh, yeah. Yes, she is. I was sitting with Lisa here at the table when Nancy was here knitting a baby hat."

"Is she married to that guy she talks about? I think his name is Neil."

"Ummmm, no. No, she's not," Kelly answered, profoundly glad that Jennifer had already had the "sex ed" discussion with Cassie.

"She really looks upset a lot of times. Sounds like she wants to get married but that guy doesn't."

Bull's-eye. "You hit the nail on the head, Cassie. This guy Neil sounded like a creep to me. Nancy said he acted all loving and attentive until she told him she was pregnant. Then he didn't want anything to do with her. Rejected her at an Old Town bar in front of other people even."

Cassie screwed up her face. "Eeeuuuuu! He really was a creep."

"Yep. You got that right." Kelly glanced up at Cassie, who was clearly starting to discern why some people behaved the way they did. "There are a lot of creeps out there in the world, Cassie. Sad to say. But it looks like you're learning to spot them."

Cassie shook her head. "I hope you're right. I'm trying. Some people start off acting really nice and fun. Then suddenly they kind of . . . change." She gave a teenaged shrug.

"I know what you mean. All we can do is try to hang around with the good guys. And girls."

"Like Steve and Marty and Greg and Pete, right?"

"Yeah. And Eric. He's a good guy, too," Kelly added with a wink.

Cassie grinned. "Oh, yeah. Definitely a good guy."

Fourteen

Steve gulped down the last of his coffee. "I'll be up at that mountain property near Evergreen today and probably to-morrow. Got a meeting with the Rural Electric Cooperative representative. I'll stay over in Denver tonight, so don't wait up." He leaned over and gave Kelly a quick kiss on the lips.

"You should go to our favorite steakhouse for dinner," Kelly said before finishing off the yogurt cup.

"That's a great idea. I'll appreciate a good steak after talking all afternoon." He rolled his eyes.

Kelly grinned. She knew Steve missed getting his hands on some wood and actually building something. "Hey, you can probably find something to do on that building site. Who's your foreman? Maybe he'll let you hammer some boards together." She gave him a wink.

"Dutch is mother hen on this site," Steve said, eyes

lighting up. "You're right. All these meetings are draining the life outta me."

"Plus, you won't get to whack any balls tonight at the game. You'll be gone."

Steve grimaced. "Yeah, darn it. I should be back for our last game, though. Don't want to miss that."

"We'll plan on it." Kelly tossed her empty yogurt cup in the trash. Then she walked over to Steve, leaned up, and gave him a real kiss. "Drive safely, okay? And watch out for crazed tourists hurrying home from vacation. They're starting to clog the roads already."

"Oh, yeah," he said with a smile as he backed away. "Count on it."

Kelly admired the rows of knitted stitches on her white alpaca sweater. Looking good, she nodded to herself. Slowly adding the inches in length she needed. Then she reminded herself to buy another skein before Mimi ran out of that yarn.

She started another row, sliding the needles through the familiar movements. This last hour of uninterrupted knitting time had been very productive. Too often Kelly found that she would get distracted by other people's conversations and her knitting productivity would suffer. At least, that's how Megan phrased it.

The familiar sounds of chairs scraping backward on the wooden floor in the workroom next door told her that Rosa's knitting class was over. Kelly would not be alone for long.

Within a few moments, women began drifting in from the workroom and classroom area, chatting about their projects. Two of them settled at the table and continued their conversation. Kelly recognized the woman Geraldine whose cousin's daughter had had an unfortunate encounter with the recently deceased Neil Smith.

Geraldine sipped from one of Eduardo's iced drinks and glanced around the table. Clearly recognizing Kelly, she gave a smile. "Hello there, Kelly. How're you doing?"

"I'm trying to stay cool. That's why I'm here in the shop. These thick stucco walls really keep out the heat," Kelly said as she slipped another stitch off her needles.

"Well, stucco only goes so far with summer heat. Air-conditioning is why I'm here," Geraldine said with a laugh.

"Oh, yes," her friend agreed with a nod, fingers continuing to knit the scarf that folded down into her lap.

"The only good thing we can say about August heat is that it's not as hot as July," Kelly added.

Kelly and the others knitted quietly for a couple of minutes, then Geraldine's friend spoke up. "Please let me know if anything more happens with your cousin's son, Geraldine."

"I will. I'm trying not to worry," Geraldine said in a quiet voice.

Kelly's ears perked up at that. "Is your cousin's son all right, Geraldine?" Kelly asked, trying to phrase her question as carefully as she could.

Geraldine shook her head. "I don't know. I surely hope so. The police came to my cousin's house this week to question Reggie about Neil Smith. I'm sure they'd heard about his run-in with Smith a year ago after that lowlife assaulted Reggie's sister, Mary. Reggie told them that he hadn't seen Neil Smith."

Kelly could hear the worry and anxiety in Geraldine's voice. "That's good, Geraldine. That way the police won't think Reggie is involved."

Geraldine chewed her lip for a second. "I'm not sure about that. Reggie confessed to me that he had actually run into Neil Smith one night recently, and they got into another argument. All about what he did to Mary. Of course, everyone in the bar witnessed it."

"Uh-oh," her friend exclaimed.

Kelly noticed Geraldine's expression. "Something's still bothering you, isn't it, Geraldine?"

Geraldine nodded. "Yes. I'm . . . I'm afraid that Reggie may not be telling me the truth. He acted really nervous when he was talking to me. Now I'm wondering if maybe Reggie did something rash. Maybe he followed Smith. I don't know."

Kelly watched the anxiety move across Geraldine's face. "Now I understand why you're so worried." She paused. "Have you told anyone else about this, Geraldine?"

"I'm going to tell Burt. Maybe he can talk to Reggie. I can tell Reggie is scared, but the police are bound to find out about that argument in the bar. He needs to talk to them first."

"I agree. Check with Burt. He may be out doing errands for Mimi this morning, but he should return soon." The familiar music on her cell phone sounded, signifying an incoming call. She glanced at the screen and recognized Don

Warner's name. "Gotta take this call, Geraldine. Burt should be here soon," she said as she quickly rose from the table. Heading toward the front door and the privacy of outside, Kelly clicked on. "Hello there, Don. How's it going with your troops?"

Don Warner's laughter sounded. "I'm not certain any of them are disciplined enough to be called 'troops' but they're efficient enough."

Kelly pushed through the heavy front door and aimed for the empty chair in the front shaded seating area. "Ooooo, damning with faint praise. You are a harsh taskmaster, Don."

This time Warner's laughter was so loud, Kelly had to hold the phone away from her ear.

"Hey there. How's Greg doing?" Kelly asked over the phone while she slid a tray of sliced beef from her fridge's meat compartment.

"He's feeling better, thank goodness," Lisa answered. "The physical therapy is going better now that his bruised and battered muscles are starting to heal."

"That's good. Now things will go easier. He needs a break." Kelly placed the mustard then the mayonnaise on the kitchen counter then reached for the plastic container of sliced roast beef.

"Boy, doesn't he ever," Lisa agreed. "He's trying as hard as he can, I can tell. Beads of sweat pop out on his forehead during every one of those PT sessions."

Kelly opened a loaf of dark rye and smeared a healthy amount of mayo on one slice of bread, then smeared mustard on the other slice. "Wow, he really is working. It wasn't that hard when I had to rehab my ankle if you remember."

"Yeah, poor Greg has to rehab a broken leg as well as a broken arm. I confess I've never had any patients with that many injuries for several years. Years ago I had a patient who'd been in a car wreck. That was bad."

"I bet. Are those other therapists a little intimidated with your sitting right there, watching them?" Kelly's knife cut out two bright red tomato slices then she placed them and the roast beef on the bread and closed up her sandwich. She took a big bite and savored while she listened to Lisa chuckle over the phone.

"No, they're not. We've all known each other for years, and have been in therapy practice for the same length of time, just about."

Kelly took her time swallowing. "I didn't drop the connection. I just took a bite of my roast beef sandwich. Steve's staying over in Denver for another meeting on that mountain property tomorrow."

"Sounds good. Tomatoes looked divine last time I was in the store."

Kelly picked up on that admission. "Lisa, when's the last time you ate something?"

"Ummmm, a couple of hours ago. I'm good."

"Sure you are. Tell me what you ate. Don't lie."

Lisa's soft laughter came over the phone. "You're beginning to sound like Megan. Megan in Mom Mode, that is."

"Don't try to deflect my attention. It won't work," Kelly warned then took another bite of her delicious sandwich.

Lisa laughed louder. "Okay, okay. I had a bag of peanuts

from the hospital vending machine. And before that, I had a bag of potato chips. Satisfied?"

After a slight delay for savoring, Kelly countered, "Not in the slightest. You head over here right now and have one of these great sandwiches. Visiting hours are probably over anyway."

"I'm okay, really—"

"Don't argue with me."

Lisa gave a short laugh. "All right, all right. I'm too tired to argue with you."

"Wise decision. Besides, you get to pat Carl when you come. Rubbing doggy heads makes everyone feel better in stressful times."

"Scientific study, huh? What's the big guy doing?"

"Right now, he's sitting and staring at me eating this roast beef sandwich. Obviously hoping I'll drop a morsel. Not a prayer, Carl." She took another bite and watched Carl's attention never deviate from the sandwich.

Carl, for his part, exercised remarkable restraint. Patiently watching the delicious-looking sandwich disappear. *Oh, no!* It was almost gone. Carl's anxious expression intensified. Rottweiler eyebrows crowded together in consternation.

"Awwww, give the big guy a morsel, you old meanie," Lisa scolded.

"You want a taste? Do you, Carl?" Kelly asked, then pulled off a piece of roast beef from the tray. Steve wasn't here to watch her blatant spoiling of The Dog.

Carl jumped up from his sitting position, stubby tail wagging. He could tell his pitiful pose had worked. Food was forthcoming!

"Here you go. But first, sit." She held the half slice in the air.

Carl's bottom hit the floor quickly. Head up, long pink Rottie tongue licking his lips in anticipation.

"Making him work for it, huh?" Lisa teased.

"You bet. Good dog, Carl. Here you go." And she dropped the luscious piece of roast beef into Carl's waiting mouth. He closed his eyes, clearly enjoying the treat.

"Okay, I'll come over for a few minutes for a sandwich and pat Carl. Then I'd better get back and try to study a little before I go to bed."

"Sounds good. I'll pour us a glass of wine."

"Better not. I'll never get any studying done then," Lisa said with a laugh.

Kelly pulled her car into an open parking space in front of the Lambspun shop. Midmorning and she'd finished a conference call with Don Warner's staff and checked on an investment property for Arthur Housemann. Not much was happening in either business. Probably the late summer August doldrums attacking. Kids getting ready to head back to school and school shopping were the prevalent activities on most people's minds.

Parents and merchants. Schoolteachers and sports coaches. Everyone was gearing up for a whole new school year. Football games were scheduled. Other fall sports teams had also started practice in mid-August. Cassie's softball team and Eric's soccer team had games scheduled twice this coming week. Friday night football games were on everyone's calendar. Let the season begin!

Kelly stepped out of her car and flipped the lock. Spying Burt walk out of the garden café area, she called out, "Hey, Burt, how's it going?"

Burt beckoned her over as he headed for his parked car. "Hi, Kelly. I'm glad I caught you. Geraldine told me all about her cousin's son Reggie yesterday. She said she'd spoken to you earlier. I thought you'd be interested to hear that Dan and his partner went to talk to Geraldine yesterday evening after she'd gone home."

"Oh, good, good. I could tell she wanted to get all that off her chest, even though it involved Reggie. She told him he should speak to the police first. But I guess he didn't."

"Well, that's hard for most people to do, Kelly. Especially hard for a young guy who had to admit he'd gotten into an argument with Neil Smith at a bar. He knew he'd get on the detectives' 'watch' list after that."

Kelly watched Burt's expression. "What do you think so far, Burt? It certainly sounds damning. Geraldine admitted she's worried that Reggie actually went after Smith with his car."

"I don't know, Kelly. We'll have to wait and see what Dan thinks. He'll be questioning Reggie. I could tell that Geraldine was really worried about him. She said he's only in his mid-twenties, so he's young. Sometimes young guys do impulsive things. Reggie certainly had a good reason to be angry at Neil Smith, considering Smith assaulted Reggie's sister."

Kelly remembered something else she wanted to ask Burt. "Have the police had a chance to talk to the few businesspeople along that street? I think there are also a couple of small older houses along that stretch of street, too."

"Matter of fact, Dan did say he sent a couple of his officers out to canvass that entire street again. Starting with the corner where Greg was hit and farther back along that stretch to where Neil Smith's body was found. They also did another peripheral check around the location. So far, Dan said only a handful of people admitted being in the vicinity that night. And none of them saw or heard anything. Just like the others that were interviewed earlier."

"I'm not surprised. Not many people actually live along there anymore. In fact, if I remember Fort Connor history correctly, the last time a lot of people actually lived there was probably at the turn of the century. The twentieth century, that is. We did turn another century a few years ago."

Burt chuckled. "You're right. After all, it used to be a quasi-industrial area with the flour mill and some other small businesses bordering it. Most of the people the police interviewed said they were walking to their cars that were parked closer to the flour mill or other businesses. Some worked on that new construction. I do recall some old-timers who lived in a few of those tiny houses along Cherry Street, near the corner. But those buildings were torn down last year with the start of the new construction on Taylor Street and Abercrombie."

"Progress. Well, that new building is turning out really well so far. Especially with the rooftop café right next to the original streets of Old Town. Boy, if that café had been open and full of people, you'd have a whole bunch of witnesses. And all those side streets would be lined with parked cars, which means people would be out in the streets walking to their cars."

"You're right. But right now, it's still a construction area and not many people are walking the streets at night."

"When do you think Dan and the department will question Reggie?"

"Pretty soon, I would think. After all, Reggie is the second lead they've gotten on the case. Felix Marsted being the first. I know Dan, and he will definitely follow up soon."

Fifteen

Kelly was headed down the corridor leading from Pete's Café into the Lambspun shop when a small tornado whirled around the corner. *Cassie.* Kelly quickly leaped to the side to avoid a collision. "Whoa! I didn't know a cyclone was in the shop."

"Ooooops! Sorry, Kelly. Didn't mean to run you over," Cassie said with a short laugh. "One of my friends from the team. You know, Carla. She's having a bunch of us from the team over to her house for a sleepover. But first her mom is going to take us all to the mall to a movie! Then we're going to check out that new sports store."

Kelly heard the excitement in Cassie's voice. "Wow, Carla's mom is one brave woman. It's hard enough to handle all you guys on the field. No way would I try to take all of you to the mall. It would be like herding cats."

Cassie laughed out loud. "Oh, that is funny! I gotta tell them you said that. Coach Flynn thinks we're a herd of cats."

Kelly continued walking down the corridor into Lambspun shop. "No way are cats a herd. They're too independent. One is hanging on to a tree limb, another is hiding beneath a bush waiting to jump out at you, and another one would be sleeping in the sun on the porch. That's you guys." She stepped into the central yarn room, Cassie beside her.

"Love it. I'll tell them. Are you going to see Greg at the rehab center tonight?"

"Yeah, we all thought we'd meet for an early taco and burrito dinner at that new Mexican café off Jefferson near Old Town. Then we can all go to see Greg. We'll have to go into his room in shifts, but that's okay. Have you been to see him again?"

Cassie nodded. "Lisa took me over this morning. Just the two of us. Greg's still got purple splotches all over, but they're starting to fade a little, I think. I wasn't up close to him before, but Eric and I got a good look from the doorway when he was first in the hospital."

"Bruising takes a long time to go away entirely," Kelly said. "You can tell how deep those bruises were from the color. Deep purple is a pretty bad bruise."

"You know, you were right. Greg wanted to hear how my games were going. He halfway smiled, I think." Cassie started to head back toward the corridor. "Gotta run. Carla and her mom are going to meet me outside in the patio garden near the parking lot."

"School starts in a couple of days. You're excited, I can tell," Kelly said. "You'll all be high school freshmen."

"Oh, yeah." Cassie bounced a little from side to side. "High school at last! Yay!"

Kelly laughed softly, watching Cassie's excitement. "Lots of new people to meet, and new friends to make. It'll be exciting for sure."

"You bet. See you later, Kelly," Cassie said then headed down the corridor once again.

Kelly strolled through the yarn room on the way to the knitting table. Stroking an especially luscious shade of deep turquoise blue yarn, she noticed a bright shamrock green skein of the same wool. To the left of that was a bin brimming over with skeins of burnt orange. Admiring how the Lambspun elves had started incorporating fall colors into the remaining bins and shelves of summer bright yarns, Kelly meandered through the room, sipping coffee and stroking yarns.

"Oh, good. I was hoping I'd find you here, Kelly," Burt's voice sounded behind her.

"Sneaking up from behind, eh, Burt? You didn't make a sound. Are you wearing sneakers or something?" Kelly teased as she continued toward the knitting table. Dumping her briefcase, she pulled out a chair.

"I guess I'm getting sneakier in my older years," Burt said with a big smile.

"Now, now. None of that talk about getting older," Kelly scolded, wagging a finger at her mentor. "You and Mimi are ageless."

Burt gave a little snort. "Ha! Nobody's ageless, Kelly. Age cometh to all men in time."

"Are you quoting the classics or the Gospel according to Burt?" Kelly teased, leaning back in her chair.

Burt laughed out loud. "Gospel, huh? I'll have to tell Mimi. That's a good one."

Kelly simply saluted Burt with her coffee mug then took a big drink. "How's Dan doing on that investigation?"

"That's what I wanted to tell you. I heard from Dan this morning, and he said he was able to question Geraldine's cousin's son yesterday evening regarding Neil Smith. And it sounds like Reggie didn't do well at all. Dan said he was really nervous and jumpy and squirmed around in his chair."

"That doesn't look good."

"You're right, Sherlock. And as of right now, he still has no alibi. Reggie claims he was at a party that night, but he couldn't remember anybody's name who was there. Naturally, he's going to attract Dan's and the other detectives' attention."

"That's for sure. Does Reggie even remember where the party was that night?"

"He sure does, and that doesn't help him at all. It turns out the party was at Linden's Bar and Grill right there in Old Town. Only a couple of blocks from the Halftime Bar, where Neil Smith liked to hang out."

"Oh, brother," Kelly said with a crooked smile. "It looks like Reggie will move front and center on Detective Dan's radar screen."

"For right now," Burt said, cocking his head to the side. "But that might change. If Reggie happens to remember someone who was at the party with him *and* gets that person to give a statement to police, then bam! Reggie's got an alibi. And we are back to square one. Unknown hit-and-run driver."

Kelly frowned. "And there's been no sign of a car with that kind of front end damage. It would certainly be noticeable because the driver ran down Neil Smith *then* hit Greg on the bicycle. That's a lot of damage."

"I agree with Dan, Kelly. The driver has that car locked away in a garage somewhere. It may never see the light of day again."

"You mean the driver would just let it sit there and rot?"

"If it means the difference between going to prison and being a free man, you bet. That's an easy choice for some folks."

Kelly nodded. "Yeah, I think you're right, Burt. Fort Connor may never see that car again."

"**Whoa,** you *are* looking better," Steve observed as he and Kelly walked into Greg's room at the rehab center. "That sure is an improvement."

"The bruises are slowly getting less purple," Lisa said as she sat beside Greg's bed where he lay at an incline. Left arm wrapped from armpit to wrist in a combination cast. His left leg hung suspended from a metal stand on the other side of the bed. A thick cast encased Greg's leg from the top of his thigh down to his foot.

"Looking good, Greg," Kelly said. "Definitely looking good."

"Getting pretty?" Greg joked in a voice that sounded a little less hoarse.

Greg was starting to make jokes again. That was a very good sign. "We won't go that far," Kelly said with a laugh. "Ruggedly handsome is more like it."

"You were pretty scary looking for a while," Steve said.

"He's definitely looking better. I've been watching those bruises fade a little every day," Lisa added.

Greg pointed to Lisa with the thumb of his good hand. "My therapist. She doesn't let me get away with anything."

Kelly laughed. "Well, if you're causing trouble now while you're lying in bed with one leg hanging in the air, I don't even want to know what will happen when you get that scooter chair you're thinking about."

Steve and Lisa both laughed with Kelly. She could tell Greg was trying to laugh, but all he managed was a low chuckle.

"Megan and Marty were here before you guys," Lisa said. "Marty keeps bringing books for Greg to read." She pointed to a stack of five books sitting on the bedside table. "Mostly history. But with the pain pills, Greg falls asleep pretty quick." Lisa laughed and rubbed Greg's good arm. "But he'll have more time to read as he gets better. Plus, he won't be on those pain pills for much longer."

"When do you think they'll let you come home, buddy?" Steve asked as he peered down at Greg.

"Don't know," Greg said. "Doc won't say."

Lisa looked at him with a raised eyebrow. "Oh, yes, he did. The orthopedist Dr. Madan told Greg that he would be doing at least six weeks in rehab. There's a *lot* of work to do."

"Slavedriver," Greg said with a crooked smile.

Kelly recognized Lisa's schoolmarm voice. "She's a physical therapist, Greg, so just go along with it. The docs and the PTs know best. I had to rehab my broken ankle for six weeks before it was totally back to new. And, you've got . . ."

She made a sweeping motion with her hand. "You've got *way* more injuries than I had. Way more serious ones, too."

"At least this didn't happen until we'd played the league finals," Steve said with a smile. "You hit in a lot of runs for the team."

"Jennifer and Pete brought Cassie and Eric the other day," Lisa said. "They were telling Greg all about their league's final games, too."

"They both played really well," Kelly said. "Eric even hit some home runs. And Cassie was knocking out double plays regularly."

"Yeah, both of them put in a lot of time with the ball machine and batting practice. It really shows," Steve added.

"That's great," Greg said with a smile.

Greg's smile was getting closer to normal, Kelly noticed. "Who else has been in to see you here in rehab? Other than all of us, that is. You know, the gang."

"The cops came," Greg said.

"What?" Steve gave a short laugh. "Don't tell me they're giving you a ticket."

"No, no," Lisa replied instead. "A detective came to ask Greg if he remembered seeing anyone on the street that night. Anyone walking to a car or something. Or, did he see anyone driving a car when he left the bar."

Kelly immediately focused on Greg, watching him. "I bet that was Burt's former partner, Detective Dan. Burt said Dan was investigating this hit-and-run."

"I would not want to be that driver," Steve said.

"I'd like to get my hands on him," Greg growled. "In a few weeks, that is."

"I think the cops are going to get their hands on him first," Kelly said. "And he's in for way more trouble than hitting Greg. It turns out there was another hit-and-run that night."

"*What!*" Steve exclaimed. Greg simply screwed up his face.

"Yes. Right down that same street, they found a guy lying there, dead. Burt says Dan and the cops think the driver hit and killed that guy first, then maybe panicked and ran into Greg as he drove around the corner. The victim's name was Neil Smith."

"How do you know all this?" Steve asked, clearly surprised.

"Because a grad student I know at Lambspun was dating that guy, Smith," Lisa said.

"Was he a student at the university, too?" Steve asked.

"It appears so," Kelly said. "Both Lisa and I heard all about Nancy's problems with this guy. It appears this Neil Smith was a real scumbag. And some Lambspun regulars told me that a year ago he used a date rape drug on another girl. He got in trouble with that girl's brother, too." She deliberately did not share any more details of the many relationships of Neil Smith.

"What a bastard," Steve said with a scowl.

"Maybe someone got even with that guy, Smith," Greg said.

"Wouldn't be surprised," Steve commented.

Once again, Kelly decided to deflect her friends' attention from Neil Smith. "So, the cops have been to see you, and we've come to see you, Greg. Who else has come to visit?"

"Let's see," Lisa said. "Mimi and Burt, of course. Curt and Jayleen came. And all of the people from Greg's office. All the IT folks plus students."

"And the Pack," Greg spoke up. "The guys from my cycling group. All the riders."

"Some of them looked pretty shaken after they saw how bad Greg's injuries were." Lisa rubbed Greg's arm again. "I'm sure they were all thinking it easily could have been them. They're all riding around in the dark, too."

"Fort Connor's grown a lot over the years," Steve observed. "There are a lot more cars on the road and a helluva lot more drivers. The good, the bad, and the dangerous."

Kelly nodded. "You're right about that. Every weekend night in Old Town we see cyclists late at night. Years ago with less people driving around, it was safer. But now . . . it's like Steve said."

"Well, Greg knows I'll slash all his bike tires if he tries to ride at night again. No more. I'd chew my fingernails to the bone, worrying."

"See there, Greg. No more night riding. You don't want Lisa to have all those scraggly nails, do you?" Kelly teased, then decided to change from that worrisome subject. "By the way, Greg, exactly where in Old Town was that party you went to that night?"

"It was at the Halftime Bar, over on Taylor Street." Then Greg glanced up at Kelly. "You sleuthing?"

Kelly didn't say a word, but she gave him a big grin. Lisa rolled her eyes, while Steve shook his head and laughed. Greg simply chuckled softly.

• • •

"Hey, Kelly," a deep male voice called through the empty café patio garden.

Kelly snapped out of her focused concentration. "Hi there, Curt," she said, recognizing Curt Stackhouse's voice. "What brings you here this morning?"

Colorado rancher and Kelly's all-around business advisor, Curt strode through the patio to her table. "Buying supplies, that's all. So I thought I'd check on Greg while I'm here. When did you see him last?"

"Last night, and he's looking better. Of course, he's still covered in bruises and bandages, but he's able to talk. And laugh, which is good."

Curt pulled out a black wrought iron chair and settled across the table from Kelly. "That boy is damn lucky." Curt fixed her with a stern gaze. "Riding around those Old Town streets at night with all those new college students wandering around. Finally away from their parents, half of them head to the bars. And half of those get drunk." Curt frowned. "Damn fools. No wonder some of them get hit by cars or worse."

Curt sounded like the stern grandfather that he was, Kelly thought. No surprise. He had grandchildren to worry about. "What's worse than being hit by a car?" she asked with a smile.

"A train. They run through the city at night about the time those kids are staggering out of bars. I know, because I can still hear the trains' horns blowing in the middle of the night. Those train tracks go right through Old Town."

Kelly's smile evaporated. "Good Lord. I'd forgotten about the trains. You're right, Curt. I hear their horns at night." She screwed up her face. "That would be a ghastly death for sure."

"I sure hope this incident has convinced Greg to stop riding his bike at night."

"Ohhhh, yes. Lisa told him she would slice his bike tires if he rode at night again." She laughed lightly.

Finally a smile erased Curt's frown. "She'd do it, too. I don't doubt it."

"You betcha. Lisa is a woman of her word."

"Changing subjects, how are Jennifer and Pete doing on their wedding plans? Jayleen and I both got the invitations, and are looking forward to it. Mimi and Burt's backyard is a pretty little spot. It will also help them in getting legal custody of Cassie."

"I agree. And it'll be easier for Tanya to agree to it."

Curt gave another snort. "Talk about another damn fool," he said in a disgusted voice.

"You're right about that, Curt. What is it Jayleen says? 'You're right as rain.'"

Curt chuckled in reply.

Sixteen

"Everything's looking good for August, so far, Arthur. Summer doldrums quiet," Kelly said over the phone as she closed her cottage door and walked through the small front yard.

"Oh, yes," Arthur said with a chuckle. "People have been away on vacations and rushed home to get the kids into school. It's hectic, that's for sure. Things will quickly change after Labor Day."

Kelly admired the still bright yellows and reds and oranges of the annuals she'd planted in May. Now, they filled the planters that lined her tiny cottage walk.

"You're right. Everyone will jump back into business mode and want things done right away. Immediately. I used to have clients like that back in Washington. That was before

I found you and Don Warner. You guys rescued me from that corporate treadmill."

"Don and I were lucky to get you, Kelly. I still think the only reason you left that Washington, DC, rat race was because you returned to Fort Connor and rediscovered what a great place it was to live." He chuckled. "That's why I started buying more of the rental housing. Fort Connor keeps growing."

Kelly crossed the driveway and walked toward the garden patio behind the café. "You are so right, Arthur. In fact, sometimes I think it's growing too much. I don't know. Too many people on the roads, now. Traffic gets clogged in some areas in the middle of the day."

"Don't mention traffic. That has gotten to be a sore spot with me."

Kelly heard the annoyed sound in her client's voice as she walked into the garden. She'd spotted an empty table near the fence and headed straight for it. Late morning, and the breakfast crowd was starting to thin out. Perfect timing. She plopped her briefcase bag and coffee mug onto the table and pulled out a chair.

"Me, too. But, you know, maybe we should change our attitudes, Arthur."

"Oh? How do you figure?"

"All those cars are filled with people. And more people mean more customers looking at your rental housing. More business, Arthur." She deliberately left the teasing tone in her voice.

Arthur Housemann laughed loudly. "I walked right into that one, didn't I?"

"I simply couldn't resist." Kelly saw Jennifer pouring coffee for customers at another table and waved to catch her eye. "After all, we're both on the same frequency, Arthur. We think alike, especially about business. That's why we get along so well."

"You're right about that, Kelly. And it looks like my secretary is signaling me, so that call I've been waiting for has finally come in. I'll talk to you later."

"Later, Arthur," Kelly said then clicked off her phone as Jennifer approached.

"Smart move to claim a nice place to work," Jennifer said as she extended the coffeepot toward Kelly's empty mug. "I also have iced coffee, if you want it." She held up the pitcher in her other hand.

"I'll have iced coffee later, thanks," Kelly said as her friend poured a hot black stream into the waiting mug. "Tell Cassie I have to see the new clothes she chose on your school shopping excursion. Fashion show time."

"We did really well," Jennifer said with a smile. "All the department stores and boutiques had sales going on, and they were packed with shoppers. All doing the same thing. Crowds everywhere. And the stores are just buzzing with excited girls."

"You have my blessing for the bravery exhibited," Kelly teased before taking a big sip. She held up her hand.

Jennifer laughed softly. "I have to admit, it was a lot of fun. I mean, shopping for teenaged girls is like stepping back in time. They get *so* excited when they find something new. Or something really, really cute."

"Really cute beats just about everything," Kelly added, then remembered something. "Hey, Jen, can you put down the two coffees for a minute? I want to ask you a favor."

"Sure. What's up?" Jennifer placed both hot and cold pots on the table.

"I wondered if you would accompany me on an early evening trip to the Halftime Bar?" Kelly waited for Jennifer's reaction. It came quickly.

Jennifer looked surprised for a second, then smiled. "Lisa told me you and Steve visited Greg in rehab last night. And you were asking him questions. She's right. You're sleuthing again. What's this all about?"

"Do you recall a woman coming in from the shop and asking questions about operating a bar in Fort Connor? Her name's Geraldine."

Jennifer settled into the chair across the table. "Yes, I do. A little over a year ago. Nice gal. She and her husband had never run an operation like that before, and they really needed some guidance. I gave them a general rundown of what they could expect and also sent them to the right people who could get them started. You know, beer distributors, food wholesalers. All that. Did you meet her?"

"I met her around the table a couple of weeks ago. We were talking about the guy who was killed in a hit-and-run in the same area as Greg. His name was Neil Smith."

"Oh, yeah. I remember that. Did Geraldine know him or something?"

"No, but her cousin's son Reggie had a run-in with Smith the year before. It turns out that Smith assaulted Reggie's sister a year ago. Gave her a date rape drug. Anyway, Reggie went after Smith at the Halftime Bar. That's where he hangs out apparently."

"And you're interested in all of this because?" Jennifer arched a skeptical brow.

Kelly leaned back into her chair. "Have you ever met the grad student who's come into the shop with Lisa sometimes? Her name's Nancy. She's got shoulder-length brown hair."

Jennifer nodded. "Sounds familiar, so I must have."

"Well, it seems Nancy got mixed up with this Neil Smith, and she believed all his talk about their being a couple. But when she told Smith she was pregnant, Smith rejected her at the Halftime Bar in front of lots of people. He said the baby wasn't his and accused her of sleeping around."

"Bastard," Jennifer said with a disgusted expression.

"Yeah, that's for sure. Well, Nancy ran home in tears. Her father was understandably furious when she told him what happened. Then one night, her father went out looking for Neil Smith. He admitted he found Smith in a bar and argued with him.

"The next night Smith is hit by a car and dies. Unfortunately, her father is also a recovering alcoholic. Naturally, Nancy is all worried that her father was responsible, because he also fell off the wagon at the same time and started drinking again."

Jennifer closed her eyes and shook her head sadly. "Oh, no. That is bad. Very bad."

"Yeah, I agree. So, I wondered if one of those bartenders at the Halftime Bar might remember if someone came in looking for Neil Smith."

Jennifer stared out into the garden for a few seconds.

"Sure, Kelly. Tonight would probably be best, if that works for your schedule. Pete's going to Denver later this afternoon and won't be back until tonight, poor thing. He's got one of those quarterly meetings with Grandpa Ben's skilled care staff. I told him to stay and have dinner with some college friends of his. No need for him to get in that rush hour traffic."

"That's for sure. And it turns out Steve is staying over in Denver again tonight. He phoned and said he wanted to continue at that condo building site and go over plans with his foreman, Dutch. Of course, Dutch will let Steve get his hands dirty. I told him to enjoy himself."

"Okay, it looks like both our guys are away. So why don't we try out that new café that's open on Mountain Avenue," Jennifer suggested. "After we let you sleuth around at the Halftime, that is."

"Sounds like a plan," Kelly said with a grin.

Kelly nosed her car into a parking space and shut off the engine. "Okay, five o'clock. It shouldn't be too crowded now," she said as she climbed out of the car.

"Don't be too sure," Jennifer said as she slammed her passenger's side door. "Serious drinkers don't pay attention to the clock."

"Thanks for checking on the bartenders' schedule. This guy supposedly worked the night when Neil Smith was killed," Kelly said as they walked along the sidewalk toward the bar. She glanced around at the old buildings along that side of the street. A pizza shop, a cigar store, a vapor den, a used clothing shop. "Repeat Performance, that's a cute name for a used clothing shop."

"Have you been inside? There are some nice things there," Jennifer said as they approached neon-lit windows. The word "Halftime" was outlined above the entry door.

"Not yet. I'd better check it out soon," Kelly said as she opened the wooden door. "I predict once that new construction behind the old feed store is finished, this entire block will suddenly start to change."

"You're sounding like a real estate agent," Jennifer joked as they entered the bar. "Oooooo, good air-conditioning."

The bar crowd noise hit Kelly the moment she stepped inside the Halftime Bar.

"Boy, this is a reminder of why I don't miss the bar scene anymore. Wall-to-wall noise," Jennifer said as she started toward the bar.

Kelly scanned the football-themed decorations on the walls while she followed after Jennifer. The décor was simple and clearly designed for comfort. Booths lined three walls, and the long bar dominated the fourth wall. Only one bar stool was occupied by an older man who was drinking a beer. She spotted a young guy in a white shirt with rolled-up sleeves wiping the bar farther down. He glanced over at them.

"Well, I'll be damned," he said as he strolled their way. "I haven't seen you in a long time, Jennifer. Where have you been keeping yourself?"

"Hey, Jimmy," Jennifer said with a bright smile as she settled on a bar stool. "I've been so busy selling real estate, I don't get out to the bars anymore. Plus, I'm still working at Pete's Porch Café. Breakfast and morning shifts. Can't be out late working those hours." Jennifer gave him another winning smile. "This is my friend, Kelly. She's a CPA."

Jimmy smiled Kelly's way. "Hey there, Kelly. I wish I made enough money to need a CPA," he said with a laugh.

Now that Kelly was up this close, she could tell that Jimmy the bartender wasn't as young as she thought at first. It made sense since he knew Jennifer from her barhopping days. "That's okay, Jimmy. I'm an equal opportunity CPA. You don't have to be rich to afford my services. But it helps." She gave Jimmy her brightest meet-the-client smile.

"Kelly and I are trying to help out a friend," Jennifer said. "She's a young college student and got mixed up with a real sleazeball. She met him here at the Halftime a few months ago. The guy's name is Neil. Our friend thought he was serious about her, but . . ." Jennifer gave Jimmy a world-weary look. "He was just stringing her along these last few months. Anyway, now she's pregnant."

Jimmy shook his head with a sardonic expression. "An old familiar story," he said, wiping down the bar again.

"Yeah. Well, she said she came into the Halftime and told this Neil about the baby. Then that bastard basically dumped her right here at the bar in front of lots of people. Told everyone that he couldn't be sure the baby was his. And then he turned his back on her. Cut her off."

"You know, I think I remember that little scene. It wasn't pretty. The girl was crying and everything. I don't remember names or anything. But those barroom dramas are hard to forget."

"That sounds right," Jennifer said.

"Why are you two asking questions about it? Is the girl trying to sue for child support or something?"

Kelly couldn't even imagine how humiliating that barroom confrontation must have been for Nancy. "It turns out Neil Smith was a hit-and-run victim a couple of weeks ago in Old Town one night," she said.

"Whoa! That was *him?*" Jimmy said, clearly surprised.

"Yeah, that was Neil Smith. And it turns out, our friend wasn't the only one looking for him. She told her father what happened, and he went looking for Smith later that night."

"Uh-oh. I think I know where this is going," Jimmy said. "I do remember an older man coming in here one night and getting in a fight with a younger guy. He looked like he wanted to punch that guy's lights out. Me and another bartender had to hold him back."

"That sounds like our friend's father. Was it a couple of weeks ago when this all happened?" Kelly asked.

Jimmy shrugged. "That sounds about right."

"Have police come in to talk to you, Jimmy?" Jennifer asked.

"They've tried to catch me here at the bar, but my boss keeps changing my schedule. He told me the cops stopped in a few days ago and asked him questions. But Dave didn't see anything. He's too busy at the front to watch the bar. That's our job." He flicked the white towel over the bar once more. "I told the cops that later tonight would be a good time. Another backup bartender is coming in. Back-to-school crunch time." He gave them a wry smile.

"Oh, yeah. I remember that well," Jennifer said with a knowing nod.

Jimmy peered at both Jennifer and Kelly. "Are you two thinking maybe the older guy was the one who drove his car into this Neil Smith?"

"We don't know, Jimmy," Jennifer said. "That's why we're asking questions. Our friend is too scared, as you can imagine."

Kelly continued, embroidering the story. "She says her father would never do anything like that. But a father will definitely try to protect his daughter." Kelly knew this was true from experience. Her dad always stood up for her, no matter what.

"You're right about that," Jimmy said, glancing down the bar.

Just then two college-aged guys walked up to the bar and grabbed a couple of stools. Jimmy glanced their way. "Gotta go. Oh, yeah, I just remembered. One night another guy came into the bar and said he saw a guy lying on the street about a block away. And a girl was kneeling beside him."

Kelly stared at him. "Really?"

"Yeah, I remember that. Gotta go. Good to see you, Jennifer. Drop in again." Jimmy started walking toward the new customers.

Jennifer looked at Kelly. "Well, what do you make of that, Sherlock?"

Kelly shrugged. "I don't know. But it sure makes me curious. I'm going to call Burt when I get back. Tell him all this."

"You do that. We want to stay on the good side of the

law." Jennifer gave her a crooked smile. "Now, why don't we try out that new café on Mountain."

"Definitely. I think I just felt my stomach growl," Kelly said jokingly.

"**So** there you go, Burt," Kelly said, relaxing back into a lawn chair in the cottage backyard. Carl was snuffling through the few shrubs Kelly had planted along the chain-link fence. "Bartender Jimmy said police were coming to ask him questions later tonight. He's had scheduling problems apparently. Hard to meet with the cops, I guess."

"Or unwilling," Burt's voice came over the phone. "A lot of young guys don't like to talk to police about other guys they know. It feels like snitching to them."

"I have to admit his story really makes the picture of Nancy's father a lot more damning."

"Yeah, it sure does. By now, Dan and the guys will probably be talking with that bartender. I'll wait until morning to give Dan a call."

"You should go to bed, Burt. You sound really tired."

"Right you are, Sherlock. Talk to you tomorrow." Burt's phone clicked off.

Seventeen

"**Hey** there, Kelly," Geraldine said as Kelly walked into Lambspun's main room. Glancing up from the lemon yellow wool she was casting onto her knitting needles, Geraldine asked, "Have you finished that sweater yet?"

Kelly plopped her knitting bag on the library table and pulled out a chair. "I'm getting closer. It all depends on how much uninterrupted knitting time I have."

"Isn't that always the truth," Geraldine said, shaking her head as her fingers worked quickly. "The problem is there are so many other things we have to take care of, our knitting gets shoved to the bottom of our to-do lists."

Kelly pulled out the white alpaca wool sweater. She had an hour before she had to make a client phone call. She slid another soft white alpaca wool stitch off the needle in her left hand and onto the needle in her right hand. She was in the home stretch of finishing this sweater finally. Kelly had just settled into a knitting rhythm when Geraldine spoke again.

"I heard some good news, Kelly. About my cousin's son Reggie. He told me he actually found a friend who was at that party the same night Neil Smith was hit by a car. And his friend will tell police that Reggie was at the party with him."

Surprised, Kelly looked over at Geraldine. "Really? Oh, that's wonderful news, Geraldine. His friend's statement should definitely take Reggie off the police radar screen."

Geraldine let out a big sigh. "I can't tell you the relief I feel. I was so worried about Reggie."

"I could tell. You had this worried expression all the time. And with good reason." Kelly caught a glimpse of Burt walking through the central yarn room and called out, "Hey, Burt. Come on in and hear Geraldine's good news." When Burt turned around, Kelly beckoned him over.

Geraldine gave a short laugh. "You're reading my mind, Kelly. Burt was next on my list to share the good news."

"What news is that, Geraldine?" Burt asked as he approached the knitting table.

She looked up at Burt with a wide grin. "Reggie found a friend who was at the same party he was that night when Neil Smith was killed. And Reggie's friend remembers seeing Reggie there."

Burt's face lit up. "That's great news. And the friend is willing to talk to police?"

Geraldine nodded. "Reggie said they were going there today. Thank goodness. I was so worried."

"I know you were," Burt said solicitously. "You should go up front and tell Mimi."

"I'll do that right now," Geraldine said, jumping up from her chair. "I'm so relieved. I'm going to call all my friends." She dropped her lemon yellow yarn onto the chair and scurried out of the room. Her excitement was palpable.

Watching Geraldine hurry off, Kelly said, "I bet we'll see her an hour from now, sitting in the shady front patio making calls."

"It's certainly good news for Geraldine," Burt said as he settled back into the wooden chair. "But now police are back to the second guy who got into an argument with Neil Smith at the Halftime Bar."

Nancy's father, Felix, Kelly thought to herself. She glanced up at Burt. "You mean the guy who works at AA?"

"Yes, it sounds like he was the only other guy who got into an argument with Smith at the Halftime Bar. The bartender wasn't close by so he couldn't hear what they were saying, but he could tell the other guy was really angry with Smith. The bartender didn't recognize him and neither did the waitresses. So he definitely wasn't a regular."

Kelly continued with her stitches, working the row. She felt sorry for Felix. He'd worked hard to turn his life around. But if he deliberately killed Neil Smith, that changed everything.

From the back of her mind, a forgotten thought wiggled forward. "You know, when Jennifer and I spoke with the bartender, he mentioned that someone at the bar said they saw a young woman kneeling beside a guy who was lying in the middle of the street that night."

Burt peered at Kelly. "You mean the night Neil Smith was killed?"

Kelly nodded. "Yes, that same night. The bartender knew Jennifer so he was certainly comfortable talking with her."

"You know, I wonder if that bartender told Dan about seeing a girl," Burt said. "Dan didn't say anything about a young woman in the street."

"I wonder who she was?" Kelly pondered out loud. "Maybe it was simply someone coming back from a party or some bar in Old Town."

"Who knows, Kelly?" Burt said, rising from his chair. "But whoever it was, Dan needs to know about her. I'll talk to you later." He started to turn away then glanced back at her. "Thanks, Sherlock. You've got a great nose for sniffing out clues."

Kelly laughed as she slid a stitch from the left needle onto the right needle. "You make me sound like that hound from a Sherlock Holmes mystery. What was it?"

"Right again, Sherlock. That was the Hound of the Baskervilles."

"That's right. And if I recall correctly, it was not a nice dog. Not like my sweet Rottie boy, Carl," Kelly teased.

"Not at all, Kelly," Burt said with a laugh as he walked away.

Kelly relaxed back into her chair. Quiet time again. Excellent. She glanced at her watch. One half hour until she had to return to her cottage and make that business call. Maybe she could finally finish this sweater at last. She slid another stitch from the left needle to the right. Another neat row of stitches formed. One sleeve was done, and she was halfway finished with the other.

Kelly was still surprised to see how much her knitting had improved over the years of coming to Lambspun. Simply sitting and knitting with her friends while they all relaxed around the table and talked about what was going on in their lives. Stitch after stitch, row after row.

Julie walked into the room then, her arms filled with skeins of bright red yarns. "Hey, Kelly. It looks like you're finishing that winter sweater." Julie dumped the bundle of yarns on the other side of the table.

"You're right. I'm in the home stretch. And stop using the word 'winter,' please. I don't like to be reminded that summer will be over," Kelly joked.

Julie laughed as she removed some yarn skeins from a bin on the wall opposite Kelly. "Summer girl Kelly," she teased. "Okay, no mention of the colder weather. Is it okay if I put some new warm weather yarns here? You don't have to look at them."

Kelly glanced over at the yarns Julie was stacking in the bin. Fire-engine red. "Hey, that's my favorite color. Toss one of them over here, would you?"

"Sure." Julie tossed a skein across the table. "You know. Bright red mittens would go great with that white sweater."

Kelly picked up the bright red skein. Soft, soft. Eighty percent wool and the rest mohair, the label read. She fingered the red yarn then compared the feel to the white alpaca sweater yarn. Similar but firmer, Kelly decided. That would be good for mittens.

"You know, you're right, Julie. I think I'll make some mittens with this after I've finished the sweater. Since I knit slower than you guys, I should have both sweater and mittens finished by the time cold weather arrives." She smiled at Julie.

"You are so funny, Kelly," Julie said with a laugh as she started to walk from the room. Stopping at the archway leading into the central yarn room, Julie turned around. "You know what would look really great? You're only halfway through that white sweater. Why don't you make the other half with the red yarn? That'll be perfect with those red mittens."

Kelly immediately pictured herself wearing the red mittens with the half-white, half-red sweater. "Hey, that's a great idea, Julie. Thanks. Are there enough skeins of the red to do both?"

Julie pulled out the bin and started counting skeins. "Oh, yeah. There are over ten skeins here. No problem."

"Do me a favor, would you? Count up how many skeins I'd need for both mittens and this sweater, and let's put them on reserve for me right now. I don't want to risk someone else buying the yarn."

"You got it," Julie said, walking from the room with the yarn bin.

It was hard to think about winter when it was still August and still hot outside, Kelly thought as she returned to her stitches. The sweater was coming along. Perfect timing for Julie's great suggestion.

"Hey, Kelly," a familiar young girl's voice sounded from the workroom doorway.

Kelly looked up and saw Cassie walking into the room, and she was wearing a cute outfit that Kelly didn't recognize. "Hey, Cassie. Is that some of the new stuff from your back-to-school shopping?"

"Sure is. You like it?" Cassie held up her hands and spun around. "I love the colors."

"It's adorable. And it's your favorite blue and green, too. How could it miss?" Kelly teased with a laugh.

"I know. We also found a couple of other new tops and pants, too. Really cute." She bounced a little side to side. "I love school shopping."

Kelly laughed softly watching her. Cassie's excitement was contagious. "I think Jennifer enjoyed it, too."

"It's *so* much fun! And I had a lot of fun with Jennifer, too. We even went out for ice cream afterwards."

"I'm going to take a wild guess and say that you're excited," Kelly joked.

"Oh, yeah. Only two more days. Yay!" Another little side step and bounce.

"Do you have any more outfits you can show me? I'd love to see them. That way I don't have to go shopping and brave the crowds at the mall."

Cassie rolled her eyes dramatically. "Ohhhhh, wow. Kids were everywhere! Moms were digging through piles of clothes. And all the dressing rooms had waiting lines. It was crazed."

Kelly wondered if that was a new teenage term, but she didn't have time to ask. Jayleen strode into the room then.

"Well, hey there! Good to see two of my favorite girls in one spot," Jayleen declared, breaking into a grin.

"Jayleen! Look at my new outfit for school!" Cassie twirled

around again while Jayleen made suitable appreciative noises.

"You're as pretty as a shiny new penny," Jayleen said with a short laugh. "Come over here and give me a hug!" She opened her arms wide.

Cassie headed straight into Jayleen's embrace. Kelly watched Jayleen close her eyes and hug Cassie tight. To Kelly's mind, Jayleen was another grandmother-in-waiting like Mimi who finally got to lavish her affection on a youngster. Different stories. Different lives.

"Jennifer and Cassie went school shopping with all the hordes and hordes of kids in town. Cassie was about to show me the other things they bought. Join me and enjoy a fashion show with all her new school outfits."

"Well, I'll be happy to do it. Besides, I can use a little sit-down about now." Jayleen pulled out a chair on the other side of the table from Kelly.

"Okay, Cassie, what's next?" Kelly played along.

Cassie grinned. "I'll change and show both of you. This will be fun!" She sped from the room.

Both Kelly and Jayleen laughed lightly. "'Fun' is the operative word, you notice," Kelly said to Jayleen.

"Bless her heart," Jayleen said. "I love her to death."

"I can tell." Kelly caught her eye. "Isn't it amazing how Cassie came into our lives suddenly and brought something we didn't even know we needed. More love, something."

Jayleen nodded, then said simply, "Joy."

Cassie bounced back into the room then and spun around to show off another new outfit. "Oh, I like that," Kelly said in admiration. "And those are new colors for you. Bright red and shamrock green."

"I know. I almost didn't choose them, but Jennifer said to try them on and see what they look like." Cassie grinned. "Jennifer says the mirror never lies."

Kelly laughed. "Well, she's right about that. Sometimes I wish it would."

Jayleen threw back her head and laughed loudly. "Whoooeee! Jennifer said it straight. And that outfit looks real pretty on you, Cassie girl."

"Thanks, guys!" she chirped and raced from the knitting room once more.

Kelly glanced over at her friend and couldn't help noticing Jayleen's continued worried expression. "Something else is bothering you, Jayleen. What is it?"

Jayleen looked up. "Yes, it is. Felix admitted to me that he was so upset and angry about what happened to his sweet innocent daughter and this scumbag who turned his back on her, well . . . Felix said his normal resolve weakened and he stopped in another bar and had a drink. For the first time in over five years. Then, of course, he had another and another and another." Jayleen sighed wearily. "Felix confessed he can't even remember when he left the bar, let alone what he did afterwards. His car was parked near the Halftime Bar. Now Felix is scared that maybe he waited for Neil Smith to leave and then . . . maybe he ran him down with his car."

Kelly stared into Jayleen's eyes and saw the doubt and worry there. "Oh, brother. He can't remember anything?"

Jayleen shook her head.

Maggie Sefton

"Well, then, maybe he's just afraid that he did it. The alcohol gave him nightmares, or something. Maybe this Felix didn't do it."

Jayleen's mouth quirked downward. "Unfortunately, it wasn't a nightmare. Felix told me he found his car in the garage like normal, but there was a lot of damage to the front fenders and the front end."

Kelly just stared at Jayleen. "Oh, brother. That is bad, Jayleen. Really, really bad."

"That's for damn sure. I know I have to tell Burt, but I still feel sick inside about it."

"I'm sure you do, but you've gotta tell him. Burt will help Felix go to the police. He'll probably go with him, and explain what a great asset to the community Felix has been."

Jayleen shrugged. "I don't know. Lord, Lord, I just don't know."

Kelly reached over and gave her friend's arm a squeeze. "Don't worry, Jayleen. Burt can definitely get Felix to the help he needs."

"Lordy, Lordy . . ." Jayleen breathed softly.

There was nothing Kelly could add to that.

Eighteen

"I'll take another look at those capital expenses and give you a call, Arthur," Kelly said as she closed the cottage door behind her and walked down the sidewalk beside her small flower gardens.

The August afternoon heat had slowly tapered from the July highs in the upper nineties at the first of August then lower, until now at the end of August, temperatures were in the moderate eighties. Moderate to Kelly, at least. The eighty-degree temps were pleasant especially in Colorado, where the humidity was much lower than along the East Coast or in the Midwest. Kelly still remembered some of those July summers in Indiana when she was a teenager. Temps over one hundred were common in July and humidity to match—in the high ninety percent. Brutal, especially when you were playing softball.

"Don't bother checking today. Wait until tomorrow morning. You should go outside now and enjoy this gorgeous weather."

The business call with her client Arthur Housemann had taken less time than she thought. So Kelly figured she had enough time to relax in the shade of the garden café and finish up. Arthur was right. It would be a shame to waste a beautiful late August day by staying inside.

"I think I'll do that, Arthur," Kelly said as she walked into the garden and headed for one of her favorite café tables in a shaded corner. Green, green foliage all around. Late summer blooms still proclaiming their beauty.

"Good for you, Kelly. The wife and I are going to head up Poudre Canyon to one of our favorite fishing spots and relax. Nothing like standing in a mountain stream and watching Rocky Mountain trout leap in the rushing water."

Kelly could instantly picture the vivid image Arthur had described. "That sounds wonderful, Arthur. You and your wife enjoy." She plopped her shoulder bag on the table and settled into a chair.

"We'll do that. I'll talk to you later." His phone clicked off.

Kelly slipped her phone into the pocket of her capri pants, pulled out her laptop, and popped it open. There was no better place to enter Arthur Housemann's real estate revenues and expenses than a shady Colorado garden in the summer. She remembered how she hated being locked inside an office all summer when she worked in a CPA firm back in Washington, DC. Summer kept beckoning to her outside the window.

Waitress Julie headed Kelly's way. "Hey there, Kelly.

What can I get you this gorgeous afternoon? And please don't say hot coffee." Julie gave her a wicked grin.

Kelly chuckled. "You're so right, Julie. I'll take a large iced coffee, please."

"That's more like it," Julie said and headed back toward the café.

Kelly started entering Housemann's expenses but only got as far as the first five columns when Jayleen's voice called behind her, "Hey there, Kelly. Mind if I join you?"

Kelly threw in the towel on the expense spreadsheet, and clicked her laptop into sleep mode. "Sure, Jayleen," she said as the Colorado cowgirl strode over to the table and pulled out a chair. Spying Julie approach with her iced coffee, Kelly asked, "I just ordered an iced coffee. Do you want some?"

"Lord, no," Jayleen said with a dismissive wave as she settled into the chair. "I've had too much coffee already today."

"Is there such a thing as too much?" Kelly teased as she accepted the ice-cold drink.

Jayleen laughed. "Maybe not for you, Kelly. Nothing for me, Julie. Thanks," she said to the waitress.

"So what's up? I can tell something's on your mind. You have that same worried look you had this morning. Didn't you talk to Burt?"

"Yes, I did. And Burt spoke with Felix on the phone and told him he would be glad to accompany Felix to the police department. Burt said Felix should go to the police and tell them everything. Felix needs to tell them before they come looking for him."

"I agree. Did Felix agree to go with Burt?"

"Felix said he told Burt he would go with him tomorrow morning. He wanted to take the time tonight to tell his daughter, Nancy, what he was going to do." Jayleen looked out into the garden.

"You still look worried, Jayleen. What's up? Are you afraid Felix will chicken out on going to the police? Do you think he'll try to run away?"

Jayleen shook her head. "No, no. That's not it. It's something else he said that keeps bothering me. It was kind of an offhand comment."

"What was it?"

Jayleen sighed. "Earlier today when I was talking with him, Felix stared off into the trees outside and said he wished Nancy had never gotten involved with Neil Smith. Then all of this would never have happened."

"That sounds like a worried father to me," Kelly observed. "He's probably talking about how Nancy is about to add the demands of motherhood onto her already busy graduate school life."

"That's what I thought, too. So I told him, just casual like, that young women make mistakes about men all the time. Then Felix looked at me with this serious expression, right into my eyes, and said, 'Not like this. This mistake can change her life forever.' I tell you, Kelly, the way he said it and the way he looked into my eyes, well . . . I got a bad, bad feeling afterwards, and I can't shake it." Jayleen looked over at Kelly and caught her eye. "Would you do me a huge favor, Kelly? Would you come over this afternoon and talk to Felix with me? I want someone's opinion who's not involved. Who can listen and hear what Felix has to say."

Kelly saw the worry in Jayleen's eyes. "Sure, Jayleen. Why don't we go over now? It's a good time for me because I haven't gotten into my accounts yet." She clicked out of sleep mode and closed down her laptop.

"Oh, thank you, Kelly girl! I really appreciate it. Felix is such a good man and totally changed his life when he quit the drinking. He deserves another good ear to listen to his story." Jayleen quickly rose from her chair.

"I'll take my car and follow you. We're going over to the AA office in Old Town, right?" Kelly slid her laptop into her bag and slipped it over her shoulder.

"Yes, indeed. Just follow me, Kelly. I promise I won't go too fast," Jayleen said with her trademark smile.

"Nice to meet you, Felix," Kelly said, shaking the tall, slender, gray-haired man's hand. "Jayleen speaks highly of you."

Felix gave a hint of a smile. "Jayleen's a good person and she's always there for us here at AA." He gestured toward a small empty table in the corner of a large meeting room. No one else was there at the moment. "We've got the room to ourselves for a while, so grab a chair."

Kelly settled into a chair across the table from Felix, while Jayleen grabbed another chair and pulled it to the table, straddling the chair backward in her usual fashion.

"Felix, I wanted Kelly to meet you and hear your story herself. She's a CPA and is one sharp cookie," Jayleen said.

Felix listened attentively, then glanced at Kelly. "A CPA, huh? That brings back memories of when I managed a company here in Fort Connor. Before I had to take an early retirement, that is. They suggested I might want to leave early, because my work was suffering." He gave another tiny smile. "That was before Alcoholics Anonymous changed my life."

"Amen to that," Jayleen said, nodding.

"It's saved many people over the years, Felix," Kelly agreed. "Before I even returned to Fort Connor, I remember when one of my mentors at the Washington, DC, CPA firm had to, uh, retire early, as you said. He finally joined AA and changed his life. I only wish he'd done it earlier. By then, his wife had left him, too. Sad." She wagged her head.

"Good for him," Felix said, then glanced down at his cup, half filled with coffee. "You want some more coffee?" He gestured to Kelly's half-filled iced coffee take-out cup.

"No, I'm good. Why don't I ask you a couple of questions, Felix. Kind of bring you back to this whole story. How long ago did your daughter start seeing this Neil Smith?"

Felix exhaled a long breath. "It was a few months ago. At first, this guy sounded like the perfect gentleman that you would want your daughter dating. Polite, smart, treated her like a lady. He was even getting an advanced degree like Nancy was. Sounded perfect. At first." Felix's mouth twisted. "Then, several months later, when Nancy discovered she was carrying Neil Smith's child . . ." Felix gave both Kelly and Jayleen an intense look. "And believe me, that baby was *his*! Nancy had *never* been with another man. Anyway, that's when everything changed. And that low-life bastard refused to even listen to Nancy. He accused her of sleeping around with other men! In front of all these people in a *barroom*!"

Felix's voice had risen with his obvious anger. He glanced over his shoulder and lowered his voice. "He even turned his back on her! *Bastard!*"

"I'd say low-life bastard is putting it mildly," Kelly agreed.

Felix gave a disgusted snort. "Nancy called me while I was here at AA that night. She was weeping, poor girl. Completely distraught. Naturally, I left the meeting and went home to see her." His mouth tightened. "I tried to comfort her the best I could. And I started calling friends in our local community health services and made an appointment for Nancy with an obstetrician at the community clinic the next day. That way she could see a doctor right away." He tossed down the rest of his coffee.

Jayleen leaned over the table, looking at Felix. "You were being a good father, Felix. Taking care of your daughter. Nancy's lucky to have you. I lost custody of my son and daughter years ago because I couldn't stop my drinking. You are stronger than I was back then. I'm proud of you." She gave him a supporting pat on the shoulder.

Kelly decided to share her brief acquaintance. "You know, I do remember Nancy coming into the Lambspun knitting shop one day, and she was all upset. My friend Lisa had met Nancy in one of her graduate school classes, and they had become friends. So I got to meet Nancy myself. She's a really sweet girl. Nancy came rushing into the shop to find Lisa. That has to be the day after she had that confrontation with that low-life Smith." Kelly deliberately didn't add that Lisa had revealed her conversation with Nancy.

Felix's eyes lit up. "You're right. That must be the next day. She told me she wanted to talk with her friend Lisa. I'm so glad you met her, Kelly."

Kelly paused, wondering how to phrase her next question. Then, in her usual forthright manner, she asked, "Jayleen did tell me that you went looking for Neil Smith one night. Is that right, Felix?"

Felix glanced down at the empty cup in his hands. "Yes, I did. I wanted to see if I could talk some sense into him. Convince him to do the right thing." He slowly wagged his head, his mouth tightening into a scowl. "Nancy had already told me Smith was usually at his favorite bar, the Halftime, on the edge of Old Town. Over near the new construction."

Kelly nodded encouragingly. "I know where it is. Lots of people hang out there, I've heard."

Jayleen made a none-too-genteel snort. "A pickup bar, from what I've heard."

"Did you find him at that bar?" Kelly continued.

"Oh, yes. He was there, trying to charm some other girl. I walked up and told him, 'I'm Nancy's father, and we need to talk.' He stared at me, and for a moment I thought I glimpsed a flash of fear in his eyes. Then he gets this nasty expression on his face and says that my daughter was lying to me. Said he wasn't the only guy she slept with, so the baby could be anybody's. Then he had the nerve to turn his back on me! Just like Nancy said he did to her." Felix's eyes narrowed. "Well, when he said that, I have to admit I lost it. I grabbed Smith by the shirt, and I swore I was gonna beat him to a pulp! And I would have done it, too, except several guys at the bar grabbed me and pulled us apart. Then the bartender told me to leave."

Felix crushed the empty cup in his hand and tossed it into a metal trash can beside the table. The cup made a thumping sound against the metal as it fell.

"What did you do then?" Kelly asked in a quiet voice.

Felix stared down at his hands, which were folded on the table. "I left the bar and walked toward my car. I was still furious. And . . . and that's when I went to another bar in Old Town and had a drink of whiskey. First drink in five years." He released a long sigh. "I stayed and had another drink and another, then I left. I don't remember much after that except walking to my car."

"Do you remember getting into your car? Did you drive somewhere?" Kelly probed.

"I remember getting into my car, but not much more." He shrugged, still staring at his hands. "But clearly, I must have waited for Smith to come out of that bar, then followed him and hit him with my car. The next day I saw the damage to the front end of my car. I wasn't sure if I'd hit something or someone until the newspaper had the story of Smith's death. Hit-and-run. That's when I knew I must have killed him."

Kelly watched Felix, watched him stare at his hands. His voice was flat, without emotion. He didn't look up at Jayleen or her. Just kept staring at his hands. Then . . . out of the back of Kelly's brain a thought wiggled forward. *He's lying.*

That surprised her, such a blunt statement coming out of

the blue. But Kelly had learned over the years to pay attention to those little thoughts that wiggled from the back of her mind. They always turned out to be true.

She pondered, wondering what to ask Felix next. Then another thought wiggled forward. *Ask him where Nancy was that night.* Kelly paused for a few seconds before speaking.

"Where was Nancy that night?"

Felix glanced up quickly. He appeared startled by her question. "Why do you ask that?" he said sharply.

"Just curious. Did she know you were going to see Neil Smith?"

"Uhhh, no . . . I didn't tell her."

Fascinated now by the sudden change in Felix's behavior, Kelly probed again. "Really? I seem to remember Lisa saying that Nancy had spoken with her and was very worried because you had gone out looking for Neil Smith one night."

Again, Felix looked startled. "Oh, well . . . I'm sure she was upset when she learned that I had started drinking again."

Kelly nodded in agreement. "That's totally understandable."

Felix glanced between Kelly and Jayleen, then glanced at his watch. "You two will have to excuse me. I have to leave now." He shoved back his metal chair on the tiled floor and stood quickly. "Jayleen, thanks so much for all your help. And Kelly, I appreciate your coming down here and listening to my sad story. I told that former police detective Burt Parker that I would be going with him to the police department and turning myself in tomorrow morning. Meanwhile, I want to go home now and spend time with my daughter."

"It was nice meeting you, Felix," Kelly said, giving him a warm smile.

Jayleen jumped up from her chair. "We totally understand, Felix. Please come back here tomorrow afternoon, and we can help you find a lawyer. You're gonna need one."

"We'll see about that," Felix said as he started backing away. Then he swiftly walked out of the room.

Jayleen stared after him for a minute then peered down at Kelly. "What was that all about?"

Kelly looked up at her. "I think I hit a nerve. Did you see how fast his whole demeanor changed when I asked about Nancy?"

"A blind man could see it with a cane," Jayleen decreed. Then she looked at Kelly. "I have a hunch you were poking around, seeing what you could find. Am I right?"

Kelly drained her iced coffee then rose from her chair. "Right as rain," she answered, using one of Jayleen's own expressions.

Jayleen simply laughed out loud in reply.

Nineteen

"Keep track of those squirrels, Carl," Kelly told her dog as she slid the patio door closed. Carl, for his part, was already bounding into the cottage backyard, heading toward the back chain-link fence. No squirrels in sight, however. Brazen Squirrel and his friends were nowhere to be seen.

Kelly slipped her briefcase bag over her shoulder, grabbed her coffee mug, and headed out the front door. As soon as she stepped down to her sidewalk, she spotted Burt across the driveway near the café garden patio. He beckoned her over.

"Perfect timing, Kelly," he said as she approached. "I was about to call you. Got your message late last night."

"I figured you would. Are you accompanying Felix this morning when he goes to see the police?"

"Yes, I am, but I'd like to hear what you thought when

you went with Jayleen to meet him yesterday." He gestured toward an empty outside table near the bushes in the garden.

Kelly walked over to the table and deposited her bag and mug. "I'd say Felix Marsted appears to be a good man who is a solid citizen and who's managed to stay sober for five years until he and his daughter encountered that sleazy, slimy, piece-of-trash Neil Smith." She sank into the black wrought iron chair and took a deep drink of coffee.

Burt gave her a wide smile. "Tell me how you really feel," he teased.

"Judging from some of the things I've heard from others, this Smith has been a real bastard in several women's lives. Frankly, it sounds like it's 'good riddance' that he's gone."

"That sounds like the opinion of everyone who had anything to do with this guy," Burt said. "But I'm curious what you thought of Felix. He made it sound over the phone like he was going to confess to the police that he drove the hit-and-run car that killed Neil Smith."

"That's exactly what he's going to do." Kelly sipped from her mug. "I started asking him questions, and Felix freely admitted that he went looking for Smith after his daughter, Nancy, had a confrontation with him at an Old Town bar. Smith refused to accept that the baby was his, and Nancy became 'distraught' in Felix's words. One night, Felix found Smith at the Halftime Bar and confronted him, but Smith totally rejected him, too. And he accused Nancy of sleeping around. That's when Felix admits he 'lost it.'" Kelly took a deep drink of coffee.

Burt's expression turned solemn. "That doesn't sound good."

"No, it's not," Kelly said with a sigh. "Felix admitted he

grabbed Smith and was going to teach him a lesson but the bartender told him to leave. That's when Felix went to another bar and started drinking."

Burt closed his eyes. "Oh, no."

"Oh, yes. Sad story. I asked him what he remembered when he left the bar. Did he remember getting into his car, for instance. Felix said he did remember being in his own car, but he doesn't remember what he did after that. Then the next morning he found the damage to the front end of his car, and he concluded he ran his car into Neil Smith the night before."

Burt stared off into the garden. "That is a sad, sad story, Kelly. And I wish I could say it's not a familiar one. But alas, it's all too similar to other recovering alcoholics who fall off the wagon. Sad. Really sad, especially when people are rebuilding their lives."

Kelly took another deep drink of her strong morning coffee. Not as good as Eduardo's but good enough to start the day. That little thought from yesterday wiggled into the front of her mind, claiming her attention.

Tell Burt how Felix acted when you mentioned Nancy.

"There was one other thing I noticed while listening to Felix. When I asked him where Nancy was while he was out confronting Neil Smith at the bar, Felix looked really startled. 'Why do you ask that?' he said. I told him that I was just curious and wondered if Nancy knew he was going out looking for Smith. Felix said no, he didn't tell her, which I thought strange because I remember Lisa saying Nancy was worried because her father had gone looking for Neil Smith one night."

Burt's gaze narrowed. "That's interesting."

"Yes, it is, and so were Felix's reactions whenever I asked about Nancy." Kelly leaned back into the wrought iron chair.

Burt peered at Kelly. "Okay, I'll bite. Why exactly did you ask about Nancy?"

"Because I remember the Halftime bartender telling Jennifer and me that another guy came into the bar that night and said he saw a girl kneeling next to a guy sprawled in a nearby street. So I've always wondered who that girl was. Was she a stranger who was walking back from an Old Town party or a bar? Or, was she someone else? Maybe she was Nancy."

Burt's smile spread across his face. "Good sleuthing, Kelly. I'm going to call Dan and tell him Felix is coming in this morning. And I'll tell him what Felix told you yesterday." Burt pulled his cell phone from his pocket and sprang from his chair. "I'll let you know how this morning turns out, Kelly." Burt started to walk away from the table when he suddenly turned around and smiled at Kelly. "Good job, Sherlock." He winked.

"Anytime, Burt," Kelly said with a smile as she slid her laptop out of her shoulder bag. Once the familiar spreadsheet appeared on the screen, Kelly returned to the peaceful world of numbers. Balancing accounts, revenues, expenses. Obeying their own laws of logic. No matter how unbalanced and difficult the numbers appeared, she could always solve the problem. Everything had to be in balance at the end. Assets had to equal liabilities plus equity. Always. If only people and their behaviors could be as logical as the numbers.

Several minutes passed while Kelly disappeared into the

numbers, her coffee mug being discreetly refilled without her even asking, and the spreadsheet columns growing in length. Then another familiar voice came from across the garden.

"What a great spot to work, Kelly," Lisa called as she walked down the flagstone path. "Mind if I join you and study for a test?"

Kelly beckoned her friend over. "Sure thing. You can also catch me up on Greg's rehab. You said his leg is getting stronger."

"I can spot a difference. The other PTs aren't saying anything yet, but I know Greg and his body. And I think I saw a tiny bit more movement when he's doing those stretches. A week from now, I bet it'll be noticeable."

"Atta boy, Greg," Kelly said as she saved her spreadsheet and clicked her laptop into sleep mode. She shoved it to the side. "You know how Greg is about personal challenges. He's probably going to be the fastest-improving PT patient in the orthopedic center."

Lisa laughed as she settled into a chair across the table. "Absolutely. He'll even get the PTs themselves involved." She withdrew a textbook and notebook from her oversized bag. "I'd better follow your example and work on these assignments while I have some time between classes."

"Work beckons," Kelly said, reaching for her laptop again. However, she never had the chance to click it back to life because another rather familiar voice sounded from the driveway.

"*Lisa! Lisa!*" Nancy called and waved as she hurried from the driveway and into the garden patio.

"Ohhhhh, goodness," Lisa said, her voice revealing her disappointment even if her face did not.

"There goes the study time," Kelly said, shoving her laptop aside once more. "Nancy is bound to be upset, considering her father has gone with Burt to the police department."

"It was late when I heard her phone message, so I couldn't call her last night," Lisa said quietly.

Nancy rushed up, breathless. "I'm *so* glad to find you here! My father has gone to the police department. He's going to tell them *he* ran into Neil with his car!"

"Oh, no," Lisa said, looking at Nancy. "Your *father* ran into Neil Smith? I could barely understand your phone message last night."

Nancy sank into the chair beside Lisa. "That's what he's going to tell them! He left with Burt just a few minutes ago!"

Kelly couldn't help noticing Nancy's choice of words. She didn't directly answer Lisa's question. "I'm sure your father wants to get this off his chest, Nancy," Kelly offered. "I met your father yesterday afternoon with Jayleen. He's a good man. I'm sure he didn't deliberately try to kill Neil Smith."

Nancy stared at Kelly, and Kelly could see the fear in Nancy's eyes. "Of course he didn't! My father would *never* hurt anyone!"

Lisa waved at waitress Julie. "You need to calm down, Nancy. You want to be able to give your father all your support. Why don't you sit back and take a deep breath. I'll order your favorite drink, okay?"

Julie walked up, notepad in hand. "What can I get you folks?"

"My friend will have a cherry-flavored cola, please. And I'll have an iced tea. No sugar," Lisa said.

"And I'll have an iced coffee, Julie, if you would be so kind," Kelly added. "And one of Pete's wonderful cinnamon rolls if any are left. Put all of it on my bill, please."

"You got it," Julie said, scribbling as she walked away.

Kelly glanced at Nancy and saw that her whole body seemed tense. Her eyes darted right and left, from Lisa to Kelly to the café and back. Kelly observed Nancy for a long moment. Something was out of sync with Nancy's reaction to her father's confession to the police. It didn't feel right, and Kelly suspected she knew why.

Nancy was feeling guilty. Guilty that her father was taking the blame for a crime he did not commit. Kelly's suspicions about Nancy pushed forward again, demanding her attention. Nancy felt guilty because she knew her father didn't kill Neil Smith. She killed him. Deliberate or not, Nancy drove her car directly into Smith that night. And Nancy was the young woman seen kneeling beside Smith's body as he lay dead in the street.

Kelly leaned back in the wrought iron chair and listened to Lisa try to soothe and relax Nancy in her best professional psychologist and therapist manner. Julie returned with Nancy's cherry cola, Lisa's iced tea, and Kelly's refilled iced coffee and cinnamon roll. Kelly savored the yummy cinnamon pastry then took a deep drink of the cold liquid before she spoke.

"Your father is a good man, Nancy. I saw that when I met him. He would never intentionally hurt Neil Smith. He was simply being a protective father."

Nancy chewed her lip. "My dad would never hurt anyone. *Ever!*" she swore.

"I'm sure he wouldn't," Lisa concurred in a soothing voice.

"And your father loves you very, very much," Kelly continued in a calm voice. "And I'm sure he would do anything for you."

Lisa glanced at Kelly with a quizzical expression. Nancy didn't answer. She just stared into the garden, then took a sip of her cherry cola.

"He would try to protect you from any harm, if he could. Wouldn't he, Nancy?"

Nancy chewed her lip again. "Yes, of course," she said in a quiet voice.

Kelly paused for a few seconds then ventured, "In fact, I suspect your father would even take the blame for something so you would not have to suffer."

Lisa stared at Kelly then shifted her gaze to Nancy. Kelly kept her gaze directly on Nancy's face, watching the different emotions flash across it. Nancy didn't speak, just kept staring into the garden.

Finally, Kelly spoke again. "You drove the car that hit Neil Smith, didn't you, Nancy?" she asked gently.

Nancy immediately bent her head and stared at her hands. Finally, she answered in a soft voice. "Yes. I ran into Neil that night. I waited for him in my car, hoping to talk to him again. But when he came out, Neil had a girl with him. She got into her own car and left, but I heard him telling her the same things he told me months ago. And . . .

240

and I got mad. Just seeing him sweet-talking her and kissing her . . . just like he did with me. It made me so mad that I wanted to pay him back."

Nancy suddenly looked up, her anxious gaze shifting between Lisa and Kelly. "I just meant to hurt him. I didn't mean to kill him! *Honest!* When I saw him lying in the street, not moving, I got out of the car and ran over to him. I . . . I was hoping to see him open his eyes or something . . . see me. But he didn't."

Her anxious gaze sought her lap once again. "That's when I got scared. Really scared. I ran back to the car and drove off. I just wanted to get home and . . . and hide from everything. I was so scared . . . I didn't even see the guy on the bicycle at the corner. Until I heard that awful sound." Nancy raised her head again and stared at Lisa, her gaze pleading. "I swear I didn't even see Greg on his bike, Lisa! I swear! I would never have hit him if I had. I'm *so* sorry! So very sorry!"

Lisa reached over and placed her hand on Nancy's arm. "I know you didn't mean it, Nancy. You didn't hit Greg on purpose."

"No, I would never do that. You know that! I . . . I was just so scared! So very scared." Nancy stared down at her lap again.

Kelly chose that moment to catch Lisa's eye briefly then said, "You'll have to tell the police all of this, Nancy. You know that, don't you?"

Nancy's shoulders drooped; in fact, her whole body seemed to droop at Kelly's words. "Yes, I know," she said softly.

"You won't have to go alone, though." Kelly caught Lisa's glance again and watched the light of agreement appear in her friend's eyes.

"That's right, Nancy. You won't have to be alone," Lisa said in her calm therapist's voice. "I'll go with you."

Nancy's head jerked up quickly. She stared at Lisa, gratitude unmistakable in her gaze. "You'd do that for me?" she asked, clearly incredulous.

"Of course I would, Nancy," Lisa said, giving her a little smile. "I'm your friend."

"Ohhhhh, thank you, *thank* you, Lisa!" Nancy said, heartfelt.

Kelly slowly pushed back her chair. "I'll go phone Burt and ask him if he could stay at the police department and meet you both. He can shepherd you through the process. Burt knows everyone. He'll make sure you have a sympathetic ear, Nancy."

Nancy looked up at Kelly, her eyes starting to glisten. "Thank you, Kelly. I appreciate that more than you know."

Twenty

Three weeks later

Kelly reached into the pocket of her dress for a tissue. She tried to move inconspicuously so the rest of the guests standing in Mimi and Burt's backyard wouldn't notice. She'd put several tissues in her pocket before she and Steve left their home this afternoon. Kelly knew she'd need them. She was right. Watching Jennifer and Pete standing beneath the flower-bedecked arbor in the shade, Kelly felt the tears form behind her eyes. Out of nowhere.

Jennifer looked beautiful in the ivory silk dress she'd had made for the wedding. The gifted seamstress had met Kelly and Jennifer during one of Kelly's many sleuthing adventures. The dress was a simple and elegant style that could easily be used for other social occasions. Pete was also handsome in his dark blue suit.

Both Jennifer and Pete fairly radiated, Kelly thought to

herself. As if a special light was shining inside them. Jennifer had confided in Kelly that she'd wanted to wear a lovely pastel green but decided on an ivory color so as to be traditional. One of the few times in her life she'd ever been traditional, Jennifer joked.

Of course, that thought brought more tears to Kelly's eyes, which she stealthily wiped away. Steve slipped his arm around her waist. He leaned over and whispered, "Check out Cassie. She can barely stand still."

Kelly glanced over at Cassie, who was beaming at Jennifer and Pete beneath the arbor. Cassie and Eric had decorated the arbor with flowers from Mimi's backyard and the café patio garden. Cassie held a small bouquet of flowers that matched Jennifer's bouquet of colorful late summer blooms—bright yellow daisies and red roses. Cassie almost danced in place, her happiness was so obvious.

The minister spoke the familiar-sounding words of the marriage ceremony. Both Jennifer and Pete had written their own vows. Kelly looked around at all of the people standing in a semicircle, watching Jennifer and Pete. If Mimi and Burt smiled any wider, their faces would crack. Megan and Marty beamed. Eduardo's huge smile was contagious. Even Greg was grinning beside Lisa. He'd gotten permission from his doctor at the rehab center to come. His broken leg was stretched out on a jumbo-sized scooter chair. Somehow Greg was able to manage over the grassy backyard. He had vowed he wasn't going to miss the wedding cake.

Kelly felt her eyes misting again as she watched Jennifer and Pete pledge their love to one another. Steve drew her closer to his side, then she felt his warm lips on the side of her cheek.

At that moment Pete and Jennifer kissed and all the guests broke into spontaneous applause. Kelly used that moment to quickly wipe her eyes again. Now it was time to celebrate. Cassie jumped up and down several times and ran into the swarm of friends surrounding Jennifer and Pete, who welcomed her into their embrace. Marty and Megan joined Kelly and Steve as everyone crowded around the newlyweds, waiting to congratulate the happy couple.

"Now it's time to party," Marty teased. "When do you think they'll cut that yummy-looking cake?"

Megan simply rolled her eyes as Kelly and Steve laughed out loud.

"Oh, wow, my feet are sore from these shoes," Megan said, rubbing the sole of one foot. "I don't understand. They've always fit perfectly."

"Is this the first time you've worn the shoes since you had Molly?" Mimi asked as she held one of the chocolate brownies Cassie had made for the wedding reception.

"Yeah, I think so," Megan said. "Why?"

"Well, pregnancy often makes our feet get a little bigger." Mimi grinned at Megan before taking a bite of the brownie. Then Mimi closed her eyes and emitted an "Ummmmmmm" sound of enjoyment.

"Oh, wow, I didn't know that," Megan said before sipping her Fat Tire ale.

"How's that leg doing?" Steve called to Greg, who was

steering the scooter chair toward the group seated in the shady patio.

"Coming along," Greg said as he steered his scooter chair to a stop at the edge of the group of friends. "Hey, Marty, have you sampled that lasagna Julie made? It's some of the best I ever tasted."

Marty jerked up in his chair. "Where? I didn't see any lasagna."

"Julie just brought it out of the kitchen," Greg said with a wicked grin. "I got the first slice."

"You dog," Marty said, jumping from his chair as Lisa walked up. "Here, Lisa, take my chair. I'm hitting that buffet table again." And he was off.

"Sounds like old times," Steve joked, then tipped back his Fat Tire ale. "You guys want to get together and watch the Broncos game tomorrow?"

"Not sure they're going to let me jump ship two days in a row. Boss Nurse was staring at me and shaking her head when I left." Greg frowned.

"Hey, why don't we watch the game over at Greg's rehab center?"

Lisa looked dubious. "I don't know if a whole bunch of us could gather there like that."

"Yeah, we're a rowdy crew," Megan said. "Boss Nurse would probably throw us out."

"Or maybe we could ask if there's a family room at the facility," Steve suggested. "We could rent it if we had to. That way we wouldn't be disturbing the other patients."

"I think there are some open areas at the end of a couple

of hallways," Lisa offered. "There are TVs, too. But we'd have to be quiet."

"*Quiet?* Our gang?" Kelly asked, incredulous.

"Hey, we can do it," Megan said. "Consider it a challenge."

"What's a challenge?" Marty asked as he walked up to the group. A half-eaten slice of lasagna sat on his plate.

"Greg probably won't be able to get away from the facility two days in a row, so we thought we might watch the game from there tomorrow." Lisa grinned. "If we can manage to be quiet, that is."

Marty's impish grin lit up his face. "Piece of cake."

Kelly joined her friends' laughter, leaning back into her chair. She sipped her Fat Tire and listened to Marty and Greg exchange verbal jabs and challenges.

"Just you wait a month," Greg vowed.

"Excuses, excuses," Marty replied before downing another delicious-looking bite of lasagna.

Kelly relaxed, watching her friends and listening to their fast-paced repartee. Glancing at the large cottonwood trees above, she saw that the leaves were still green. Now that it was September, there would be a gradual changing of the seasons. Cooler nights would signal the sap in the trees to slow and gradually stop. Leaves would turn from green to bright yellow, orange, and red. Then, in November at the latest, they would crumble and fall. Leaf raking would become a standard weekend activity. Then much as Kelly hated to admit it, winter would arrive. There would be the first snow. And then more. Colder temperatures would force wearing of coats and scarves. *Brrrrr.*

The passage of the seasons. Days turned into weeks. Weeks turned into months. The eternal passage of time. Kelly sipped her craft brew and watched Cassie roll a ball to little Molly, who was crawling as fast as she could manage across the green grass. Still green for a while.

Then out of the back of Kelly's mind, a tiny thought wiggled. *It's been over a month.* Kelly let it play through her mind. What a strange thought, she mused. And then . . . then Kelly let the entire thought play through her mind. Center stage. She stared out into Mimi and Burt's backyard gardens.

Is that possible? It's been over a month. Can that be? What if it is? Good Lord!

Kelly continued to stare out into the backyard while her friends' repartee and laughter flowed by her. Obviously a quick stop at the drugstore on the way home was in order. She glanced around for Steve and spotted him at the buffet table chatting with Burt. Then she saw Jennifer and Pete walking toward the group and pushed the way-ward thought to the back of her mind. Now was the time for celebration.

Kelly held up her Fat Tire. "To the bride and groom," she saluted.

All of her friends joined in as a beaming Pete and a radiant Jennifer joined the rest of the gang.

Kelly stared at the test strip in her hand. Positive. Again. She had tested twice, and the results were the same each time. She was pregnant. Definitely pregnant. *Good Lord.* She continued to stare at the strip as a jumble of thoughts bounced around her brain.

Pregnant? Her! Good grief! How was that possible? Well, she knew how it was possible, but . . . but her? Good grief!

A loud thumping on the bathroom door broke through Kelly's thoughts. "Hey! You falling asleep in there? I've made coffee. Come and get it," Steve called from the other side of the door.

Kelly disposed of the test strips, splashed some water on her face, and stared at herself in the mirror. *Her? A mother?*

Still slightly dazed, she left the bathroom and walked toward the kitchen. September sunshine was streaming through the windows. Steve was sitting at the kitchen table, reading the Sunday Fort Connor newspaper.

"I've already poured you a cup. We've got doughnuts. That should hold us until we get to the hotel for the wedding brunch." He grinned at her over his mug before taking a sip.

"Thanks," Kelly said as she zeroed in on her coffee. Taking a large sip, she closed her eyes and let the caffeine rush start. She'd need some caffeine for the conversation she was about to have. A tiny thought in the back of her head wiggled forward. *Caffeine. Caffeine.* Good Lord. She needed to go online and research. Right now, she needed the coffee.

"I've already put the wedding gifts in the car," Steve said as he returned to the newspaper.

Kelly looked over at Steve, innocently reading the Sunday newspaper, clueless.

Of course he's clueless. How could he know? Kelly's inner voice jabbed. She gulped down more coffee.

Maggie Sefton

Steve glanced back at her. "What's the matter? You have a funny expression on your face."

Kelly opened her mouth to say something, but she didn't know what to say. Should she try to work into it? Or lead up to it? Or . . . or . . .

"What?" Steve started to laugh as she stood there with her mouth open.

Finally, Kelly's natural instincts took over. *Just go for it.*

"Steve . . . I'm pregnant."

Steve just stared at her for a few seconds as his grin disappeared. "Are you serious?" he asked, his brown eyes wide with surprise.

"Yeah," Kelly said, nodding her head. Dazed and confused, that was her.

Steve let his mug drop on the table as he leaped from his chair. *"Fantastic!"* he yelled as he raced over and grabbed Kelly in his arms, lifting her up as he spun her around the kitchen. "I can't believe it! Are you sure?"

Kelly laughed as he set her back on the floor. "Yes! I tested twice, and it was positive twice."

Steve stared into her face. "How do you feel? I mean, are you happy, or . . ."

Kelly didn't have to think. She could feel a warmth inside her chest. A good feeling. "I'm happy, I guess. I'm just . . . I don't know . . . shocked. I mean . . . whoa . . ."

Steve grinned as he pulled her close. "Whoa. Oh, yeah." And he lowered his lips to hers. Kelly encircled her arms around his neck and kissed him back. *Oh, yeah.*

• • •

"Marty, if you take any more bacon, I swear, you're going to grow a snout," Megan teased as she watched her husband deposit yet another full plate of breakfast food on the dining table.

Marty just grinned and made a snorting sound before he gobbled another slice of bacon.

"The hotel staff are staring at you, too, Marty," Lisa said as she returned to her chair beside Greg. "They're incredulous."

"We ought to come back here for breakfast when I'm in fighting shape," Greg said. "Then we can really horrify them." He poured some cream into his coffee.

Kelly looked around the hotel dining room Jennifer and Pete reserved for their wedding brunch. It was packed with people. Everyone who had attended the wedding showed up this morning for the wedding brunch. Friends and family all surrounding Jennifer and Pete with their love and affection. It made Kelly feel good inside, and somewhat eased that nervous feeling of excitement she had. She felt weird. Kind of excited and a little confused. And definitely dazed. Dazed and confused. Still.

Steve leaned close to her ear and whispered, "I'm dying to tell everyone. How about now?"

Kelly turned to the most important man in her life and smiled into his dark brown eyes. "Go for it. This will be fun to watch."

Steve gave her a quick kiss. Then turned to Pete, who was seated beside him. "Watch this." Then he glanced down the table and called, "Hey, Burt, why don't you turn on your video camera. I'm going to say a few words."

251

"Sure," Burt said with a smile and grabbed his cell phone from the table.

Steve rose and clanged his fork against the water glass beside his plate. "Everyone!" he called out.

Kelly watched all her friends and acquaintances turn their attention to Steve.

Steve held up his newly filled champagne glass. "Another toast to the newlyweds. To Jennifer and Pete! Happiness always!" He raised his glass and drank to accompanying cheers and calls of agreement.

Kelly sipped from her champagne. She'd never really liked champagne. She watched Steve hold up his glass again, then he glanced to her with a big grin.

"I don't have another toast, but I do have an announcement. Kelly and I both. We're going to have a baby." Steve tossed down the rest of the champagne in his glass as the dining room went from silence to raucous uproar in a matter of seconds.

"Oh my God!"

"I can't believe it!"

"Damn, dude!"

"Whoa, so cool!"

"Wheeeeeee!" Cassie squealed.

"Oh my, how wonderful!"

"Oh, wow!"

Kelly laughed as she was suddenly swept up in the outpouring of her friends' affection and their love. Showering over her. Her friends hugged her and laughed and cried and squealed and congratulated and kissed her on the cheek. Sweeping her up in their love. Kelly let herself be swept up. With family. Her family.

Llama Headband

FINISHED MEASUREMENTS IN INCHES:
Approximately 4" wide x 20" long

MATERIALS:
100% Hand-dyed Baby Llama (~100 yards)

NEEDLES:
Size 4–5 needles or size needed for gauge.
  Removable marker
  One button

GAUGE:
5–6 sts per inch

ABBREVIATIONS:
K = knit; **P** = purl
YO = yarn over
K2tog = knit 2 together
SSK = slip two stitches one at a time knitwise, knit them together through the back.
SK2po = slip one knitwise, knit 2 together, pass slipped stitch over.
St(s) = stitch(es)
RS = right side
WS = wrong side

LLAMA HEADBAND

INSTRUCTIONS:

Cast on 9 stitches.

Next Row (RS): K4 place marker, K5.

Knit 9 more rows.

Row 1 (RS): K1, YO, knit to 1 st before marker, SK2po, knit to last 2 sts, YO, K2.

Rows 2 and 4: K2, purl to last 2 sts, K2.

Row 3: K2, YO, K1 into the hole 2 rows below, knit to 1 st before marker stitch, SK2po, knit to last 2 sts, K1 into the hole 2 rows below, YO, K2.

Repeat last four increasing rows until there are 23 stitches.

Repeat Rows 1 and 2 until piece measures 15 inches from cast on.

Row 1: K1, YO, K2tog, knit to 1 st before marker stitch, SK2po, knit to last 4 sts, SSK, YO, K2.

Rows 2 and 4: K2, purl to last 2 sts, K2.

Row 3: K2, YO, knit to 1 st before marker stitch, SK2po, knit to last 2 sts, YO, K2.

Repeat last 4 rows until 9 stitches.

Next row (RS): K3, bind off 3 sts, knit to end.

Next row (WS): K3, cast on 3 sts, knit to end.

Knit 2 more rows. Bind off. Sew in all loose ends. Sew button for decoration.

Pattern courtesy of Lambspun of Colorado, Fort Collins, Colorado. Designed for Lambspun by Larissa Breloff.

This bread is quick to make and cranberries can be found year-round. I kept tinkering with recipes until I came up with the flavors that I especially like. Give it a try and enjoy!

Cranberry Orange Nut Bread

2 cups all-purpose flour
1½ teaspoons baking powder
½ teaspoon baking soda
1 teaspoon ground cinnamon
½ teaspoon salt
1½ cups white sugar
1 cup orange juice
¼ cup melted butter
2 eggs
1 cup fresh cranberries (not frozen)
1 cup chopped walnuts
½ cup grated orange peel

Preheat oven to 350 degrees F. Grease one regular-size bread loaf pan (or two small loaf pans). Dust pan lightly with flour, dumping excess. Combine flour, baking powder, baking soda, cinnamon, and salt in large mixing bowl. Combine sugar, orange juice, melted butter, and eggs in another bowl, mixing well. Stir into flour mixture along with cranberries, walnuts, and orange peel. Mix well, blending all ingredients. Pour into prepared loaf pan. Bake for 50 minutes or until knife inserted into center of loaf comes out clean. Remove pan to wire rack to cool for 10 minutes, then run knife around edges of pan and turn out onto rack to cool completely.

Keep reading for an excerpt of
the first book in Maggie Sefton's
New York Times bestselling Knitting Mysteries . . .

KNIT ONE, KILL TWO

Available from Berkley Prime Crime!

Kelly Flynn nosed her car onto the gravel driveway and pulled to a stop in front of the familiar little house perched beside a golf course. Everything looked the same. Aunt Helen's beige stucco, red-tile-roofed cottage looked as cozy and inviting as always. Golfers were scattered about the lush greens, doggedly working to improve their games. In the background the Colorado Rocky Mountains, still snow-capped in late spring, loomed over the entire scene. It was all picture-postcard pretty, just like Kelly remembered, except for one thing. Aunt Helen was dead—murdered a week ago in her picturesque cottage.

A "burglary gone bad" the police called it. Kelly's gut still twisted at the thought. Aunt Helen would have fought back. Kelly knew she would. Even though she was thin as a stick and a foot shorter than Kelly, she was wiry and tough.

And she had spirit. Spunk. She'd never go down without a fight. Not Aunt Helen. No way.

Kelly felt tears rise to her eyes again as she remembered her aunt's favorite admonition: "Never give up, Kelly-girl. If you want something bad enough, don't you ever give up." The tears escaped, running down Kelly's cheeks, and she swiped them away with the back of her hand. She'd never even had the chance to say good-bye. At least with her dad, Kelly'd been able to tell him how much she loved him. Cancer might be an ugly way to die, but it was slower. Murder was a thief in the night, creeping in to steal away valuable loved ones. And this thief stole the only mother Kelly had ever known.

A cold, wet nose shoved against Kelly's neck, and she turned to pat the shiny black Rottweiler head resting beside her shoulder. Carl always sensed her moods. "Don't worry, boy, I haven't forgotten you. You're looking at that grass, right?" She pointed to the manicured golf course, stretching from her aunt's property all the way to the river that meandered diagonally through the scenic college town north of Denver.

Kelly let herself gaze. It had been six months since she'd returned to Fort Connor, where she spent her early childhood. Every time she returned, she wondered how she'd ever make herself leave again. The sky was bluer here, the air was cleaner, and the sun was brighter by a mile. "A mile high to be exact," as Aunt Helen used to say. What a gorgeous day. If her aunt was still alive, she and Kelly would take one of their favorite hikes along a trail in the nearby Poudre Canyon. How could it be so beautiful with Helen gone?

Carl whined to get her attention, clearly eager to explore. "Okay, boy, but you can't run on the course. The greens-keeper wouldn't appreciate your lifting a leg on every tee." Carl rolled his soft brown eyes to her in pleading mode.

"Nope. You'll just have to make do with the yard." Kelly opened the car door and slid out, grabbing a leash as she did.

Carl's ears perked up at the magic jingle, and he gave an excited yelp. That meant outside and play. Snapping the leash to his red collar, Kelly headed toward the small backyard. Tall cottonwood trees surrounded the property, shading both house and yard. Flower boxes were already planted, even though Kelly knew the frost date in northern Colorado was a yearly gamble. Somehow, Helen always won out. Her green thumb or gardener's luck could overcome even Colorado's capricious weather.

Kelly made a mental note to water the plants that evening. She wasn't about to let Helen's plants die with her. She swung the back gate open and ushered Carl inside. "It isn't the golf course, boy, but it's bigger than your yard for sure," she said, referring to her postage stamp–size townhouse yard on the outskirts of Washington, DC. Carl didn't waste time. He took off the moment his leash was unsnapped, nose to the ground.

The sound of another car coming down the gravel driveway caught Kelly's attention, and she turned to see a red minivan drive up to the larger stucco and red-tile-roofed house across the drive. A woman exited the van and entered the sprawling mirror-image of Helen's cottage.

Both houses and the assorted outbuildings nearby occupied a pie-shaped wedge of land that clung to the corner of a busy intersection. Kelly remembered when both streets were country roads cutting through fields of sugar beets and sheep farms. Now, a big box discount store swallowed the opposite corner and townhouses clustered across the street.

At least her aunt and uncle had sold their farmland to the city for a golf course and kept only the cottage and its yard. If she squinted her eyes hard enough, Kelly could block out the golfers and picture her uncle heading to the barn years ago when he was still alive.

"Kelly, is that you?" a woman's voice called.

Kelly shut the gate, knowing Carl would be occupied for hours identifying scents. She turned and recognized Mimi Shafer walking across the driveway. Mimi owned the knitting and needlework shop that now occupied what was once Aunt Helen's and Uncle Jim's farmhouse. Her aunt had been ecstatic about the arrangement, since she was an expert knitter and quilter, but Kelly had always felt vaguely resentful. She remembered when the house was filled with Aunt Helen and Uncle Jim—and memories. But Uncle Jim's long illness changed all that.

Now, Kelly felt nothing but gratitude. Mimi had been Aunt Helen's closest friend and had never left Kelly's side during yesterday's service. She gave names to faces and helped Kelly stand and sit through a liturgy that was no longer familiar.

Kelly straightened her white blouse and navy skirt. Not as tailored as her usual CPA firm attire, but sober enough for a lawyer meeting. She couldn't wait until she could change into a casual top and slacks, maybe even shorts if it stayed warm. Ever since she got back, she'd been dressed up and meeting people. Just like the office. But Colorado meant sunshine and mountains and freedom to Kelly. And that meant shorts, a T-shirt, and sneakers.

She brushed her chin-length dark-brown hair behind her ear and checked the barrette in back. Kelly'd rushed through her shower and dressing in order to fit in a morning run along the trail that ran beside the motel. She'd barely checked the mirror. After yesterday's tears, she needed to clear her head. Running always helped her think.

She waved to Mimi. "I just thought I'd let Carl use Helen's backyard today while I go to all those . . . you know, meetings. Lawyer, banker, and all that."

"That's a great idea. I'm sure he's tired of being cooped up in the motel room," Mimi said with a bright smile. Her sun-streaked brown hair feathered softly around her face. Fifty-ish, slender, and pretty, she wore a powder-blue straight dress that accentuated her trim figure. But what really drew Kelly's attention was the open-weave vest she wore on top; the loosely fixed knots held the yarns together. Varying shades of blue traveled all the way to green and back again. The effect was stunning.

"Do you have time for a cup of tea or coffee?" Mimi asked, obviously hoping for a yes.

Kelly hesitated, running through her mental daytimer. That and the Greenwich Meridian time clock in her head kept Kelly on task. She depended on that clock. Back in the firm, everyone kept track of their time in tenths of an hour—six-minute intervals—billable hours. Consequently, Kelly was seldom late. "I have a few minutes. My appointment with the lawyer isn't until ten."

Maggie Sefton

"Oh, darn, I was hoping we'd have more time," Mimi said, her smile momentarily missing. "I've been dying to show you the shop, but I guess it'll just have to wait until later today. Why don't we step over to the café?" She gestured toward the pathway leading around the farmhouse.

Kelly completely forgot that a bistro-style café had opened in the former kitchen and dining room of the farmhouse since her last visit. As they followed the flower beds and flagstone path, Kelly was astonished to see the café also spilled out into the shady backyard. Surrounded by high stucco walls, the entire patio was private, secluded from the outside. The whole setting was delightful and charming, Kelly had to admit.

Mimi chose a table and sat down, motioning to a nearby waitress as Kelly settled into a wrought iron chair. "This is really quite nice. I like what they've done here," Kelly surprised herself by saying. Noticing the many tables filled with customers lingering over late breakfasts and brunch, she asked, "How's it doing? Financially, I mean. I know how hard it is for small restaurants to make it." As a beginning accountant years ago, Kelly had had several restaurants to worry about. "Shoe box clients" she used to call them, because they always kept their accounts in shoe boxes for some reason.

"Actually, quite well, according to Pete," said Mimi. "He's the young man who had the idea of turning this whole area into a restaurant. Somehow, he managed to convince the management company that owns it to invest in used equipment, and he volunteered all the labor. He put his heart and soul into this place." She shook her head.

"Let's hope all that hard work hasn't been wasted . . . for both of us."

Intrigued by the cryptic remark, Kelly was about to respond when the waitress appeared. She had shoulder-length reddish-brown hair that curved around a pretty face. "Hi, Mimi," she said with a bright smile, then turned a warm gaze to Kelly.

"Kelly, this is Jennifer Stroud," Mimi introduced. "She was also a friend of Helen's."

"Kelly, I just wanted to say how shocked we were at Helen's death. She was a wonderful lady. I used to see her over at the shop almost every day, and she was always so sweet and loving. We'll all miss her a lot."

The comments caught Kelly unprepared, and she felt her eyes grow suddenly moist. She glanced down at her napkin. "Thank you. You're very kind."

Jennifer reached out and patted Kelly's arm. "Hey, that's okay. Let me bring you something. I know Mimi's order already. Earl Grey, cream. How about you?"

"Coffee, black and strong," Kelly said with a smile, which helped chase away the tears.

"Down with decaf, right?" Jennifer winked as she flipped the notepad closed. "Be right back."

"I think she was at the funeral yesterday, but I really can't remember too much," Kelly said as she watched Jennifer skirt between tables, glad for the chance to compose herself.

"Oh, yes, she was there with the other knitting shop regulars."

"Regulars?" Kelly asked. "Who are they?"

"We've got lots of knitting and needlework groups that

meet regularly at the shop during the week. Some are organized, some just happen, like Jennifer's group. They're a bunch of women, many of whom are around your age, who meet after work a couple of times a week or more. Of course, anybody who shows up is welcome to sit in with any group. That's how Helen met Jennifer and the others."

Kelly could easily picture that. Helen was always knitting, and loved nothing better than to share her passion. It was a shame Kelly had proven to be such an unwilling student. Now, she was sorry she'd always feigned impatience whenever her aunt had tried to coax her into learning to knit.

"I know Aunt Helen enjoyed that," Kelly mused. "She loved meeting new people. And living across from the shop, she could make new friends almost every day. Every week when I'd call her, she'd always tell me something funny she'd heard, usually from some friend." Kelly would miss those phone calls.

"Helen had lots of friends, as you saw yesterday at the service. Everyone loved her, and we want to help you in whatever way we can, Kelly. Several people have offered to help go through the house when you're ready."

Kelly groaned inwardly. That unpleasant chore had almost slipped her mind. Whenever it had appeared, she'd shoved it away. At least having people with her would make the task easier and less painful. "I confess I've deliberately not thought about that chore," she admitted. "I guess I'm avoiding going into the house after, well, you know."

"I understand, Kelly."

"Thanks so much. I really appreciate your help. I remember how hard it was going through my dad's things, and I'd been prepared for his death."

Mimi reached out and patted Kelly's arm. "Well, you're not alone this time, Kelly. We're here to help you."

Jennifer's cheerful bustle and the inviting tray of coffee and tea arrived just when Kelly felt her eyes grow moist again. After the funeral yesterday she thought she'd cried herself dry. Apparently there was a well inside her that ran deeper than she knew.

There was no one left anymore. Her dad, three years ago. Now, Aunt Helen. Her entire family was gone.

"Here you go," Jennifer announced as she set the tea and coffee in place. "Pete even threw in one of those wicked cinnamon rolls on the house."

"Ohhh, that's cruel," Mimi groaned. "He knows I can't have the sugar."

Kelly eyed the tempting coil of golden, flaky, sweet dough slathered with a sugary cream cheese icing that drizzled down the sides. She'd forgotten Fort Connor's community weakness for these oversized breakfast buns. The bakery that specialized in making them kept the calorie count a secret.

"It's still warm," tempted Jennifer with a grin.

Her normal willpower was either sound asleep or stunned into silence at the sight of the huge pastry. So, with no nagging voice in her head, Kelly picked up the fork. "What the heck. I'll need it for all those meetings. Lawyers are depressing."

"Absolutely," Jennifer concurred, clearly enjoying Kelly's quick capitulation. "Besides, you're tall and slender. It'll never show. On me, it'd be on my hips in five minutes."

"Oh, right," Kelly retorted with a grin. "Why don't you share it with me?"

Jennifer rolled her eyes. "Don't tempt me. I was born with a sweet tooth."

"Seriously, I can't finish this monster all by myself." She sliced the bun in half and pushed one half to the side of her plate.

Jennifer glanced at the pastry. "We're not supposed to eat with customers."

Kelly sensed weakness. She took a big bite, closed her eyes, and let out a dramatic, *"Mmmmmmmmmm!"*

"That's it. Priorities." Jennifer laughed and grabbed her portion.

"Which are?" Mimi teased.

Jennifer paused after swallowing. "Right now, sugar. It's gonna be a busy day."

Kelly polished off her share and reached for the coffee, which was surprisingly rich and dark. She drank in the blissful enjoyment of the strong brew. "Yum, this is really good for the plain stuff. My compliments."

"That's Eduardo's doing. He's our cook and insists on making the coffee every morning. I think he throws in espresso or chicory or shoelaces or who knows what. But it'll wake you up, for sure."

"Bless him, and tell him I'll be back." The timer went off inside her head, and Kelly drained the cup. "Speaking of that, I have to go. Lawyers get all pinched around the edges if you're late." She scooted back her chair and brushed telltale sugar flakes off her skirt. "Oh, Mimi, I almost forgot.

Could you fill a bowl with water for Carl, please? I fed him this morning, but I forgot to grab his water dish."

"No problem. I'll give him some food come dinnertime, too, so don't rush. And make sure you stop in the shop when you return. I can't wait to show you everything we've done. You haven't been in since we opened four years ago." Mimi exuded pride. "You'll be surprised, I think."

"I look forward to it. Thanks, Mimi," Kelly said as she backed away from the table. Glancing at Jennifer as she headed for the pathway, Kelly waved. "Nice meeting you, Jennifer."

"Oh, you'll see me later at the shop. With the others. Good luck with the lawyer."

Kelly hastened to her car. She'd dutifully let Mimi show off her shop, for Aunt Helen's sake, if nothing else. Kelly couldn't knit her way out of a paper bag. So all that knitting stuff would be lost on her. Her aunt had tried several times to instruct Kelly when she was growing up and even as an adult, but it never seemed to take. Kelly would fumble the needles and drop the yarn—whatever it took to appear completely incompetent. There were so many more fun things to do outside on the farm, she just couldn't sit still long enough to learn.

Besides, all those different kinds of stitches looked complicated to Kelly. Knitting here, purling there. All that yarn, needles busily working away, stitch after stitch, row after row. Looked like a lot of work to Kelly. She just didn't have that kind of patience. The only patience she'd ever had was for numbers. Numbers stayed put on paper. They didn't fall off the end of the needles.

Oh yes, Kelly thought, as she backed her car out of the parking space, numbers were far less confusing than knitting.

Lawrence Chambers tapped his gold-rimmed pen against the leather desk pad as he scanned the documents before him. Kelly used the opportunity to study the lawyer, who was the same age as her aunt. His gray hair shone silver as a stray morning sunbeam crossed the desk. Chambers had been Aunt Helen's trusted lawyer and close friend for a lifetime.

"Thanks to Helen's foresight, you should have no problem handling any expense involved with the estate," he spoke up. "You're cosigner on both bank accounts, checking and savings, as well as the safe-deposit box. It was a smart move, considering you're her only heir."

"Aunt Helen told me four years ago what her wishes were. I've always tried to oblige her in whatever way I could."

Chambers glanced up from the papers in his hand and smiled across the large walnut desk. Kelly noticed his faded blue eyes were kind.

"Helen appreciated everything you did for her. She told me so many times."

Kelly glanced away. "She was like a mom to me, Mr. Chambers. You know that. Besides, when my dad died three years ago, I promised him I'd take care of her. She was his only living relative." Guilt twinged inside. She'd never broken a promise to her dad in her whole life.

Chambers set down the papers, watching Kelly, then gestured to the wall. "That's hers, you know."

Kelly studied the framed quilted scene that had caught her eye earlier. Deep, rich browns and greens portrayed a small house nestled in the mountains, surrounded by tall evergreens. "I thought that might be her work. It's so vibrant."

"Yes, she did that from a photograph of the mountain cabin our family has had for years." He smiled. "She surprised us with it on our anniversary. That was Helen. Always doing for others. If she wasn't stitching for someone she knew, she'd be knitting for the homeless shelter."

"Yes, I know. I'm the one who used to buy the yarn online to save her money." A spark of anger flared suddenly. "It doesn't seem right, does it, Mr. Chambers. My aunt was murdered by some vagrant, exactly the sort of person she tried to help. Where's the justice in that?"

Chambers clasped his hands on top of the documents. "There is none, Kelly. This is one of those horrible, awful acts of random violence."

Kelly stared at the floor-to-ceiling walnut bookcases that lined one wall. "The officer told me this was a 'burglary gone bad.' She said this guy came into Helen's house that night, saw her purse and grabbed it. Then, supposedly Helen came out and saw him, screamed, and he strangled her. Then he ran off."

"Yes, that's exactly what the police told me. Apparently this man was a drunk and a vagrant and was always getting into trouble. He must have come into the house, grabbed her purse, and when Helen came out," his voice became strained, "he killed her for it." He sighed. "Thank goodness he was too drunk to be smart. The police saw him run away from the scene, so they caught him right away."

Kelly leaned forward in her chair and eyed Chambers. Something he'd said. "That's a little different from what the police told me. They said they'd seen this guy 'near the house,' not coming from it. Are you sure that's what they told you?"

Chambers pondered. "I'm fairly certain the detective who spoke with me said they captured the suspect fleeing the scene. Yes, that's exactly what he said. 'Fleeing the scene.' And I took that to mean he was coming from the house."

"Do you remember who you spoke with, Mr. Chambers? The woman who called me was a community relations officer and wasn't involved with the case."

"Oh, yes, I spoke with Lieutenant Morrison. He's in charge. A very experienced detective, from what I've heard. Very thorough."

Kelly opened her portfolio and wrote the name on a legal pad. "I'm sure you're right, Mr. Chambers. I mean, this guy had to be lurking around Aunt Helen's house before he came in. Looking in the windows or something." She closed the portfolio with a snap. "He must have been drunk. Why else would he have tried to steal from a woman who never carried more than twenty dollars in her purse?" A bitter note crept into her voice. It felt good to release it.

Chambers peered at Kelly over his glasses with a worried frown. "Well, uh, she may have had more in her purse—"

"Oh, no, sir," Kelly countered. "She never had more than

twenty bucks and change at any one time. She always used her debit card because it kept her on a budget. And I should know, Mr. Chambers, because I drew up her budget and kept her accounts every month. She was still paying off some of Uncle Jim's medical bills, so she was very careful."

Chambers' lined face creased even more. "Didn't she tell you about the . . . the, uh, money she was borrowing?"

Kelly blinked. Surely she couldn't have heard the lawyer right. "Borrowing? Helen wasn't borrowing any money. Remember, I kept her accounts. I would know."

"I'm afraid she did. Just before she died."

Kelly stared back at him, incredulous. "*What?* Where . . . I mean, who . . . how much?"

"Twenty thousand dollars," Chambers said in a pained voice.

"Twenty thousand dollars!" Kelly sat bolt upright. "But why? And . . . and where would Helen borrow that kind of money, anyway? She was living on Jim's state pension and Social Security."

"The only place she could, Kelly. She refinanced her house. And went to one of those predatory lenders to do it." He shook his head sadly. "I advised her against it, but she wouldn't listen. She said she needed it and would talk to me later. I assumed she was giving it to you, that you needed it for something."

"*Me?*" Kelly shot back. "I'd never ask Aunt Helen for money. I'd starve first."

Chambers sank back into his leather armchair. "Oh, my . . . oh, my," he said, clearly troubled. "I thought the money was for you, that's why I didn't worry too much when she said she needed it. After all, you're her only living relative."

Kelly stared at the diplomas that lined the wall behind Chambers' desk. This was impossible. It made no sense. Her aunt wouldn't even consider such a risky move without consulting Kelly. "This is crazy, Mr. Chambers. Aunt Helen was a sensible woman, you know that. She'd never do such a thing. Why . . . why, we just refinanced her house three years ago to pay off most of Uncle Jim's medical bills. We got a really low rate. Perfect for her. I was going to help her pay off the mortgage so she'd have it free and clear in ten years." Her hand shot out in frustration. "She wouldn't . . . she couldn't have done this stupid thing."

Chambers took off his glasses and rubbed his eyes but said nothing.

Anger flashed through Kelly, right up her spine. "Wait a minute. Do you think some sleazy con artist got his claws in Aunt Helen? Tricked her into some wretched investment scheme? I'd told her not to even talk to those weasels if they called."

"No, no, Helen was too smart for that." He dismissed the threat with a wave. "She and I frequently discussed some of the scams out there for the unwary, especially vulnerable seniors."

"When did she talk to you? When did she tell you what she was going to do?"

"About three weeks ago. She called to tell me she was refinancing the house because she needed money and asked my recommendation for a lender. Apparently she'd already been turned down by her current mortgage company and two others. There was no more equity left."

"I know, we used it all three years ago."

"Well, I asked how much she needed, thinking I'd lend it to her myself. When she told me twenty thousand dollars, I was shocked and told her so. I asked what on earth she could need that much money for, and she refused to answer. Said she'd talk to me later and hung up. I didn't even hear from her again until last Friday, the very day she was killed."

"And what did she say then?" Kelly probed.

"That's when she told me she'd found some Denver mortgage company that was only too glad to write up an above-value mortgage. She wouldn't tell me the interest rate. It must have been awful. But she did say she got the check for twenty thousand dollars. It never occurred to me she'd cash it." Chambers leaned over his desk and sank his head in both hands. "Good Lord. That's what got her killed. All that money sitting in her purse. Oh, Helen, why? *Why?*" His voice cracked this time.

Kelly pondered for a moment, giving Chambers time to collect himself. She was still trying to make sense of everything she'd heard. Her logical mind didn't want to accept her aunt's illogical actions. It was totally out of character. Why would she put herself upside down in her mortgage at her age? Especially since she'd had to refinance only three years ago to pay off most of Uncle Jim's medical bills. And why on earth would she take all that cash home with her?

The shock of her aunt's murder had been enough to occupy Kelly's thoughts the entire two-thousand-mile drive to Colorado. But now that the funeral was over and she had more time to think, Kelly began to notice details. Details that didn't belong. After all, that's what she did for a living. In her consulting role with a large accounting firm, Kelly analyzed a corporation's financial statements looking for anything that jumped out and made her buzzer go off. She'd never imagined that she'd have to turn that same concentration on uglier matters so close to home.

Waiting another moment, Kelly gently asked, "Mr. Chambers, have you spoken to the police? Did you tell them all this, I mean about the money and all?"

He lifted his red-rimmed eyes and cleared his throat. "No. I would never divulge Helen's private business. That's privileged." He sniffled.

"Then I think they need to know there was a lot more money stolen than they originally thought. I'll call this Lieutenant Morrison as soon as I leave here." Picking up her portfolio, Kelly stood and deliberately let her voice assume the official business tone she used so often. That would give Chambers something to hang on to. "Thank you, Mr. Chambers, for everything you've done and everything you've tried to do to help my aunt. I'm going over to the bank right now and check the accounts. And I'll look into this new loan as well."

Chambers straightened and rose. "That's a good idea . . . oh, wait a minute. I think I wrote down the name." He paged through the daytimer on his desk, scanning the pages. "Yes, here it is. U-Can-Do-It Mortgage in Denver." He peered at the daytimer while Kelly wrote the information in her notebook. "Ohhh, yes . . . there is something else. Here's the note. Helen also said she was coming in soon to talk about her property. She wanted to make sure it all went to the city for gardens in case you didn't want to live in Fort Connor. But she didn't want to donate the land. It was to be sold, with you receiving all the proceeds."

Kelly stared blankly at him. Another surprise. "Gardens? Really? She never mentioned that."

"Yes, that surprised me, too." Chambers shook his head. "But, of course, she never got the chance to come in for the appointment. So you're free to sell the property if you choose."

"But that was her wish, apparently," Kelly mused out loud.

"Apparently so. She loved you very much, Kelly."

With that, Kelly knew she had to leave. If she misted up, Chambers would lose it again, and that would be embarrassing. Not so much for her, but for the older gentleman. "Thank you, again, Mr. Chambers," she said, and headed for the door.

"You're welcome, Kelly. And, I'm sure you'll find those mortgage papers in Helen's house. Take care, my dear."

Kelly waved and made a swift exit. She was sure she'd find the papers in the cottage, but the thought of going into the house where Aunt Helen was murdered still chilled her. Kelly hastened to the parking lot as she searched her cell phone's directory for the number of the Fort Connor Police Department.